PRETTY LITTLE KILLER

PRETTY OBSESSIONS
BOOK TWO

AJ MERLIN

AUTHOR'S NOTE

Pretty Little Killer is a dark romance that contains some content that may be problematic for some readers including murder, graphic violence, **some graphic torture**, serial killers, kink, sex work, knife play, and light breath play, mentions of past abuse, and on-page **sexual assault from outside of the relationship.**

CHAPTER 1

"*All passengers should remain in their seats while we taxi to the gate.*"

My thumb scrolls through the messages on my phone, finally accessible after the four-hour flight from Indiana to the St. Augustine airport. I'd gotten lucky and found a direct flight from Indianapolis, instead of an out of the way layover. But the flight was still long enough to cause a crick in my neck and an ache in my lower spine. Thankfully, I know it will be chased away once I can find a tub to sink into and fall asleep in.

Hello? Are you ever coming back?

My eyes snag on the message from *evan82*, and my heart clenches like it's being gripped in icy fingers. There's nothing wrong with *evan82*, I'm sure. But the fact that Rob of *fuck Rob* fame had started just like this before he'd attacked me has made me too afraid to stream again, or answer any messages like this.

Plus, it isn't like I'm hurting for money. Thinking about that twists my stomach into something like guilt and I sweep

1

away the thought that Rook has basically been my sugar daddy ever since I'd left to go home for Christmas.

Another message from *user3245* makes me roll my eyes. His platitudes and well wishes are nice, if more than a little overboard. But at least his intentions are... good? Well, more whiny than good, and I know it isn't actually me he's worried about. It's the fact that he missed jerking off to my body and my stream.

When I remember that, it's easier not to feel bad about ditching the men who'd tipped me so well I hadn't had to worry about getting a different job last semester. They didn't care about *me* when they sent these messages.

Just what I offered them.

The plane shudders to a stop and I wince, wishing I could effectively rub the aches out of my neck and back now, instead of having to wait to get home to take care of them. My teeth grind as the man beside me jolts into me as he stands. His low rumble of an apology does little when his jacket flaps against my face for the second time.

Shrugging, I wait for him and the others to move until I get up. I'm not trying to beat anyone to the door, and I don't have anyone waiting that I want to be timely for. It's just me, and the Uber I'm going to call when I have my duffel bag out of the baggage carousel.

Everyone else can fight it out for a five minute start to their heart's content. Two passengers do, and with eyes closed and the top of my head resting against the low ceiling over my seat, I listen to their raised voices intertwined with that of a flight attendant. It doesn't take long for them to realize the door is open, however, and the verbal combatants shuffle for the door at max speed. Which unfortunately isn't much faster than what I would consider a snail's speed.

Still, I wait until there's enough space for me to sidle out of the seat with my backpack in my hand. I won't throw it over my shoulder for now, since hitting someone in the face with it could be seen as an act of war in some areas of Florida. I keep pace with the person in front of me until I get to the door; the flight attendant's smile is empty below her tired eyes as she wishes me well on my travels before turning to look at the next person in the ever shuffling line of passengers.

When I'm free of the crowd and my feet are safely on the concourse, I let out a heavy breath, tilting my head back to loosen some of the strain in my neck and shoulders. I don't love flying, and the Dramamine I took still drags at the edges of my brain and pulls my thoughts to the sluggish side. It's not enough to slow me down, however, and my steps open up as I follow the baggage signs. I'm barely paying attention to my surroundings except to weave around other people as they rush for their flights or shuffle to the baggage claim as well.

My legs are burning by the time I find the sign proclaiming I'm there. I let out a huff of air and look for my flight number on the lit up boards above each carousel, eyes skimming over the people milling around them in groups without actually looking at anyone.

But when my eyes find my carousel and the bags already moving through it like tubes on a lazy river, I stop. I blink once, then again, my brain telling me in that drowsy, medicine-affected way that I've missed something important. *Really* important, though I have no idea what it might be.

I look up and see a group of passengers I recognize, including one of the loud, irritated women from the front of the plane. Her attitude doesn't seem to have improved, and she scowls at the baggage carousel like the force of her will can make it go faster.

But that's not it. I don't care about her.

My eyes flick from face to face, and I ignore the people

coming and going as I scramble to figure out what my brain has missed as it screams its importance to the back of my mind.

Until my gaze lands on my dark purple, slightly beat up bag that I've had for the past four years. I'd bought it specifically for these trips, to be easy and light when I travel to and from school.

Only, it isn't on the carousel where it belongs.

Long fingers clamp around the black straps, and I follow the hand up to a black-clad arm and over to the front of a hoodie that reads *Wickett University* on its front in big, blocky letters. Finally I look up, blinking a few times at a face I haven't seen in over a month, and a smile that hits me harder than it should.

"Welcome back, Blair," Oliver greets, all enthusiasm and golden retriever energy as he makes his way toward me, still carrying my duffel in one hand. "Want me to take your backpack? You look pretty–"

"How are you here?" I ask, barely acknowledging what he's saying or that I've interrupted him. Not that he looks upset about it. In fact, his smile hitches wider across his full lips, eyes dancing in a face that could break the hearts of any woman with a taste for adorable men.

"I drove," he tells me slowly, like it's understandable I might need the clarification. "Then I looked for your flight and waited here for you."

"But I didn't tell you that I was coming back today."

"You're right."

"And I definitely didn't tell you what flight or airline I was taking."

"You most certainly did not."

I bite my lower lip, let it go, then do it again. Even in my tired state, it's impossible to miss the way his eyes flick down to my mouth, his own lips parting slightly like he'd much rather be the one with his teeth sunk into my flesh.

"Are you stalking me long distance?" I ask at last, prompting him for some kind of explanation.

His gaze flicks back up, widening in surprise and something like confusion or hurt.

But God, it can't be *hurt*. Oliver doesn't get hurt feelings.

Right?

"That's a strong word," he says finally, smiling apologetically. "Maybe I've been coming here every day and checking flights from Indianapolis for you."

"That's obsessive," I can't help but point out slowly, though there's no real heat in my words.

He shrugs, his gaze sliding to the side like he's a kid caught doing something he shouldn't. "You're not exactly the first one to say that."

"Yeah, that doesn't really shock me." But insults don't feel correct, even though my skin prickles with both fear and anticipation at his closeness. "Thank you," I say in a rush, taking a last step closer to him. "Though I'm not sure I'm worth all that effort."

His smile is suddenly blinding, and he closes the last of the distance between us before leaning forward, one hand coming out to gently, oh so gently, press against my hoodie-covered hip. "You're worth more," Oliver agrees, and kisses me sweetly in a way that begs me to drop all my worries and fears that have come back in full force.

I reach up as well, the hand not on my backpack strap finding his arm and gripping lightly until he suddenly flinches. A grimace crosses his features and makes me spring back like I've hurt him somehow with my light touch. "Oliver?" I scan his features, worry replacing enough of the fear to turn my thoughts away from my own problems. "Are you okay? Did I…"

I trail off when he licks his lips, and this close I can see the split in them and a bruise on his temple. "You're hurt."

"You don't have to worry about it," he assures me, not stepping away.

"It wasn't..." I know my words are dangerous, but curiosity gets the better of me. "It wasn't Professor Solomon, right?"

His snort is all the answer I need, but the incredulity in his gaze seals the truth of it for me. "Absolutely not."

"Then what—"

"Do you want to go? It's kind of loud in here." He looks around for emphasis. "And cold. My car has *heat*."

Despite it being much warmer here than back in Indianapolis, heat sounds embarrassingly good right now. Even though he still stirs fear through my chest with every look and glance towards me, I follow him without a word. I almost have to trot through the airport to match his longer, more confident strides. I watch him while I do, studying his reactions and expressions.

There's something wrong with him.

But I've known that for months now, and it isn't what fascinates me now. What fascinates me is the fact that if I didn't know better, I wouldn't have been able to tell at all. He's just so perfect at his act. At proving himself to be the friendly twenty-something year old who's unassuming, non-threatening, and so normal it makes my teeth hurt.

Is it even an act? It has to be, when I've seen the truth. When I know what he looks like when the mask falls and he does the unthinkable. Images of his face the night he killed Rob flash through my mind like stop motion animation, the movements in my inner eye not entirely smooth or realistic.

I don't realize that we've made it outside until he stops at the car he'd driven last semester as well. The sleek, dark outside is unobtrusive in the parking garage, and he pops the trunk, gently settling my duffel bag in it. Any potential protests die in my throat at the sight. And when he reaches out a hand for my backpack, I give it to him without a word, happy that I'm not being thrown in the trunk along with them.

When the trunk slams closed, I walk like a zombie to the passenger side, sliding into the seat and buckling my seatbelt with trembling fingers. He's only a second behind me, and by the time the heat is on and warming up the light chill that's chased us in from the parking garage, I've remembered all the reasons this really is an awful, terrible idea.

He's a murderer.

A serial killer who'd murdered women who looked like my roommate because she'd pissed him off by cautioning me. But here I am, sitting beside him like everything is fine and I'm not bothered by any of it.

But I am. I am, especially in the small confines of his car and when I'm here, breathing in the scent of his cologne and *his* scent under it, that draws me in almost against my will.

In fact, I don't realize I'm leaning toward him until he turns, one hand coming up to brush my hair back from my face. "How about I take you home, wonder girl?" he breathes, his green eyes sweet and earnest. "So you can get some sleep and relax. Does that sound okay?"

Fighting not to lean into him as my stomach churns, I nod. "Yeah," I agree. "That's, umm. I'd really appreciate that, Oliver. Thank you."

CHAPTER 2

"Hey, Blair?" Oliver's voice is impossibly kind, and his hand on my shoulder is gentle, his fingers trailing over my hoodie. "We're home."

I let out a breath through my nose, but don't open my eyes. He's not waking me up. I've been awake for a few minutes now, and it had been immediately obvious to me that we are *not* in fact home.

Well, not my home at least.

I shake my head and bury myself more firmly in my hood. "Did you forget something?" I murmur into the soft fabric. "This isn't *my* home."

"Well, I didn't specify, and you didn't correct me," Oliver replies, a hint of wickedness in his tone that makes something in me stir. It's fear, definitely. I won't accept anything else, especially when his hand moves to tuck my hair behind my ear. "Do you want me to carry you?"

"Do you want a repeat of the last time you carried me into your house?"

"Depends on how much of a repeat. You, uh, kind of

knocked yourself out last time," he reminds me, not unkindly. Though, if he really meant to be nice about it, he would've 'forgotten' about that incident.

"I meant the kicking, punching, and hitting you." My eyes open at last, falling on the brown-tinged grass of his yard that waves in the light breeze as if begging for water from the sky above. The trees are less full than they will be later in the year, and I turn my head just enough to look at the front of his and Rook's large, grandiose house.

I could never afford something like this, no matter what kind of art history job I obtain in the years to come. "How does Professor Solomon afford this?" I ask, blinking a few times to clear my eyes of sleep. Then I rub them as well, dragging my palms against my face to chase away the itch of sleep. "I didn't think professors made *this* much. Maybe I should change my career ambitions."

"Maybe you shouldn't." Oliver chuckles, unbuckling both of our seatbelts and politely making sure mine doesn't smack me in the face. "This isn't from his professor's salary. His photography work is incredibly well-known, and he was paid well to take portraits a few years ago. But it bored him," he adds, in answer to my next question. "He said being that being well-known wasn't good for his hobbies, so he 'retired' and started teaching instead."

"He's a terrible professor," I point out, stretching my legs as much as I can in the seat. My leggings slide against my skin, the fleece lining soft and giving me the warmth that I wouldn't have gotten in a thinner material.

"He's a great professor," Oliver argues, opening the door and allowing the light chill to seep into the car, ruining my cocoon of comfortable warmth. It saps the drowsiness from me and I straighten as well, running my fingers through my hair.

"Are you going to take me home?" I ask, more casually than

I feel, belying the pounding of my heart in my chest and the way my hands shake. "Or am I being kidnapped?"

"You're not being kidnapped," he laughs, flashing me a quick grin. "We've already played that game. Though..." he trails off thoughtfully, and I know that can't be good. "I'm into that, and last time wasn't exactly *sexy*. Do you want to try again?"

"No."

"I bet you'd like it."

I throw him a pained, exasperated look. "Are you going to take me home, or am I going to have to knock you out and take your keys?"

He blinks, looking thoughtful, and mulls over my words. "I'll take you home in the morning," he says finally, and when I glance at the clock in his car, I see that it's almost eleven at night. "Juniper isn't back yet—"

"God, you're such a stalker—"

"And once she's back, she's going to convince you to play it safe around me again." A shrewd, unhappy expression crosses his features, and it sets my entire being on edge as the hairs at the back of my neck prickle with concern.

"She hasn't done anything to you," I remind him in a rush, my tone breathy. "She doesn't hate you, and she isn't actively trying to get me away from you, Oliver. You can't—"

"Kill the rest of the population that reminds me of her?" His head tilts to the side, the look in his eyes almost inhuman in its cold, calculating feel. "Is that what you were going to say?"

It's so jarring when he reminds me what he is, but validating, too. Because I sometimes forget that under his sweetness and his enthusiasm, this is the real him. "Yes," I say, refusing to look away or give him my fear or my trepidation. I won't beg for him to be kind when I don't think he knows how to be kind to those he doesn't care about. "I won't be around you if you do."

"Oh, but Blair..." He reaches out, a smile catching his lips and dragging them upwards into something both amused and cold. "You're implying that as long as I *don't* hurt her or anyone else that reminds me of her, that you won't leave me. Is that true, wonder girl? You won't leave me?"

For a moment, I can't speak. My breath catches in my chest, and the chill that creeps up my spine is less from the cold and all from *him.*

At last, after a few long moments that feel like centuries, I knock his hand away with a scowl and pull back toward my door. "I'll leave you if I want to leave you," I say, and open the door so I can step out onto the driveway, trying not to look like I'm running from him.

Oliver hops out with much more grace than me, and less urgency. But before I can think to grab my bags, he does it for me, shouldering my backpack and hoisting my duffel bag over one arm while I watch.

"Rook missed you," he tells me conversationally, the cruelty sapped from him like the cold has simply whisked it away. "He won't say it out loud, but I can tell. He was worried, too, since you weren't streaming or messaging us."

"Well, I kind of had a good reason," I point out absently, taking the time to really look around the outside of his house. It's just so... *normal.* Of course, I don't expect there to be a sign in the front yard with SERIAL KILLERS LIVE HERE emblazoned on it in large, blocky letters. But it doesn't feel right that they can look so harmless to their neighbors.

"Eh, I don't know. You were never in any danger from us, Blair. You will *never* be in any danger from us." His voice gains an edge to it at the end, but I don't get a chance to say whatever it is that bubbles to my lips when he opens the door and strides inside, confident that I'll follow.

Though since he has my things, it is kind of obvious that I'm not going anywhere else. I close the door behind me, the warm, spicy scent of candles curls up my nostrils as I glance around the house. It looks the same as the last time I was here. Though, as I've only been here three times, I find new details as my eyes flick through the living space.

The television in the living room is on, though muted, and I let my attention linger on whatever reality show takes up the screen before following Oliver deeper into the house. In the kitchen, he rests my duffel bag on a chair and hooks my backpack over the back before stepping back with a sigh and a roll of his shoulders.

"Where's Professor Solomon?" I ask, looking around the space.

"I think he's in the living room. He doesn't leave things on when he leaves the room, but I'm surprised he didn't hear us come in," Oliver admits, turning back toward the living room and walking into the open space. I follow, eyes on the sofa until a blanket-covered shape comes into view.

He's... *sleeping*.

As I edge around to look at his face in the glow from the lamps and the lights flickering from the television, it hits me how different he looks when he's unconscious and the lines in his sharply handsome face are smooth.

"He looks so... nice," I say, surprised at myself and the fact that it's *true*. "And not very scary."

"You think so?" Oliver stands beside me, tilting his head to the side as he crosses his arms. "I don't know. I've always felt he looks like he's waiting for something."

"Or for someone to disappoint him," I quip. "That feels very him, don't you think?"

"Oh, absolutely—"

"I'm not asleep," my ex-professor says with a sigh, lips barely moving and his eyes not opening. "So I'm going to do you both the favor of stopping you now, before I hear something that requires me to get the handcuffs." My stomach clenches and unclenches, and I watch as his eyes flutter open under his dark, thick lashes that frame them so well.

God, it should be illegal for a serial killer to be this gorgeous. He stretches languidly like a cat, and his eyes finally roll to mine, making me realize I'm fucking *staring*. "This isn't an art gallery, Love," he purrs, using what I've come to believe is his nickname for me, even though it's also my actual name.

"What?" I ask, not understanding what he means as I feel a blush burn up my cheeks. "I didn't—"

"You don't have to just look." The implications settle into me, and I know there's no longer any chance of me hiding the embarrassment that stains my face like paint. Oliver snorts at my side, and Professor Solomon reaches out to snag his hand, looking up at him with concern. "Are you feeling okay?" he asks, the care in his voice drowning out the sleep. He sits up and pulls Oliver down to him until the latter is almost on his lap. "How's your shoulder?"

Oliver grimaces and glances up at me, making me feel like a third wheel. "I'm fine, Rook," he mutters sullenly, cutting his gaze to the side.

Rook looks up as well, following Oliver's glance until he meets my face. "You didn't tell her," he murmurs, trailing his fingers through the younger boy's hair. "You don't want her to know."

"Know what?" I find myself asking, unsure if I *should* be curious.

Oliver makes a sound of dissent, but Rook ignores him to say bluntly, "He dislocated his shoulder a week ago."

"Holy shit." Stupidly, I sit down on the couch, eyes on Oliver's face as he studies the wall intently. "Are you okay? Is that why your face is bruised? Did you *fall*?"

"I didn't fall, Blair," he informs me plainly, green eyes flicking to mine. "I'm fine."

"What happened?" I repeat, unable to help my curiosity and building concern. "Shit, Oliver, I'm sorry. I shouldn't have let you carry my bag. Why didn't you tell me?"

He makes another irritated noise and glares up at his boyfriend. I look up at him as well, unable to miss the play of a smirk across his features. "You did this on purpose."

"Maybe," Rook agrees, nosing Oliver's temple. "But is it really so bad if she knows the truth, Oliver? You claim to want her in our lives completely. That means you can't keep shit from her like you do from everyone else."

Oliver glances at me again, his lips parting and then says, finally, "I'll tell you if you agree to stay the night. But I don't think you really want to know."

"Curiosity may have killed the cat," I admit. "But satisfaction brought her back, remember?"

"I don't think that applies here."

"If you don't tell me, then I'll call an Uber."

He doesn't reply right away. Instead, Oliver throws a glance upward, eyes glittering with irritation at his partner, before extending a hand to me, pinky sticking upward toward me. He tilts his hand, points it at me accusingly, and cocks a brow when I don't move.

"I'll tell you," he repeats. "If you pinky swear to stay the night."

Out of all the awful decisions I've made over the past six months, surely staying here, with them, isn't anywhere near the worst of them. Trepidation churns my stomach, along with my curiosity. But it isn't until Rook shifts that I look at him, his dark eyes fixed on my face like he's trying to read me before I open my mouth.

Is he afraid of what I'll say? Or worried I'll slap Oliver's hand away and hurt his feelings to the point where he definitely won't want to open up to me?

Jun's warnings flicker through my head, and the mental argument I've had with myself at least six times over winter break follows. The words sound accusing even when they're inaudible to anyone else.

You're really going to stick around with the boy who killed girls who look like your roommate and the man who would easily do the same if given the chance?

Saying I've struggled with the idea is an understatement. Especially since the adrenaline that pumped through me last semester has long since faded, and I'm fully in control of my decisions.

If I stay, if I let this continue, there will be nothing to blame except *me*. There can be no excuses this time, or reasons to give myself that I *had* to, or my thoughts being muddled.

I've told myself for weeks that whenever the opportunity presents itself, I must break ties with them in a way that's safe for me, and safe for Juniper. There's no other option right now except to *leave*.

And yet...

And yet I can't help it when my hand lifts like it's being dragged upward by magnets. I can't seem to stop the anxious half-smile that curls my lips when I hook my finger around his and the contact jolts through me like electricity.

"Sure, I promise. Unless dinner sucks and I have to go get food," I bargain, my eyes flicking between them as uncomfortable questions claw at the back of my brain. I'll deal with them later, though. Not right now. There's only so much room in my head right now, and both Rook and Oliver are occupying every square inch of it.

"I'm cooking," Rook informs me, getting to his feet with a sigh. "So it's not going to *suck*." He glances down at our joined hands and I can't tell what he's thinking as he studies them. "What are you in the mood for?" he glances up at my face when he says it, though reaches out to smooth a hand through Oliver's hair in a surprisingly tender gesture that makes my heart twist.

When Oliver looks up, face falling and vulnerable for half a second, my heart just about flops onto the floor to pant in jealousy.

"Breakfast," I say, with only a touch of hesitation. "If I get a say, then definitely breakfast."

"Of course you get a say." His words are dry, bored, like I'm not saying anything worth his interest. He drops his hand from Oliver, eyes our hands again, then walks away with the feline grace that he always seems to possess, even when he's just woken up from a nap on the sofa.

"Your boyfriend is weird," I mutter, half to myself, though Oliver chuckles and suddenly jerks me downward, using my pinky finger as leverage until I'm on the sofa beside him.

"I missed you, wonder girl," he informs me, drawing my eyes up to a face that's lit with his glimmering green gaze. "Did you watch any of my streams while you were home?"

I screw my face up into apologetic bewilderment. "No," I lie, because I'm absolutely not going to tell him I watched every single fucking one of them. "No, I didn't. I was busy having an existential crisis over you giving me a polaroid of a dead body."

"Liar," he chuckles, rucking a long-fingered hand through his messy hair. "I have viewer logs, and you forgot to log out of your account, darling."

Shit. That was incredibly careless of me. I scowl at the oversight, pulling a laugh from him as he sits back and tugs me with him.

I try to unwrap my finger from his, but the moment I do his hand is around my wrist, and unless I *really* want to fight him, I have no choice but let him pull me into his lap. Then his legs come up to bracket my hips as he drags me flush against the warm, firm planes of his body.

Fear courses through me when I realize that I'm trapped, but so do images of the night on my stream when he'd fucked me for my viewers and helped me make more money than I'd ever seen in my life. It's not right for him to be so charming, but articles about Ted Bundy's social skills swim before my eyes, giving me proof that not all serial killers are like Rob.

Well, Rob wasn't even a serial killer, to be fair. He was just pathetic, desperate, and obsessed.

"Don't fight me," Oliver breathes, wrapping an arm around my waist. "You don't need to fight me."

"Oh, yeah?" I demand, even as he uses his arm to crush any empty air between our bodies. "Why's that, Oliver?"

"Because you can use your words and get much better results."

"Now who's the liar?"

He raises his brows, looking so like Rook for a moment that it shocks me into stillness and dries my mouth like the Sahara desert.

"Try me," Oliver invites. "Stop fighting, and use your words for me, Blair."

"Take your arm off of me," I order instantly, knowing that the result will be nothing except a laugh and him telling me to get serious.

Except... it isn't. He takes his arm off of me and I sit up, still in the v of his thighs but just far enough away that I can press my hand against the flat of his stomach if I wish.

"Tilt your head back," I go on, just to see if he will.

He does.

Oliver drapes himself back on the arm of the couch, letting his head fall back until the line of his neck is on display for me, whether I want to slit his throat or mark it up as mine. He shouldn't trust me like this. He doesn't know me. I could hurt him, or leave, or any number of things and with him not paying any attention, he would never see it coming.

"Oh," I mutter finally, unsure of how else to react.

In response, he chuckles and sits up more comfortably, legs still around me but using the armrest as a cushion for his lower back instead of draping himself along it. He reaches out, palm upraised, and finally turns his hand just so he can tuck my hair behind my ear. "Are you just going to stare at me, Blair?" he purrs, eyes dancing with mischief. He knows the effect he has on me, and it's nothing short of unfair. "Or do you want to hear what happened to my shoulder?"

CHAPTER 3

"It's not that exciting," Oliver tells me, though the way he glances towards the kitchen, as if he either wishes Rook was here or that he hadn't said anything, doesn't go unnoticed by me.

"You don't have to tell me if you don't want to," I find myself saying in the face of his unsureness. I don't want to force him to, though when I say it his gaze snaps to mine, unreadable, and his mouth twists into a wry grin.

"Don't do that," he murmurs, his expression sly.

"Do what?"

"Take it back. You wanted to know, and I said I'd tell you. Commit to the deal, wonder girl." His words prickle up my spine, but I don't say anything.

I don't know what to say, after all.

"I was adopted," he tells me, heaving a sigh as he readjusts his legs, knee bumping into my ribs. I lean on his other leg that's pressed against the back of the couch, hoping he can't see just how curious I am to hear whatever it is he did.

"And you dislocated your shoulder being adopted?" I ask, unsure why that has anything to do with this story.

He rolls his eyes in exasperation, though his smile turns apologetic, boyish.

Charming.

God, he shouldn't be so charming.

"Sometimes I go back home to, uh, see how things are going." It feels like something more than that, but I've already pushed my luck tonight and I don't know how much more I can get away with here. "Not out of love. Just out of... self interest?" He cocks his head to the side, thinking. "Whatever. I went back and someone was there that I used to know. They don't like me. He never liked me, truth be told." His eyes suddenly go flat. Like all the emotion has been sucked dry as he looks at me again.

"I was dumb," Oliver admits, shrugging his uninjured shoulder. "I should've known to *never* give someone the opportunity to hurt me once, let alone twice." My insides clench, but not in fear. No, it's sympathy that twists me up into knots, and the urge to find out just how badly he was hurt.

This time *and* before.

"It was a good thing Rook was there. He did that thing he does, where he takes someone apart so artfully and beautifully."

"I don't think murder can be pretty," I comment without thinking, earning a snort from the older boy.

"You would be wrong. He's *gorgeous* when he's covered in blood and viscera and *insides*." With my body against his leg, I feel the full body shudder that travels through him, and I watch the way he tilts his head back once more, like he can't get enough of the memory. "And what he does is just as gorgeous. It was sad, though. *I* was sad," he amends, and lets out a huff into the air over the sofa.

"Because you fucked up your shoulder and face?" I ask, assuming the most obvious reason for it.

"Because he insisted on taking me to the hospital instead of *fucking* me in the cooling blood that stained the snow red."

There's nothing to say to that. I stare at him, head tilted to the side like a confused dog, and wait for the hamster wheel in my brain to come up with *something* that isn't completely worthless for me to open my mouth and say.

In the end, I have nothing. Oliver smiles at me as he waits, beautiful with his teeth-flashing grin, and chooses not to help me out by giving me anything to work with, or adding to the conversation to move us past this impossible point.

Thankfully, Rook chooses that moment to save the day. Movement from the corner of my eye draws my attention, and I look over to see him leaning on the wall, gaze on both of us. "Breakfast is ready," he explains, when Oliver raises his brows. "What do you want to drink, Love?"

"Umm..." The question catches me off guard. I'm an adult who can get my own drink, but he asks it like it's *obvious* he should get it for me, just as *obvious* that I should stay here for dinner, and let Oliver drive me home.

It's caring in a strange way, and at odds with everything they should stand for.

"Water?" I ask, not knowing what they have, but also not wanting to ask for anything outlandish or weird.

"She drinks chocolate milk when she gets pancakes out," Oliver supplies, drawing my attention. "You can have both," he assures me when he meets my eyes, getting to his feet and pulling me up with him. He follows Rook into the kitchen, pulling me along, but I wouldn't have tried to leave anyway.

I'd promised, after all.

The table is set with three sets of plates and cups, and my brows raise at the amount of food he'd cooked in a relatively short amount of time. Scrambled eggs, bacon, toast, and fresh fruit wait for me, and I sit down just as Rook places a glass of chocolate milk in front of my plate. Oliver sprawls down beside me, a sigh on his lips as he leans gingerly back against the chair.

"You should take care of me," he informs his partner as our professor sits down in his own seat with a glass of water and another of what might be apple juice in front of him. "I'm in pain. Don't you love me?"

Rook hums into his glass as he takes a drink and gestures for me to get food. "You drove to the airport, carried her bags, and brought her home," he states dryly, without looking up when his glass is back on the table. "You clearly don't need me to *coddle* you, Oliver."

"Thank you," I break in, before Oliver can do something totally reasonable like flip the damn table. I put two pieces of toast on my plate, then move for the bacon and eggs. "This looks amazing. And I'm really grateful."

"You're welcome, Love," Rook rumbles softly, his fingers brushing over the backs of my knuckles as I pull it back. "How was your break, anyway? Now that Oliver's harrowing summary of ours is over."

It isn't exactly *over*. He'd barely told me anything at all.

I think back to my own winter break, from theorizing about the murders of those girls that have now been 'solved' by putting the wrong person away, to lying to my parents. They don't know anything about my last semester. Not more than surface level details, anyway. They don't know about my cam work, about Oliver, about *anything*.

And they never will.

"It was fine," I shrug, using my fork to cut up the scrambled eggs as I look for ketchup on the table. Given that some people think it's blasphemy to even consider, the fact that it isn't beside the butter tells me that they probably feel that way too. Asking would probably earn *me* a stabbing, and not the fun kind. "I just spent it with my parents and saw some of my extended family." Extended and held at arm's length, due to how little I *like* them.

"I notice you didn't sign up for my spring photography class," Rook goes on, his voice low. My hand tenses around the fork, but I eye him surreptitiously as I take a bite, wondering if he's upset, shocked, or just saying it.

"I'm not a masochist," I say finally, sweetly, with some kind of smile on my face that I hope looks believable. "I'm trying to keep up my GPA since I'll be graduating at the end of this semester."

To my other side, Oliver stirs, and I look at him to see him look almost... worried?

"What?" I can't help but ask, but he shakes his head.

"I forgot this was your last semester is all," he explains, one shoulder lifting and falling in a shrug.

"So no photography, then?" Rook goes on, nonchalant-ness coloring his tone.

"I'd rather be murdered," I reply cheerfully.

"Funny." He tears off a piece of his toast and puts it into his mouth, chewing thoughtfully. The look on his face, in his dark eyes, won't bode well for me in the long run, but I refuse to give in or look scared. "You didn't do *poorly* last semester," he goes on at last, finishing off the toast as I cram my last piece of bacon into my mouth. "You did really well for a beginner."

That definitely stings more than it should, and I wonder if he realizes how much of a backhanded compliment the words are.

"Cool. I'll consider it my questionable elective of the past four years," I shrug, watching him from the corner of my eye. Looking at Oliver, I realize he's doing the same, and he's being quieter than normal. "How, uh, how was the rest of your break?" I hurry to add, wanting to move him off this subject. "Did you—"

"What do you say to a bet?" Rook's not listening to me, and obviously has no intention of letting me talk him out of this particular subject.

"If I win, do I get custody of Oliver?"

"Do you *want* custody of Oliver?" He glances at me, incredulous and disbelieving.

But he's right.

Oliver makes a noise, sounding slightly affronted. "I'm not a child," the serial killer reminds us. "Not even close."

Rook smiles sweetly at him as I struggle not to scoff. "Of course you're not, sweetheart," he agrees, tone placating. "You're a big, bad adult."

"And we love you for it," I add just as sweetly. "No, I don't want custody of Oliver."

"Well, what do you want?"

"World peace."

If Rook rolls his eyes any harder, I worry they'll disappear in the back of his head for good. "You're such a brat," he informs me, but the words are too warm to be a true insult. "Don't let him rub off on you. If I catch you keying my car like him, you're not going to be able to walk for a week."

"Don't threaten me with a good time," I mutter, too tired to be as quiet or meek as I should, given the circumstances.

I'm also too tired and slow to do anything when he reaches out to grab my hair, pulling my head back just enough that I have no choice but to meet his eyes.

"You like this too much *not* to take my class," the dark-eyed professor purrs, his eyes catching and holding mine. "What can I offer you that will get you in my classroom, so I get to look at you and Oliver at least twice a week?"

When I open my mouth again, his eyebrows rise by increments, silently warning me to give him a *real* answer.

"I..." I search my brain, unable to come up with something worthwhile, or something he'd really bargain. "There's absolutely no way I can let my grades fall. So I *can't* take a class that will drag my GPA down right before graduation. I *suck* at photography."

"You don't suck," Oliver protests. "You're really good."

I turn to look at him as much as I can with Rook's hand still in my hair. "He gave me a B. *Minus*."

"I gave you the grade you deserved." He mulls over the thought. "I'll help you," Rook says finally. "I can't promise an A for no work, obviously." Releasing my hair, Rook sits back. "But I'll help you. I'll mentor you and help you with your art history final. Last semester, you wanted to add a photography component. It would set you apart from your peers to do something that different."

I scrunch my face up in thought, though I'm still not sure this is a good idea.

But he's right. And so far, I haven't come up with something better than the idea I'd had last semester.

"Fine," I say, drawing my leg up to press my heel against the seat under me and wrap my arms around my knee. "Fine. I'll sign up for your class. But if I can't get an A on the first assignment, then I'm dropping it. Deal?"

"Deal," Rook agrees, a small, half-smile on his lips that brings a very certain worry to my chest.

The worry that I'm absolutely, without a doubt, going to regret this.

After dinner, I find that all the energy I thought I had disappears in a puff of jet lag flavored smoke. I press my face against my hands, sighing against my palm and letting my eyes fall closed. "I didn't mean to be this tired," I murmur, hearing Rook get to his feet beside me. He leans over to kiss my hair, and from under my arms I can feel him pluck my plate off of the table in front of me.

"You deserve to be tired. You were traveling all day," Oliver reminds me, the sound of his chair pushing back gets me to open my eyes. When I do, I find his hand in front of my face, offered to me with patience and his sweet grin. "Come on, Blair. Want to go to bed?"

This isn't in my plan of reminding myself why I *can't* do things like this with them anymore. This isn't in any of my plans, but I place my hand in his anyway, and let him tug me away from the kitchen. I don't say anything as he does, but I stride along behind him as he leads me down Rook's side of the house. I haven't seen his office, though I try to peek in there now with no success.

Instead, Oliver opens Rook's door, showing me his king-size bed covered in multiple, dark-colored blankets and strewn with pillows.

"Why do we never sleep in your bed?" I ask curiously, stopping to peel off my hoodie and toss it to the bench at the foot of the bed. "I know you have one."

"My bed isn't as big as Rook's," he admits, picking up the blankets and jiggling them in invitation with a wag of his brows. "And my room is a mess right now." *Right now,* he says, as if it's not been a wreck before. According to Rook, or what he said last semester anyway, Oliver's room is always a mess.

I throw myself onto the bed with a groan, curling up on my side as Oliver slides in behind me, his arm over my waist. There's still a feeling of trepidation in my gut, of anxiety, but some of that fades when Oliver hooks an arm around me and drags me close.

The rest of it vanishes when Rook comes in and slides into

the bed as well, at my front instead of behind Oliver, and I can feel his eyes on me even though mine are closed.

"We'll let you sleep in," he promises, an arm over my shoulders and my face nearly pressed to his chest. His hand isn't on me, and judging by the movement I feel, that's because he's stroking Oliver's arm. Once in a while I feel his fingertips, and before long he's moving his hand between us, touching both of our exposed skin in turn.

I can't help but shiver every time he does, and a part of me stirs in excitement, though I know I'm too tired for more than this. Still, I sneak a hand up between us to curl it in his collar, moving just enough that I can press my hips back against Oliver's and my face against Rook's chest.

Is it wrong that it feels this fucking amazing being trapped between the two of them, with both of their hands on me? Any conversation between them is quick and soft, and the silence along with their presence quickly lulls me toward sleep.

Something's wrong with me, I whisper to myself, silently. *Something is wrong for me to like this so much.* Not just like it, but some part of me begs for it to go further. For Oliver to hook a finger in my leggings and pull them down enough to tease me, if not outright fuck me.

But I chase the feelings away and move again, my nose still pressed against Rook's chest and my arm hooked over his shoulders in a desperate plea for sleep.

It works, and I fade off with the sound of their soft voices in my ears, while their gentle touches and firm grip are the last things that I feel.

CHAPTER 4

P rofessor Carmine's office is just as severe as she is. The room is decorated sparsely, with only a few of her favorite pieces decorating the walls in neat, black frames and so perfectly hung that I would be willing to bet she'd used a level to do it. Her file cabinets are black and labeled, and her desk, with only a few photos and trinkets, is so orderly that it's hard to believe someone actually *works* here in the small office.

I fidget in the chair across from her, remembering the last time I'd been in one of these small offices. Rook had taken that time to give me a *B minus* for his class, and I'd felt like throwing one of his file cabinets out the window in an attempt to crush his car. Now I feel somewhat better, but with no idea *why* Professor Carmine wants to speak to me, it's impossible not to be nervous.

"I hope you're looking forward to your final semester?" My professor, who must be nearing the modest age of seven hundred and two, rests her elbows on the desk to peer at me over her glasses. With her ghostly blue eyes, pale skin, and white hair, she looks like a ghost that hasn't yet realized she died two centuries ago.

"Uh, yeah," I agree, glancing up at her from under my bangs. There's a lot more to that answer than *uh yeah* can communicate, but if I haven't told Juniper or my parents, I'm certainly not about to tell my favorite professor.

"I'm not good at small talk," my professor admits, tapping her fingers on the back of a thick textbook. "Would you want to be my teaching assistant this semester, Blair?"

"Yes," I say, without needing to think about it. I blurt out the word before I can stop myself and offer her a half-apologetic smile. "If you'll have me. I would love to be your TA."

"Have you TA'd for anyone else? I almost thought Professor Solomon would rope you in, but he's still having Oliver do all of his work." She shakes her head, like she doesn't approve of one or both of them.

"Was Oliver ever in your classes?" I ask, curiosity prickling at my tone.

"He was. The worst, best student I've ever had." She rolls her eyes, then adds, "He's amazing when he puts his mind to it. But that's so rare, and he always seemed to want to be somewhere else."

Yeah, I could guess *where*. Or at the very least, with who.

"Oh," is all I can think to say. "He's great with photography. He was kind of my mentor last semester." It's not quite the truth, but it's better than a lie.

"Just be careful with him." My professor sighs, pulling out a folder labeled with the words *Teaching Assistant*. "Everything you need is in here. Unfortunately, I'm running behind already. If you know the basic ideas?"

"Yes," I tell her, trying to sound confident and not as nervous as I feel on the inside. My heart flutters against my ribs, and the glow of pride travels up my spine to warm my face. I'm thrilled that she asked *me* out of anyone else here. "I was a TA for Professor Nicklin last year."

"Your office hours will be here in my office," Professor Carmine explains, not remarking on my comment. "We'll touch base this week about when they'll be. And I'll see you in class Wednesday."

She barely waits for my answer, but opens the door to the rest of the art department, hesitating when she does. At first I don't see why, and I pause, thinking she has something to say to me, or is waiting for some kind of answer.

Until I lean around to grab my backpack and see that the door to her office is blocked by another, broader figure.

If there's any professor I've been glad not to have, Professor Langhorn is it. Nearing retirement age, the black-haired, always-smiling man is known as 'quirky' in more polite circles of conversation.

But I've never felt that polite toward him.

I can see the irritation in Professor Carmine's posture as she looks at him, and she lets out a breath before glancing back at me. "Professor Langhorn," she greets, not seeming thrilled by his presence. "Can I help you?"

He glances up, surprise on his features moving too slowly to be real. "Oh, I am so sorry Antonia," he greets, using her first name instead of *professor*. Having been in her classes for years, even I know she prefers her colleagues to use her last name as well, and I can *feel* the disdain radiating from her when all he does is smile in the face of her dislike. "And Miss... Love, right?" he asks, gaze flipping to mine too quickly.

I settle my bag on my shoulders, offering him a half-smile that I don't feel and wishing he'd *move*. He's irritating, frustrating, and says stupid shit that all of my professors roll their eyes at. Yet somehow, he can't seem to realize that not many people here like him.

Well, except for the secretaries in the art department. For some reason, they always seem delighted when he walks in, at least every time I'm there.

"Love needs to go," Professor Carmine informs him. "If you would, Professor Langhorn...?" She gestures at him with two fingers, as if she can move him to the side with her mental powers alone.

Though if anyone could, it would definitely be her.

He smiles apologetically and mock bows, stepping to the side and letting Professor Carmine out of her office. She gestures me out as well, and I stand uncomfortably, glancing at the other side of the hallway where Professor Solomon's office is.

The door is closed, lights in the small slat windows out. He isn't in there, though if he was, I would be over there instead of here, at least until Langhorn finds something better to do.

So much for me hanging around for a while to get some work done.

I smile at both professors, pretending not to hear the stupid quote from some obscure play he throws at Professor Carmine, wiggling his brows as he does so. He's married, I know, and she doesn't look in any way impressed by his words.

"Goodbye, Love," he calls, causing me to come to a halt and look back at him so that I don't come off as rude. "If you're going to hold office hours, maybe I'll have to come to them," he chuckles. "I never was clear about that art history stuff."

I laugh in agreement, feeling less and less comfortable by the second. He's just so *awkward*, though this is definitely tame for him. "Yeah, okay," I agree, hating that he was clearly *eavesdropping* on my conversation with Professor Carmine. And by her face, she doesn't like it either. As he draws her back into reluctant conversation, obviously not seeing the pinched, displeased expression on her face, I take off down the hallway, intent on finding somewhere else to get my shit together and make sure Rook's spring photography class has been properly added to my schedule.

When my front door opens with my hand reaching towards the knob, I freeze, eyes flicking up to Juniper's face as she opens the door wider.

Her eyebrows jerk upward, then she grins in delight at seeing me. "I was trying to wait for you to get back," she says, moving away from the door so I can come in. "I'm meeting up with Jesse tonight."

"Ooooh," I wince in empathy. "How's that going?" Last I'd heard, they'd been on the outs. If that's changed, I'll be surprised. Doubly so, considering that the reason for this fight is on Jesse, and Juniper takes a long time to forgive.

"It's... going," she says, her vagueness more proof that while it might be going, it isn't going *well* by any means. She sighs and refocuses, looking me over thoughtfully.

Uh oh.

"How's Oliver?" Her words are shrewd, the meaning behind them clear, as well as her disapproval. "You haven't said anything about him since we've been back, and he hasn't been here." My phone goes off in my pocket, and her brows rise. "That him?"

"Probably," I tell her, fear rising in my throat. "Can you just...leave him alone? Please? He's not what you think he is." *He's way worse.* "Oliver's a good guy." I need her to believe it. I need her to get out from between Oliver and me, before he snaps, and killing girls that look like her isn't good enough anymore.

Doubts bubble to life in my head, thoughts fleeting and accusations thrown around like tennis balls through my skull.

He's a serial killer.

He's insane.

I should run and never let him touch me again.

But the worst one of all is one that I hear loud and clear above the others.

What kind of person am I that I haven't gone to the police or told my parents? Or Juniper... How can I let him touch me, knowing what he's done?

It bothers me, of course. It has to bother me. I refuse to let it drop or try to smooth it over in my own brain.

But I know, deep down, I'll eventually have to confront the fact that it doesn't bother me nearly enough.

"Is he?" She looks away, and I'm surprised to see both doubt and apology on her face. This fight with Jesse must really be bothering her, for her to question her opinion of someone she dislikes. But that might be a good thing for me. It means this is my chance to convince her she *is* wrong, and to leave Oliver alone before it kills her.

"He's really sweet." I try not to oversell him with my words, and absently pull my phone from my pocket, hoping to god he hasn't sent me something to the contrary.

Will you watch my stream, wonder girl? Please?

The *please* twists at my heart, but I also know instantly I can't use this as proof of his sweetness. I'm definitely not at all ready to have the conversation about my new job or Oliver's long-time career with her right now. So I stuff the phone back into my pocket, not replying to him, but also grinning up at Juniper.

"I think I'm a little in love," I tell her, though the words don't feel quite right in my mouth. Because I'm pretty sure I don't *love* Oliver, or Rook. I don't know how I feel about them, except that I know I should feel a lot worse when I think of them. But for her, I don't mind telling the lie.

"With *Oliver*?" Her eyebrows nearly disappear under her

black bangs, and her dark eyes widen. "Oliver Greer? The criminal justice major?"

"Yep."

"And he hasn't like... hypnotized you or anything?" I shake my head at her question even before she's finished asking it.

"No, Juniper," I promise her. "And weren't you leaving? You need to work this out with Jesse, don't you?" Guilt flickers in her eyes, and she glances at the door.

She sucks in a breath, teeth coming to press against her lower lip. "I owe him an apology," she admits, and when I don't respond, she clarifies with, "Jesse. And... maybe Oliver too."

Would an apology placate him? Or just piss him off more?

"I'll talk to Oliver, okay?" Glad that it seems I've mollified her towards him, maybe; at least for now. Some of the tension falls from my shoulders, and I link my hands behind my back, staring at her. "Good luck with Jesse. He's really a good guy. But you know that, or you wouldn't be considering marrying him, huh?" I wiggle my brows at her, and she ducks her head, not meeting my eyes.

For all their fights, it's obvious they were made for each other. And it's obvious they'll make it through this one as well.

"Yeah, well, if we make it that far, you're the maid of honor." She laughs, the sound brittle and humorless. "And you can't refuse."

"Fine, fine." I shoo her toward the door, flapping my hands at her like limp wings. "Go. Work through it. Have great sex while I do homework." I'm not going to do homework, and the real reason I want her to leave. Once classes start tomorrow, she'll be gone later at night than me. As she always has, Juniper picked classes for her last semester that would let her sleep in late and get home late, but I've always preferred getting out at a reasonable time of day. It means we don't see each other much, except for the weekends, but it works right now. Especially with how things are with Oliver, Rook, and me.

When she's gone, I lock the door behind her and kick off my shoes by the door before heading into my room and tossing my backpack onto the bed. I change quickly, telling myself I'm *not* hurrying to get to Oliver's stream before he starts, but it's hard to lie in the cool dimness of my bedroom.

And besides, there's not exactly anyone to lie *to*, is there? Except for myself, and that feels like a ship that's already set sail.

Finally, dressed in comfortable shorts and the hoodie that Rook bought me last year, I sit on my bed, laptop on a pillow and open as I stare at the momentarily dark screen. It boots up immediately, and I navigate to the *funxcams* site, ignoring the twelve messages I see in my inbox before heading to Oliver's page instead.

He's just started. I pull up his stream while he says something to one of his other viewers, leaning back in his chair and barely paying attention.

His mask tilts downward when I join, and I see the change in his posture almost instantly. He leans in, hands clasped on his lap, and says in an undeniably husky tone, "It's certainly been a while, *Finalistgirl*. I've missed you." The delight is obvious in his voice, and here, where there's no one to see me, I feel a smile spread over my lips.

Hi, I type into the chat bar, dragging my knees up under me to get more comfortable. *It has been a while, huh?*

Oliver's noise of contentment finds my ears, but he remembers what he is doing, and a second later replies to someone else's comment, giving them the same level of enthusiasm he'd given me. Someone tips, and I grin as *Framed_Failures* tips higher, keeping himself in first place in *letsplayjay's* stream. It has to be an ownership thing, I think. He's possessive of Oliver to the extreme, even here, where no one knows who he is.

But even though it sounds like a bad thing in my head, I can't help the slight surge of envy that tingles at my spine. Though I flex my fingers to push it away before I can stop to think about it for any longer than I have to.

If I'm envious, or jealous of them, then it'll be that much harder to figure out what I need to do to keep my head when I'm around them.

My eyes flick back to the screen, so that I'm no longer looking at my hands. I love watching Oliver work. He shimmies out of his jeans, a movement usually so awkward that it shouldn't be graceful in the least.

And yet... it is. Everything he does is so easy. So effortless. I swear that's why half of the people here are in love with him.

It's not why I've fallen for him, and my stomach twists every time I admit that to myself, but it sure as hell helps. He talks to a few others who address him, his fingers curling around his length. He's not quite as big as Rook, based on what I remember, but that certainly doesn't mean he isn't impressive here, like he is everywhere else.

He runs his fingers up and down his gently curving length, teasing the head of his cock and bucking his hips absently into his hand before settling down again.

It sends a spark of heat down between my thighs, and without thinking, I clench them together as if to create a little friction there. God, Oliver is something.

He talks as he works, his mask never leaving his face and his voice never sounding anything but engaging.

Well, until he gets excited. I see pre-cum build at his tip, and he leans back more, his hips not so willing to stay still. A big part of me wishes I was there, wishes I could do it for him or that he would fuck my face.

Even while he streams wouldn't be so bad, but I thrust the thought to the back of my head. I swear I can't be *that* much of an exhibitionist. It's most likely just the effect Oliver has on me. He could make me do anything easily, if he asks me with that sweet smile on his lips.

His voice lowers to a purr as he tries to keep his conversation going. My thighs flex again, and I watch as he jerks himself off in earnest for his viewers.

God, he's so gorgeous. Every line of his body flexes and moves, showing off his glistening skin for the viewers. I can see the edges of the tattoo that stretches the expanse of his back, and I wish so much that I could run my fingers over it.

I'm hopeless.

My teeth sink into my lower lip as I watch him, eyes never able to leave the screen until Oliver sucks in a breath between his teeth and comes all over his fingers. A flush of heat goes through me and I sit back, suddenly embarrassed by myself.

I'm supposed to be reminding myself why this won't work. Not watching his stream and having to fight not to get myself off as well. "God," I mutter, leaning back against the head of my bed while Oliver finishes up his stream and bids farewell to his viewers.

I'm still sitting there when his stream ends completely, and a groan leaves me as I throw my arm across my eyes, blocking out the view of my room.

I'm *hopeless*.

CHAPTER 5

I f I fall asleep in Professor Carmine's class, she'll skewer me alive and feed me to her two mastiffs. I know that for a fact, but it doesn't stop my eyelids from drooping as I scrawl notes onto my iPad propped on the small desk in front of me. It isn't her fault that I'm so tired. It isn't even her choice of subject matter, because I find the discussion of Viking art and imagery incredibly intriguing. I *like* my chosen path of study and most of what it contains. It's her monotone voice and the steady, not-too-bright light in the room that creates the perfect atmosphere for falling asleep, no matter how much I try to will myself to stay awake.

I hadn't meant to stay up so late. I hadn't meant to go through a few other *funxcams* streams and my messages until Juniper got home, less worried than I'd seen her in days, and told me that she and Jesse were officially back together in every way.

I should've gone to bed before four am.

The iPad pen droops in my hand, nearly falling before I jerk back upright, clenching it harder between my fingers and quickly write down the notes that I'd missed from the current slide. Honestly, it isn't like I *need* these notes. This is one of those subjects I'd studied last year, when I'd requested to work ahead for extra credit. I know these art styles and patterns fairly well, plus the nuances she points out with a capped marker to the rest of the class.

But staying awake is part of the grade in here. Personally, I've always suspected that Professor Carmine is aware of her voice, her tone, and the fact that she comes off like a radio letting out static. Frankly, I wonder if she's installed dimmer lights in this room, knowing it would weed out the weaker candidates for degrees.

Already I hear the slow, heavy breathing from the girl beside me that tells me she's dead asleep. She'd probably come in here expecting to be given a syllabus and let go, but Professor Carmine isn't like that. To her, if you're not taking up the entire time, then you're doing it wrong.

She'll work us to the end of the hour with no remorse or excuses.

Behind me, I hear soft snores getting progressively more pronounced, and when my eyes flick to our professor's again, I see that she's searching the rows, looking for the offender. She can always tell when someone is asleep, and it's the one thing that keeps me from letting myself totally relax.

Sure enough, while she doesn't stop talking, Professor Carmine walks up the tiers of the classroom. Her voice stays steady as she goes while still talking about the same artwork, without having to look at her notes or the board. Has she memorized these lectures well enough to do them without looking? I wonder how well she knows her own schedule, and if she could tell me what we'll be studying in March, but still without the aid of notes.

She stops beside the sleeping senior, and I glance back with pity at the unsuspecting fool as he snores peacefully, not understanding the danger he's in.

At least, until Professor Carmine drops the heavy planner she'd been carrying onto his desk. It smacks down hard, tumbling off of the hard surface and to the floor below. The boy jumps, the sound coming out of his mouth somewhere between a yelp and a shriek as he looks in horror at our professor.

"There you are, Mr. Finnegan," she says, still in that same tone as other students fight not to laugh. For my part, I bite my lower lip and thank God it isn't me getting woken up like that. I've seen students fall out of their chairs before thanks to the shock, but this senior just stares up at her like she's the devil, holding on to the sides of his desk in a white-knuckled grip.

While she might not have been spawned directly by the underworld, some part of me wonders if she takes some kind of sick glee out of terrifying her students.

"And just in time for the end of class." Her eyes fall on his empty notebook as she picks up her planner, and her mouth twitches in disappointment. "I see you've taken thorough notes. I assume you'll be well prepared for next Friday's quiz."

Mumbles of dislike go through the room, and someone even thumps their head back audibly into the window behind them, a groan following the action as the boy rubs the back of his skull. Professor Carmine doesn't seem to notice. She strides back to her desk and waves her hand lazily, the sign that we're free to go.

I don't linger. I love her class, and I'm thrilled to be her assistant for one of the intro to art history classes that meets Tuesdays and Thursdays. But today I need to get out of here, before she senses how exhausted I am.

My iPad is shoved into its sleeve quickly, the pen dropped in with it, and once that's back in my backpack, I stand. I sling it over my shoulder, and pull my headphones out of the pocket of my skirt. It moves as I walk, tickling my upper thighs with the two slit sides that show the shorts underneath that shine with two silver buckles.

"Professor Carmine?" I ask, going to her desk as other students stream, or run, out the door. She glances up at me, brows lifting, but still continues packing.

"You seem tired today, Love," she remarks, and I bite back a frown.

So she had noticed, even though I'd done everything in my power to stop her from doing so. "Sorry," I apologize, adjusting my grip on my backpack and shrugging my shoulders to push my sweater to a more comfortable spot where it isn't choking me. "My roommate almost broke up with her fiancé last night." I know she doesn't care for excuses, and he isn't *exactly* her fiancé, but garnering sympathy still is my best hope here.

"I hope everything worked out all right." I can't tell if she means it, or it's just a default response, but I quietly thank her, anyway.

"Are Tuesdays and Thursdays at four okay for my office hours? Well, hour," I amend. Part of my job as teaching assistant is to hold a few hours a week for her students to come ask me for help, though she herself had told me that it'll most likely rarely happen, if ever.

"That's acceptable," she agrees, after checking her planner a few times before she says it. "You're okay with using my office?"

"Yeah. It's convenient, since I just have your class before that," I point out, glancing back and seeing that all the other students have made their grand escape from the room, leaving it empty and silent.

"Great. Thanks for letting me know, Love." I've never understood why she doesn't use first names nearly as much as last names, but it's never bothered me. Though now it makes me prickle, just a little, and only because of the way one other person on this earth calls me *Love*.

Would he be upset to know that Professor Carmine does as well? The thought is silly, and I chase it away as quickly as it came as I follow her out of the room. Once we're outside, we say our goodbyes, then I pause to glance up at the news board that serves to announce events to the entire art department.

As I'd expected, there's nothing there of interest. Of the three seminars that I want to attend later in the semester, none of them are on the board yet. It's not surprising, since they aren't for another few months and the next few weeks the board will be covered with posters of recruiting clubs and welcome-back dinners for students who are into that kind of thing.

I used to be, though. Back when I didn't have Juniper, and I'd thought that college was made for partying, lying, and making friends that didn't know the real you. But that was three years ago, and now the clubs don't interest me. Neither do the dinners, the events, the sports, or whatever else I can see here. Though, of course, given this is the art department, the best spots on the board are taken by art club news and upcoming shows from the theater department.

"Tell me you aren't from around here." A jovial, masculine voice makes me stiffen, and I turn around to see Professor Langhorn behind me, his eyes not on my face but looking at my skirt instead. Immediately I want to cover myself, feeling ashamed, but I only frown and take a moment to try to process what he's just said to me.

"What?" I ask, trying to be polite. "I'm not, but... I'm not sure I understand what you mean, Professor."

Brazenly, he points at my skirt, snorting. "Does your mother know you're wearing clothes like this?"

"My mother isn't in charge of my clothing choices." There's some disbelief in my voice, and my mind is numb with it when he insults me. "Can I help you with something?"

"No." His eyes flick over me, not once coming up to my eyes, and I feel disgusting, like I'm being swarmed by flies. He's a large man, easily looming almost as wide as the door I'd just come out of. I shift my weight from one foot to the other, uncomfortable as hell when he looks me over again.

I want to leave. I want to be anywhere but here, but my boots feel glued to the carpet under me. So I look up at him, hating that I have to tilt my head back to see his face, and when I move, my elbow brushes the wall behind me, reminding me that I'd have to walk around him to go anywhere else, unless I'm prepared to dig a hole through the wall.

"I just think you should consider what kind of message you're putting out is all," he says, looking disdainful as he gives me one last, oily glance. "Because it isn't a very good one, from where I'm standing. And someone's going to get the wrong idea."

I blink, looking away from him, and suck in a breath to say, "I can't control other people's ideas, *Professor*," I tell him, wishing I could channel some of Rook into my voice. "But I hope you have a good day." With as much pride and fearlessness as I can muster, I stride away from him, nearly brushing his arm when he doesn't move and get a whiff of stale cologne and dirty laundry as I do.

How is this man still employed? I'm sure tenure is a hell of a thing to break, but this man looks like he's been here since the dinosaurs and talks like he's losing it.

I don't realize that Oliver's calling my name until an arm suddenly grabs me, pulling me to a stop. I gasp, my brain telling me it's not him and that it's Professor Langhorn instead, but the fear that claws at my stomach fades when I see Oliver, his face full of worry.

"Sorry," I breathe, stepping closer to him and gripping his shirt without thinking. It chases away the panic in my chest, shoving it back as I use my hold on him to ground myself and remind my racing heart that everything is fine. "I'm sorry, I just..." I can't help it when I step closer, dragging him towards me by his shirt. He doesn't stop me. Oliver's arms slide around my waist, and I press my nose against his shoulder, breathing in his musky scent that chases away Professor Langhorn's stench.

"What happened?" he asks, his tone sharp as he radiates sudden attention. He turns, pressing his lips against my hair, but I take another breath before I answer, not wanting to say something stupid.

I don't want Professor Langhorn to end up dead. It would be wrong, no matter how much his words had creeped me out.

"It's fine," I tell him, though I don't feel fine. His words feel stuck to me like oil, and it's hard to shake them off when they cling and echo through my skull. "Someone said something gross to me, but I'm not going to tell you what."

"You don't trust me?" There's a hint of a chuckle, like he already knows the answer.

"Uh, no," I tell him, finally pulling back. I chase away my fear, my irritation, and grin broadly at Oliver. "No, I definitely don't. Full offense intended, since we both know you."

"We do indeed," he agrees solemnly, but holds me to him when I try to move away. "But this isn't going to work if you're too afraid to tell me things, because you think I'll go off the rails."

"Yeah, but how do I know you won't *go off the rails*?" I point out, glad we're hidden between two cars in the parking lot so that no one else can see or, hopefully, hear us right now. "Literally all I have to work with is last semester." Juniper's words flicker through my brain, and I remember what I need to tell him.

"Last semester was a fluke. Kind of. Sort of," he admits, brushing my hair back from my face. I take that moment to look at him, my gorgeous spree killer, with auburn hair that the sun seems to sink into greedily, and dancing green eyes that shine with all that captured sunlight. "I'd never put you in danger, Blair."

"Okay," I whisper, hating how easily he can win me over. *Hating* how much I want to tell him; though I keep the words locked behind my teeth to spare the professor what would probably be a grisly death. "Unrelated, but..." I lick my lips, needing to change the subject. "Juniper wants to apologize. She thinks she read you wrong and misjudged you." I don't look away from his gaze as he thinks the words through, or as I add, "Even though we both know she didn't."

"Are you just pushing her to apologize to prevent a repeat of last semester?" he asks, humming as he steps close to me again. "Did you write her a script as to what to say to me, Blair?"

"You're acting like our darling professor," I accuse, the panic dull in my throat when I flick his arm. "Cut it out."

"Maybe he's rubbing off on me." He can't keep a straight face when he says it, but there's an edge to his grin that I'm sure I don't trust. "She doesn't need to apologize to me, you know. Especially when we both know she isn't *wrong* about me."

"But she needs to lay off you. And if apologizing and seeing you act like the sweetest, fluffiest golden retriever ever born will convince her you're boyfriend material?" I tilt my head to the side, expectantly. "Then she'll damn well do it, and I'll be there to watch."

He hesitates, looking away from me like there's something he wants to say. In the end, however, Oliver kisses me hard instead, his eyes still inscrutable. "Whatever you want, wonder girl," he promises in a low purr, pulling me toward his car. "Just let me drive you home, please?"

"As long as we don't stop for murder on the way," I agree, knowing I should walk instead. But I can't. Not now, not this time, while the spot between my shoulder blades itches when I think about the idea of Professor Langhorn watching me from the art department.

CHAPTER 6

I walk down the hallway through the art department on Friday, with my camera bag slung over one shoulder and my backpack on the other. The route brings back memories from when I'd dreaded this walk.

Truth be told, I still do a little. Just because he has affection for me doesn't mean Rook is any sweeter to me. If anything, I'm pretty sure it will be the opposite. Especially during his class. I walk at a slower pace when I pass his office, eyes wide and baleful as I stare at him at his desk.

As if sensing my disdain, he looks up with narrowed eyes and lets out a breath that would be impossible to miss. He rolls his eyes, shaking his head at my display, but just when I think he's going to say something to me, he goes back to the papers he's looking at and ignores my presence altogether.

"If that's you trying to get a reaction out of him, you're doing it all wrong." Oliver's lazy voice is loud, and I swear I see Rook's shoulders tense at his words. The younger serial killer slings an arm over my shoulders, holding a large drink in his other hand. "Want to share?" He shakes the mostly full

47

caramel macchiato in front of my nose, and I don't need to be asked twice. "Suck it loud," he advises, both of us still standing in front of Rook's office as I do just that, making sure to rattle the ice around the cup as well.

Professor Solomon looks up at us again, and if looks could kill, at least one of us would be on the floor, twitching, and no longer on this mortal coil.

"He's forgotten to mention something that you should both take into consideration, Love," our professor intones, just loud enough for us to hear.

"That you hate coffee, fun, and ice?" I ask, shaking the cup again and feeling too bold with Oliver's arm around me.

"That I can't fail *him*." His eyes fall to mine. "But I sure as fuck can fail *you*."

He brings up a good point, and some of the bravado fades from my chest. I take another sip of coffee, his gaze still on mine, but do so normally, so that it doesn't make much noise. Placated, he looks back down, though it's only to gather up the pile of what appears to be syllabi on his desk and stand up with them in one hand, the strap of his leather bag going to his other.

As we watch, he leaves his office, glancing around the hall like he's expecting something, and comes to a halt in front of us. Any fondness he might have for me is absent in his glare, and I find myself stepping back, suddenly unsure.

Until his hand comes up to stop me, hand cupping my jaw so briefly that I doubt anyone would know what he'd done. "Don't be afraid of me, Love," he murmurs. "I won't hurt you."

"You hurt me already," I remind him slowly. "You stabbed me with a B minus last semester. I still haven't recovered."

He rolls his eyes at my words, shaking his head before fixing Oliver with a glare. "*Don't* encourage her," he threatens. "I can *fail her*, Oliver. Don't forget that."

"I thought you said you wouldn't hurt her," he remarks, a shit-eating grin on his lips. "Doesn't that include failing her?"

Rook pauses, a muscle in his jaw twitching as I pull another mouthful of coffee into my mouth.

"Don't bring that into my class," he reminds us absently, glaring at the coffee like it's personally offended him. "One more time, Oliver, and you're both going to regret it. Understand?" He looks between us, from my nodding to Oliver's mock salute, before heading toward the classroom, and breezes inside.

"Would he really fail me?" I muse, handing the drink back to Oliver as he drops his arm and takes it from me.

"I don't think so," he dismisses with a quick shake of his head. "No way... probably. Do you think he'd fail you?"

"I think you know him way better than me," I argue, taking a last drink before dumping it in the trash can outside of the room. "I mean, I told him I'd leave the class if I didn't earn an A on the first project. So I'm kind of safe... right?"

"Right." But Oliver doesn't look too sure. And when I nudge him for an answer he tells me, "Well, Rook is kind of... anti-ultimatum. He'll go along with what he promised, but you might not like how he does, is all. And remember, don't call him Rook in class where he'll hear you, or to anyone who doesn't know."

"Like you do?"

A smile touches his lips, and his eyes glitter with mischief. "Yeah, like I do. Unless you're a masochist who likes being punished like me, anyway. In that case, do whatever you want. I sure as shit won't stop you, wonder girl."

In the end, I barely get a chance to do anything. Professor Solomon breezes through the syllabus, and the ten other students in the class, not counting Oliver, all appear to have been conditioned by him to actually listen, instead of looking bored or disdainful as they had last year in beginner photography. A few do glance at the clock, and a girl by his desk looks like she wants to proclaim her love for him any time he takes a breath.

"First project starts today," our professor announces. "I can guess who will be pairing up with who, but let me know by tomorrow over email."

"What a psychic," Oliver mutters at my side, and the remark catches me off guard enough that a snort leaves me.

It's loud. Too loud in the silence, and Rook turns on me with a look of irritation on his face that has me wanting to run for the door. I wince at my stupidity, and wish he'd stop glaring at me like he wants to set me on fire. Too late, I wish I would've turned it into a cough, since now it seems I was snorting at something he'd said.

Finally he looks away and I let out a breath, barely listening as he finishes up his speech and releases us for the day.

Immediately, I shovel everything into my backpack, fumbling for the hoodie he gave me and pulling it on so fast that I nearly put it on backwards. I just need to leave before he can be upset with me. If I can get out of his eyesight—

"Greer. Love. *Stay.*" There's no room for argument in his voice, and I groan into the fabric of the hoodie before yanking it down where it belongs. *Damn it.*

I stay, because I don't know what else to do. My heart pounds in my chest, and for a few moments I'm not looking at the serial killer who's made me breakfast for dinner and fucked me with a tail. I'm looking at my professor, who almost gave me a C last semester and looks like he wants to have me expelled.

Explanations and apologies bubble to my lips when the others leave the room, but Oliver just fidgets with boredom at my side, looking up at the ceiling above us without a care in the world. But of course he isn't afraid. Rook *loves* him, and also can't fail him like he can me.

"I didn't—" I begin, wishing I hadn't stopped and glared at him, or drank coffee so loudly in his face. He holds up a hand, one finger up, and I go silent at the obvious sign to do so. For a minute or so, he doesn't move. Professor Solomon writes something in a planner, glances at his phone, and flips the page to write something else. Only then does he put everything in his bag and get up, striding toward us while glaring down his nose at both of us.

"I didn't mean—" This time his hand touches my face, finger against my lips to make me go quiet once more.

"You're letting him turn you into a brat," he informs me, hand soft on my face. He turns his wrist to cup my jaw, gazing down at me with dark eyes that I can't read. "Come on." His hand falls instantly and he strides on past, going to the door and out it, without another word.

I scramble to my feet, followed by a much more relaxed Oliver, and walk out of the room to see him standing in the hallway, studying his phone. "I'm sorry," I say, quick enough that he can't stop me. "Please don't fail me. I'll drop if you want me to, I'll—"

"Love," he sighs my name, eyes lifting from his phone to mine. "I'm not going to *fail* you for snorting in my class." His eyes land on Oliver as the younger boy slinks by, mouth tightening. "*You* shouldn't be trying to get her in trouble." When Oliver doesn't answer, Rook reaches out to grab his arm. "Are you feeling neglected?" he purrs, making every muscle in Oliver's body tense.

Oliver's gaze slides to the side, then flicks up to mine. "If I say yes, she won't be in trouble?" he assumes, studying Rook's gaze.

The latter grins, all predatory and barely any humor. "No,

that isn't how this works. You don't get to call the shots, and she's still got a reprimand coming."

God, I wish I would've played it off as a cough. I could've done it, even if I had to actually choke myself to sound believable.

"I'm going to run to my office," Professor Solomon informs us both. "You'll come over for dinner, won't you? Oliver won't be streaming today."

"I, umm, have plans?" I try to say, but I'm sure we all know it isn't true.

"Cancel them," my professor states, breezing past me. "I'd rather you have dinner with us."

"What if they're important?" I can't help but ask, and he stops dead, making me wish I'd just shut up. Even Oliver's face, his raised brows and his half frown, makes me think it would've been better to either go along with it, or go home.

"Okay, Love, okay." Rook sighs heavily and turns to face me, looming into my personal space in a way that makes me wonder if he's afraid anyone else is looking or just doesn't care. "What are your incredibly important plans? If they're so important, I'll get it. I'll understand *completely*." He blinks once, then again, waiting for me to speak. "Unless you're lying to me, and if so, you're about to be in a *lot* more trouble than you were thirty seconds ago."

Shit. *Shit.*

Fear builds and bubbles in my throat, and my lips part as I look at him. I'm *afraid* of the man in front of me, and as I try to work past the way my throat closes around any words, I might want to say, my fingers clench and unclench in front of me.

"Rook." Oliver's voice is soft, and he slinks an arm around my waist. "Stop, okay? She thinks you want to hurt her."

Rook's gaze softens just a touch, and he steps back enough that I can breathe again. "Oh, Love," he sighs. "You make it so easy to forget that you're not already ours. To you, at least. Do you really have plans?" I shake my head as he waits. "Do you really think I'd hurt you like that?"

But I don't answer or move my head one way or the other. I don't know. I don't *know*, and I feel too flustered to even make an educated guess. Rook studies me, and again the urge to apologize bubbles up my throat.

"Come here," he says, crooking a finger at me. "Oliver, *stay*." He points at a nearby couch, and Oliver huffs under his breath before going over to sit on the edge of the creamy yellow monstrosity. "We're in the art department," he reminds me quietly, when I glance around the area. "Nothing's going to happen to you here."

He's right, I think. If I scream, everyone would hear. There's no way for him to murder me unless he does it incredibly fast. I follow him, dragging my feet along the rug until we get to his office and he half-closes the door behind me, careful not to let it fall all the way shut.

"I'm sorry," I blurt out again. "I just got... too comfortable. I shouldn't have snorted, or done the coffee thing, or—"

"Stop," he tells me firmly, sitting on the edge of his desk and leaning back on his hands. "You shouldn't apologize for those things."

"Why? You're mad," I point out, examining his face incredulously. "You're *literally* trying to get me to go home with you so you can, what, punish me? Fail me? Threaten me?" I clench my hands, trying not to let my voice raise any further than it already has.

"Well, actually, I thought I'd take you home, feed you, play with Oliver, and play with you, too. When Oliver gets this way, it's because I've been working too much. He's sensitive, Love. A lot like you. I thought you might be the same." His voice is softer than it has any right to be, and I don't know how to take his words as I stand there, feeling more and more unsure by the moment.

"You're *really* not mad?" I ask and watch him shake his head.

"It would take a lot more than your clumsy attempts at needling me to upset me, I promise you that." A small smile curls at the side of his mouth. "Do you want to go home with us?"

"Umm, I..." I suck in a breath and try to look more aloof, less like a terrified fawn. "I *guess* I can cancel my plans." Though I hadn't had any plans, apart from watching Oliver's stream. But if he's not doing that, then I definitely don't have anything else to do. "Did you know the prices for an Uber from your house to my apartment are insane? I think I'm being cheated." I watch him open and close a few drawers, storing a notebook in one and pulling a camera lens from the other.

"Do you not drive?" he asks absently, dropping the lens into his leather bag.

"I drive some. Just not here. Juniper has a car, and there's nothing wrong with public transportation. Plus, this is St. Augustine. Not the middle of bum-fuck nowhere." Back home, I would've had issues without a car. But here, it hasn't been too big of a deal.

He snorts and gestures for me to go out the door, where I wait for him as he locks up. When I glance over, I see that Oliver is still on the sofa, head tilted back to stare at the ceiling, exposing the length of his throat. Rook follows my gaze and sighs. "He's pouting," my professor observes, striding back over to him. "Get up, my love," he purrs softly, the words having an instant effect on the younger boy, who rolls to his feet gracefully. "You're taking Blair home."

Oliver turns to me and grins, green eyes warm with

delight. "What won you over?" he asks, leaning close to wrap an arm around my waist. "Did he promise to cook?"

"He promised to play with you. I'd like to watch," I reply, wiggling my eyebrows suggestively. The words seem to catch him off guard, but Oliver snorts a second later.

"We'll see you at home, yeah? You're done?" Oliver asks, his hand dropping from my waist a moment later so he can curl his fingers around mine. Rook nods, sweeping his hair back with his long fingers.

It occurs to me that they have to come and leave separately. Rumors would spread if they were taking the same car home, and there's no way no one would notice.

"I'll be right home. And so will you." His harsh, stern tone is back, and he glances between us with a look that leaves no room for arguments. "Don't stop anywhere. Don't look for ways to make me *more* irritated with you, Oliver."

If anything, Oliver stands straighter, preening at what he seems to think is praise. "Stop that," Rook admonishes, but Oliver doesn't. "I'll see you both at home." It's as much of a farewell as he seems capable of giving, and he breezes on by, heading for the stairs while Oliver and I just stand where we are, watching our professor go.

"We could make a run for it? Hide at my apartment?" I tease, some of my good humor creeping back to me with caution. "I know you don't like my roommate, but she makes a scary enemy. We could *so* survive a week before he overcame our defenses."

Oliver's delighted grin is reward enough, and my heart squeezes in my chest like it's being gripped by an imaginary fist. "As tempting an idea as that is, Blair?" He leans close, pressing his nose to my cheek. "I'm actually looking forward to this 'reprimand' of his."

CHAPTER 7

Oliver makes it home first. Before I follow him inside, I halt at the door to look up at the front of the house and the cloudy sky above it.

This shouldn't feel spooky. I don't have a reason to be afraid of them. Not like I thought I did. Though, the idea of a *reprimand* from His Majesty makes my stomach churn in both excitement and anxiety.

But he'd said he wouldn't hurt me. Not in a way that'll stick, or in an academic way. If I can't trust the serial killer who's done amazing at keeping himself and his boyfriend out of jail for so long, who *can* I trust?

"Wonder girl?" Oliver's sweet, slightly unsure voice calls me from inside, and I tip my chin down to see him in the hall, gazing back at me with bemusement clear on his features. "What are you doing?"

"Do you think it's going to rain?" I ask him, wondering if I should close the door so no bugs can get in. A car purrs into the driveway behind me, and I don't need to turn to know that Rook's SUV has arrived, blocking in Oliver's car.

Not that I think for one second that, in a moment of desperation, Oliver would hesitate to drive over the well-manicured lawn, smash into the neighbor's mailbox, and hit someone while he was at it if he was actually trying to go somewhere.

Footsteps behind me shock me out of my daydream, but before I can move, arms wrap around my shoulders, holding me against the warm, solid line of Rook's body. It's so affectionate, without any undertone of warning, that I can't help but lean back into him, if only for a moment. His hand comes up to tuck my hair behind my ear, and from the corner of my eye I see him glance up as well.

"Are we looking at something?" he asks blithely, his thumb rubbing over the pulse point in my throat. "Other than the sky?"

"Just the sky," I tell him, my voice quiet. "It looks like it's going to rain."

"It always rains this time of year," Rook murmurs in my ear. "Are you going to go in, Love?" The beginnings of a threat linger at the edges of his voice, and even though I hope he won't hurt me, it sends a shiver up my spine that I know he feels just as clearly as I do. "Or do you want me to make you?"

My first conversation with him slams back into me. How I'd admitted that CNC, or consensual non-consent, has been something on my mind for a few years. It makes me tense now, and my tongue itches to tell him yes. That I want him to pick me up, throw me over his shoulder, and take me inside.

"No," I say instead, a sigh on my lips. I don't trust him enough to tell him that, or let him. I want to walk in of my own free will and feel like I have some control over the situation.

For a moment, I think he won't listen. That he'll pick me up anyway and pull me inside, as part of the start of his punishment for the coffee and the snort. But then he just... waits. One hand skims up my arm, covered by the hoodie he'd bought me. The other drops to his side, making sure I know that I'm not trapped or obligated to be here.

It's surprisingly sweet of him, and I swivel in place to look behind me at my professor, who only raises a brow and stares back.

"Do you intend to stand here until it rains?" he asks softly, a hint of amusement in his voice. "You might have a long wait. I think the forecast said it'll be another hour or so."

"Sorry," I murmur, not sure what I'm sorry *for* exactly. Other than wasting his time; it grinds on me that I'm doing just that while my feet are glued to the ground.

Then a hand touches mine, and I look down to see Oliver in front of me, concern on his face as he grips my fingers with his. "I thought you weren't afraid of our house anymore," he breathes, pulling me inside. "There's nothing different about it this time."

But there is. As much as I'm too afraid to say it, this time is completely different than the other few times I'd come here. Because I *know* what I'm here for. I know what I'm getting myself into, and what I'm saying *yes* to. Sure, I might not know the specifics, but it'll be hard to rationalize this to myself later, since I'm walking into this with my eyes open and no misconceptions.

Don't they see how different it is, because of that one reason?

I follow Oliver inside, not bothering to look around too much. It's only been less than a week since the last time I was here. They obviously haven't built me my own wing yet, which is a true shame, and it looks exactly the same as the last time I was here.

God, I wish I could afford a house like this. My apartment is amazing, and I'm thrilled we can afford it thanks to Juniper's digging into available housing resources and being so good at getting what she wants. But this is so far beyond that it's unreal. I can't imagine this house cost less than almost seven figures, and I wonder just how famous Rook was, or is, in order to have bought it just for himself.

"Here." Rook tugs lightly at my backpack, his other hand coming up to pull down the strap of the camera. "I'm going to put them in the living room for you." He disappears when I give both to him, feeling suddenly vulnerable in the air conditioning of their house. I reach up to rub my arms, still glancing around the room, and let out a breath when I finally accept that I don't actually want to run away.

Not that it makes me any less terrified of what that means, or what I'm getting myself into by staying.

"I see you still haven't built me a wing," I comment, my voice only a little unsteady. "That's a shame. I can't tell you the amount of disappointment I feel."

"I told him to," Oliver sighs dramatically, and when I look at him, I see that he's almost vibrating with nerves.

No, *wait.*

When I study his face, I realize it isn't nervousness that's coursing through him.

It's excitement.

He tries to keep it off of his face. Tries to look anything but exceptionally impatient as his eyes follow Rook's movements. Had our professor been right? Is this really Oliver when he feels *neglected*, or like Rook has been too busy to pay attention to him? The man of my thoughts reappears at my side and gazes at his boyfriend, one brow raised as he looks him over.

"Do you want to go *sit*, Oliver?" he asks patiently. "You're as bad as her."

"No, he's definitely worse," I disagree, surprised when

Rook's hands find my hoodie and he drags me back against him. "What—"

"Take it off and put it by the door, Love," he sighs against my hair, the epitome of someone who has never once been disobeyed and isn't expecting to be now.

"What if I'm not wearing a shirt under it?" My mouth moves faster than my brain, and Rook's fingers tighten in the material.

"What if you aren't? Both of us have seen it all before, haven't we? There's nothing to be ashamed of. Nothing to hide from, seeing as you know how we feel about you."

Oliver moves, surprising me. But instead of going to *sit* or doing something crazy like making the situation worse, he closes the distance between us, creating the front of the cage Rook has already started with his body pressed to mine.

"Show me," he growls, his mouth close to mine as he grips my face. "Show me, Blair. Please? Do you know what it's been like without you? I couldn't even *touch* you since you were gone. And you haven't streamed in forever. Do you want me to beg?" His smile widens, that hint of crazy in his eyes flaring to the surface without him trying to stop it.

But why would he? We're past me not knowing. We're past the secret of what they are, and to them, I'm here. I'm theirs. I'm a *promise*.

I just have to figure out how to tell them, and myself, that isn't true.

"No." Rook hauls Oliver up by his hair, and before I can say anything about how I am *not* the problem this time, drags both of us through the house, Oliver by his hair and me, luckily by the arm.

Is this common for them? I wonder, as I nearly trip up the stairs leading to the hallway where Rook's room is. Is it common for Rook to just grab Oliver when they get home and fuck him, punish him or whatever else they do here?

God, I hope they don't murder people in their *house*.

When he reaches his room, he lets go of Oliver, only to point at the floor by the bed. "*Sit*," he orders, and while I'm expecting Oliver to make a big deal out of it or outright break a window... he doesn't. He sits, his knees coming down hard on the wood floor. I wince in sympathy, my arm still in Rook's grip until he drops me on the bed, seated near the edge of it.

"I shouldn't have to tell you how to act at Wickett," Rook sighs, walking away from both of us and going to the closet. He strips out of his long sleeve shirt, and grabs something from the shelf that he tosses onto the bedside table. "*Neither* of you." I search his face for irritation or frustration. Even anger, knowing him.

But I find something else instead.

He's *enjoying* this, I realize, tossing a glance at Oliver. He's having *fun* reprimanding us, and if I didn't know better, he likes the fact that Oliver pushed me into acting up as well. At least, that's what I think. I could be wrong. I could very *easily* be wrong, given how little I can read Professor Solomon.

There's only one way to find out if I'm right, and if I'm wrong, there's a solid possibility I'll be dead like Rob, with just a Polaroid to remember my face. "I don't see what I did wrong," I comment, looking down at the bed before glancing back his way. I pick at the blanket casually, like I'm telling the truth, and I don't expect the intensity of Rook's gaze when he looks up at me.

Nor do I expect the surreptitious, approving grin from Oliver on the floor. "You can't expect her to read your mind, Rook," he agrees, sitting back on his hands. "All she wanted to do was drink coffee. And we *like* you. Is it so weird we were waiting for you outside your office?"

Swiftly, I nod in agreement, a blithe smile on my features. "I do, like you," I agree. "I didn't know I couldn't wait outside of your office." We all, of course, know *that* isn't the problem. And the snort is being ignored, as is the glaring and the way we acted with said coffee.

"You're both *really* going to do this?" Rook asks, looking between us as if he's asking more than that. Like he's asking permission or confirmation, not just incredulous at our words.

Oliver opens his mouth, then waits. Instead, he looks at me for confirmation, his brows lifting just a little in question, as if asking if I'm *sure*, and waiting for me to take the lead.

It's not hard to figure out that he's waiting to see if I really want to push this game in the direction it's already leading. If I do, I doubt Rook will be as nice as he has been. Or at least, as polite at keeping me at arm's length.

Can I handle the way they play?

Well, there's only one way to find out, isn't there?

"Explain it to me in detail, professor?" I ask, oh so sweetly and with the best streamer-persona I can manage. "Explain to me *exactly* what I did wrong? So I don't repeat it?" After kicking off my shoes, I curl my legs up under me on the bed, staring at him like he really is about to launch into some captivating lecture.

Rook lets out a breath, his eyes closing for a half second before he strides forward, arm up so he can grip my throat in his fingers. "Clothes off, Oliver," he tells his boyfriend without looking away from me. "But don't you *dare* touch yourself." He glances over to make sure he's being obeyed, then back to me, where he's still holding me in his grip.

A tremor goes down my spine, anticipation igniting sparks at my fingertips. "All right, Love," he purrs, reaching out for the bag he'd tossed onto the bed and dragging it to him. "I'll explain it for you in a way you'll be sure to understand"—one-handed, he pulls a black collar free from the bag and dangles it in front of my face, causing my stomach to do a small flip—"as soon as I make sure you aren't going anywhere for the lecture. I know I'm not always the most interesting instructor, so I don't want you to have any ideas for escape. Oliver?"

The other man, now only in his boxers, straightens, gazing at us with unbridled *want* in his eyes. "Yeah?"

"Put this on her for me."

Oliver takes the collar without hesitation as Rook lets go, stepping back so he can watch us with heated eyes and no sign of a smile on his full lips. Oliver sits on the bed, the mattress dipping under his weight until I'm unintentionally leaning into him. He brushes my hair back, the collar in his hand, then stops.

"I can't," he says, grinning at me, then up at Rook.

I try to figure out his angle of insubordination so I can capitalize on it, but nothing is coming to mind on how he's going to play this.

Rook's brow angles upward, giving him a disbelieving look. "And why is that?"

"Her hoodie is in the way."

I realize, in that moment, that Oliver is on nobody's side but his own. Calling him a traitor would be untrue. He was never my ally, only his own.

But I still turn to glare at him, the hint of a disbelieving smile on my lips. "You would forsake me like this, Oliver?" I ask, a hand fluttering up to press against my chest as my heart races. "Me, your own wonder girl?"

"In an instant, Blair," he assures me, then glances back at Rook. "What do you want me to do?"

"I want you to put it on her," Rook repeats, hands on his hips. He doesn't smile, sure. But he can't hide the look in his eyes, or the intensity of his gaze. "If that means something needs to come off... then take it off."

I can now clearly see I have no allies in this room. Especially when Olive tackles me to the bed like I was going to put up some kind of resistance. But since he's expecting it... I do. I give him a token struggle, even as my entire being begs to help him rip off my hoodie so I can feel that slim strip of leather around my throat. Is it Oliver's collar? I can't help but wonder, though the leather looks almost too delicate for him, because I would've expected something heavier.

He pulls the hoodie over my head and quickly takes my t-shirt with it, leaving me in the black, strappy bra I'd pulled at random from the drawer this morning.

Oliver stops, his eyes flicking over the straps and the silky black material. With one hand around my throat, he reaches out the other, and strokes along the top of it, just over the swell of my breasts. "Please tell me it's a matching set," he begs huskily, glancing down at my leggings. "I'd give my *soul* to see you in something that matches."

"Oliver," Rook warns, shifting his weight from one foot to the other. "You don't get to enjoy this. Put it on her. Now."

Oliver does, sliding the warm, buttery leather around the back of my throat. He buckles it in the front, snug enough that I'll feel it there, but not tightly enough for it to choke me. My breath catches, stuttering in my throat, and my soul nearly leaves my body when he pulls a thin leather and chain leash free from the bag with delight on his face.

"You got this just for her," he accuses, glancing up at our professor, who only shrugs one shoulder. "You're so special, you know," Oliver coos, clipping the leash to my throat and giving a small tug, even though he's still holding me on my back. My heart slams in my throat, breath barely making it past my parted lips.

"Am I?" is the only thing I can think to say, and my thighs press together unintentionally as I stare up at Oliver.

"Yeah, Blair," he chuckles. "He got you a collar to match mine. I'd say that's real fuckin' *special*." When he gives another light tug, I gasp, but Rook is there a moment later, pulling the leash from Oliver's grip.

"You're still in trouble," he reminds his boyfriend, free hand reaching out to grip his hair tightly. I see Oliver's eyelids flutter—as if he can't help himself—and his mouth falls open, so he can let out a soft gasp at the rough contact. "Floor. Now." Rook lets go and Oliver sinks down like he's melting, his knees once again hitting hard enough to make me wince.

"Don't bruise your knees," Rook remarks, sitting down on the edge of the bed and looping the delicate leash around his fingers until it's tight between us. "You say you don't know what you've done wrong? Then come here so you can *listen*." He yanks on it, dragging me on my hands and knees toward him. He doesn't stop, but instead curls the slack around his hand and continues to guide me forward, until I have no choice but to lean against him, my bare upper body against his searing heat.

"I want you to sit on my lap, Love," he instructs me slowly, eyes never leaving mine. But I want you to face Oliver. Understand?" It's not a hard concept, but the way he talks to me like it might be has me flushing with humiliation.

"Of course, I understand," I can't help but snap. "It isn't difficult."

"Neither is behaving in my classroom." He keeps the leash tight as I move until finally my back is pressed flush with his chest and my legs are spread over his thighs. I was right about him liking us adding fuel to the proverbial fire. Under me I can feel his excitement, even through his jeans, but I'm too nervous to do anything about it, or even mention it.

"I don't ask much of either of you. Don't go on any murder sprees without telling me." That one is obviously directed at Oliver, and the latter grins up at him sweetly. "Don't bring coffee into my class." That one might be at me, but as I've never actually committed such a crime, exactly, I only bat my eyes at him. "And don't, for the love of God, call me *Rook* when we're there. Don't *act* like you're something other than my student and my irritating assistant. Do you know what people would think, Love? If they saw how you acted today?"

"That you... gave me a B minus last semester and I'm obviously not thrilled?" I refuse to let it go. My sweet, helpful smile must shine like a beacon as I turn to look at him, but he certainly does not return the look.

But when he grins, it's nothing so sweet as mine. It's dark, with an intent I can't read, and he takes that moment to pull back on the leash until I'm flush against his chest. "Were you always such a fucking brat, Blair?" he purrs in my ear, using my real name for the first time in a while. "Or were you holding out for me, hoping I'd play with you like I do with him? Is that what you want? For me to wreck you like I do him? Maybe you want me to *ruin* you, so that you stay with us because no one on the face of this damn earth can make you feel like we do?"

"I don't—" I don't get to finish my words. He shoves two fingers into my mouth, shutting me up, and his gaze cuts to Oliver.

"If you touch yourself, you'll regret it," he warns. "Take her leggings off." Oliver doesn't hesitate, but that isn't surprising, given how enthusiastically he put a collar around my neck. He jerks them off quickly, taking my underwear with them, which pulls a glare from Rook. "You're impatient," he remarks, one arm slipping around my waist as he spreads his thighs so that I have no choice but to spread my knees wider, as well.

Rook reaches around me, the hand on my waist gone, as

Oliver crawls closer until he's between the v of our legs. He cups Oliver's chin sweetly, Rook's thumb brushing over his lower lip as I look down into his heated, bright green gaze.

"You can't fuck her until you make her come," Rook informs him, and my heart jumps in my chest at the casual way he says it. "And she doesn't get to come until she's learned her lesson." I turn to glance at him as much as I can, but his hand on the leash keeps me from going far.

"What lesson?" I breathe, eyes drawn back to Oliver as he puts a hand on my thigh.

"The one where you know what you're not going to do at the university anymore," he replies coolly. "But if he does make you come before you've learned it, then you get to take his place being in trouble."

I stiffen slightly, eyes going wide as Oliver looks up with undisguised glee. "That's not fair," Oliver points out, his voice quiet. "To her, I mean. Do you know how fast I can get her off, Rook?"

"Do you know how fast of a learner she is, Oliver?" Rook shoots back.

"And what does, uh, being the one in trouble mean?" I can't help the tremor in my voice, or the way I'm both terrified and excited at the prospect.

"It means he and I get to play with you however we want, whenever we want, for twenty-four hours," Rook informs me. "But if you don't come before then, he's still in trouble and *he's* the one who gets to wear the collar, a tail, and nothing else for the day."

"I'm a really fast learner," I tell Oliver.

His grin meets mine, and he grips my knee harder. "Sure you are, wonder girl," he agrees, and shoves my thighs wide, forgetting the meaning of slow. His tongue licks a line up my slit, and when he finds my clit he laves attention over it, causing me to cry out at the sudden stimulation.

"Can you... explain this lesson to me?" I whine as Rook's arm slips around my waist again. When I try to lean forward, he jerks me back with the leash, holding me to his chest.

"In a minute," he chuckles against my shoulder. "Don't you want to watch him?"

"I want to *win* this little game."

"Do you? Do you want to win, Love? How *badly* do you want to win, hmm?" Finally he lets me look at him, and it dawns on me when I look in his eyes that I've fucked up.

Because I've forgotten that above all, Rook doesn't play fair. He didn't play fair with the tail last semester, and the same look graces his face now.

He has no intention of letting me win.

I suck in a breath, my heart pounding, but my words are interrupted by the soft sound of surprise forced out of me when Oliver's fingers join his mouth. He slides two into me, stretching me with them, and pushes them as deep as they can go while his tongue finds my clit once more. "You don't want me to win," I accuse, my eyes widening slightly. "You—"

"You have the bigger lesson to learn. Oliver would enjoy it either way. But I want to see how you *play*. How you handle *us* playing. Did it never occur to you that we don't play fair? Honestly, you should've been looking for ways to tilt the odds in your favor an hour ago when you knew what I wanted." The hand around my waist moves, sliding up my body, until he can deftly undo the front clasp of my bra. My breasts fall free as he tugs it off, tossing it somewhere I can't see.

"Gorgeous girl," he purrs, hand cupping my breasts and thumb teasing my nipples, in turn. "If you wanted this so badly, you only had to ask. You don't have to stand outside of my office and *beg* me for attention with those big blue eyes of yours. All you had to do was come in and ask. But if you want to do things the hard way, you need to be prepared to meet the consequences." He pinches hard just as Oliver adds another finger, and I nearly shriek at the stimulation.

"Maybe I just wanted to piss you off," I suggest, my head spinning. Heat courses down my spine, finding that place between my thighs that makes my toes curl. "Maybe it's not about the sex."

"Baby girl, it's always about the sex. Do you think he likes irritating me just to do it? No, Love. Not at all. Tell her." He moves suddenly, dragging Oliver up by his hair until he's looking up at us, breathes coming in gasps.

A grin hitches across his lips at my expression, and he chuckles. "Sorry, Blair," he admits, his voice hoarse. "I just like to push him far enough that he'll wreck me for a few days."

"Traitor," I accuse, trembling at the look on his face. His eyes dip back down to my body, and he glances at Rook with a whine.

"Let me go," he urges. "Let me go, Rook. She tastes so fucking good, and I just want to taste her when she comes."

My own hand darts out when Rook releases him, but I'm not nearly strong enough to hold him away from me, and he's back between my thighs in an instant, a purring growl coming from him as he licks at my thighs and thrusts his fingers deep once more.

This time I do cry out, lunging forward just to have Rook drag me back, both arms holding me like a straightjacket, and the leash keeping me flush against him. "It was always going to be you that lost," he tells me in a growl, nipping at my throat when I throw my head back against his shoulder. "Learn your lesson? You don't learn unless I make you. Besides, you could just tell me you had, and how would I know if you were lying?

This way, I can make sure the lesson sticks, and I get what I want out of it, too."

"To grade me on my lesson learning performance?" I pant, turning my gaze to his.

"No," he chuckles, lips brushing mine. "You here, where you absolutely fucking belong, for longer than a few hours. We kept your pretty tail, Love. We knew you'd be back for it. I'll help you put it in, since I know Oliver is a little too rough. By the end of tomorrow, you'll be so used to it that you'll *whine* for it back when it's gone. You'll whine for me to fill you up, and I don't think you'll mind too much when I fill you with my cock instead of the tail."

My breath nearly stops, head spinning, but I can't say anything. Not when I'm barely managing to breathe, and certainly not when he kisses me hard, his mouth searing mine and chasing any coherent thought out of my head.

Oliver pulls away while Rook kisses me, but I don't get to see where he's gone. If Rook knows, he isn't letting me find out. He keeps me there, my mouth against his while Oliver does whatever it is he's doing. A drawer opens and closes, and I hear him thump back down to his knees just as the sound of something being turned on makes me jump.

"I know I said I wanted to taste you while you come," Oliver huffs, one hand running up my thigh. "But I decided I'd rather see you lose it completely."

Rook stops kissing me, his hand forcing me to look down at Oliver just as he presses the vibrator against my clit.

I scream. There's no other word for it; no way I can't when he rubs it up and down my slit, focusing more on my clit than anywhere else and sending me into orbit with pleasure. My orgasm tears through me, matching the shrieks that hurdle out of my throat as Rook murmurs encouragements in my ear.

"Stop-*stop*," I gasp, wishing I could shove at him as the

pleasure becomes too much and edges on pain. "I can't—I came already. *Stop,* Oliver."

"Come again," Oliver argues. "Come on, wonder girl, you can come again." He moves the vibrator to focus it over my clit, his fingers sliding into me to curl against that sweet spot inside of my body and rub against it.

"I can't, I *can't,*" I argue, writhing in Rook's hold. "Professor—"

"I'm not going to help you," he says with a laugh, holding me tight. "Come on, Oliver. You can do better than this. You're being too *nice* to her. Too gentle."

Oliver looks up, eyebrows raised, a grin playing on his lips. "You're right," he agrees happily, and flips the vibrator up to its highest setting.

When I scream again, I don't stop. I can't go anywhere at all, and the desperation feeds into how turned on I am. Heat streaks down my face as I clench my eyes closed, and somehow, though I have no idea how, my body surrenders and I come again, clenching around Oliver's fingers as my entire body screams with how tense I am.

Finally, mercifully, Oliver pulls away, a chuckle on his lips as he stands up and leans forward to kiss me, thumb swiping over the tears on my cheeks. "You're so good, Blair," he purrs. "And you'll totally hold up your end of the game, right?"

"What?" I ask, opening my eyes to look at him. I can't remember anything right now, and the only thing I can focus on is how wrecked I feel.

"You lost the game," Rook purrs against my cheek. "That means for the next twenty-four hours, you're ours to play with, and take care of, and *keep.*"

"Don't worry," Oliver adds, grin turning sly. "I'll take care of you, wonder girl. You won't have to worry about a thing."

CHAPTER 8

"I'm asleep." The words are slurred as they leave my mouth, and I curl up more tightly on my side as fingers stroke along my arm. "I'm so asleep that you're never going to wake me up."

"Well, that's just not true, objectively speaking." Rook's purr in my ear has me shuddering, and he nips the skin of my throat, making me shiver under his touch. "Relax for me, Love." He pushes my thighs apart just enough to pull me back against him, and it doesn't take an A student to know what he's going to do, even before I feel the brush of his cock against my slit.

"You cannot fuck me again," I moan, burying my face in the pillow even though I'm thrilled that even hours later, he still wants to be inside me. "I'm fucked out."

"You're not," he promises, a low laugh evident in his words. "You just need to relax." I'm pretty sure that I'm so wrecked from the last eight hours that it doesn't matter how much I do or do not relax. He slides into me and I shudder, contentment rising in me when he wraps his arms around my body and pulls me back against his warmth. "You feel so good, Love," Rook murmurs, slowly fucking into me like I'm here, just for *him*.

Which, given the circumstances, I am. As if he senses what I'm thinking, he traces the edges of the collar still on my throat, surreptitiously checking the fit before closing his fingers over the base of my throat. I let out a sigh, not worried about him choking me. He doesn't like breath play as Oliver does. In fact, I'm more under the impression that he just likes to see his hands on me.

"Fuck," I breathe, hand curling in the pillow under me as he hits a spot deep in me that still has me seeing stars even though he and Oliver have made me come at least four times after the two from the 'lesson.' If I'd thought I wouldn't be able to come again after this long, I'd been mistaken. Rook seems to take delight in proving me wrong, and I can't help the soft, low sound that leaves my throat as I turn harder into the pillow.

"Let me hear you," he orders, pulling me up by the leash. "Come here, Love. Sit up for me." I don't know why he wants me to, especially since it means it leaves me empty and him *not* fucking me, but I sit up and gaze down at my professor, who lies naked on the bed with Oliver passed out and snoring on his other side.

It reminds me of someone surrounded by their favorite pets while they sleep. Though, given the circumstance, I suppose it isn't such a far-fetched analogy as it should be.

"Come on." Rook adjusts me, pulling my leg over his hips so that I'm straddling him with the blanket pooled behind my hips. "You can't tell me you don't know what to do," he adds, when all I do is press my hands against his stomach.

"You just don't seem like the kind of guy who would be

into this," I admit, lifting one hand to curl around his length. It's slick from my wetness, and I slide my fingers along his hard cock, eyes never leaving his. "This is rather un-top-ly of you, don't you think?"

"No," he says, no hesitation in his answer. "I don't think that at all. I can still top from here, and you'll still do everything I say, Love." It must be nice to go through life with the unwavering confidence he has, and I sigh in envy at his audacity.

God, to be an attractive, murderous man.

A hand on my leg surprises me, and I glance over to see Oliver not as asleep as I'd originally thought. He blinks blearily at me, smiling sweetly, and lets his gaze slide to Rook. "Isn't it a little early to be up, my love?" he murmurs, his voice husky with sleep.

"I'll rejoin you in dreams as soon as our darling girl does what she's so good at," Rook purrs, turning so that he can kiss Oliver sweetly. The latter sits up when he's done, turning and kissing me with lips that taste of Rook and his own sweetness.

Kissing them has become an addiction, and my heart twists when I realize that when I inevitably break it off with them, I'll never get to taste this again. But I chase the thought away as Rook re-clips the leash around my throat, using it to pull me down to look at him.

"As much as I love watching you with him..." my professor purrs, a warning in his eyes. "I want you to ride me, Blair. I'll give you to him afterward."

"Is that a threat?" I ask slyly, rising up to my knees and sinking down onto his length. The change in position pushes him deeper into my body, and by the time I'm sitting more comfortably on his hips again, I have to close my eyes in order to stop seeing stars.

He's bigger than Oliver and has no trouble fucking me deeply in any position. This one so much so that it feels unfair, especially when he gives a small thrust upward, his hands coming to rest on my hips.

"Good girl," he praises, when I can't help the small yelp that leaves my lips. Oliver leans in to kiss my arm, not seeming to mind that my body rises and falls with Rook's movements as he holds me in place over him. "That's my good, sweet girl. You're such a gorgeous little problem, you know that? So *perfect*."

"Problem?" I gasp, my fingers curling against him as he picks up his pace. "How am I a problem?"

He doesn't answer. Not right away. Instead he fucks me, with Oliver behind me, caging me against his body as his hands rove my entire body with ease and he murmurs the sweetest, filthiest things in my ear that have my blood racing.

Before long, Rook loses patience. It's not much of a surprise when he growls and flips us over again, nearly knocking me into Oliver, who laughs and moves out of the way. "I *mean*," he growls, lips inches from mine, "that you're my perfect problem, Love. You aren't like Oliver. You aren't like us." He gives a particularly harsh thrust that has me yelping, then drags my legs up over his hips.

"Stay like that. I want to feel you come around me." His hand dives between us in the scant space, fingers effortlessly finding my clit. "You're the problem I never want to get rid of. And I will figure out how to make you want to stay, instead of us having to almost kidnap you like this. You hear me, Blair?" The use of my name continues to send a jolt of surprise through me, and I can't look away when he stares into my eyes like he can see my soul.

"I-I'm close," I breathe, chest rising as I pant. He grips the leash more tightly, forcing me to arch my back for him and keeping me in an almost uncomfortable position. "Rook—"

"Then come for me," he chuckles. "Come around my cock, gorgeous girl, while I make you a promise." I don't want to hear it. I don't want to come when he's like this, but he's not giving me much of a choice. Especially when every thrust has my eyes crossing in pleasure and my lips parted so I can pant for air.

"I promise you," he growls, his voice loud in the small, quiet space, "that I'll find a way to make you come around to our side. Because Oliver's drowning for you, and I'm losing the ability to stay above water as well." His teeth click together just in front of my lips, then as if it was a warning, he lunges to bite down hard, the pain of it sending me tumbling into my release.

"I'll make you ours, Blair," he promises, though I barely know what I'm hearing as my mind short circuits from the perfect way he fucks me. "No matter what I have to do. You're perfect for us, and we'll never let you get away."

"You should stream." Oliver's voice is muffled against my throat, and I lean back against him with a sigh, my eyes closed.

"Oh, yeah?" I mutter, unable to help the way my hips buck at his touch and my skin shivers under him. Then, more seriously, I add, "I'm going to. I miss it, I think. A little. I'll start again when I'm back and I can work myself up to it—"

"I meant here," Oliver interrupts gently, his fingers dipping between my thighs to tease me. He has to be just as worn out as I am, and I hesitate, looking back at him over my shoulder. "I meant here, with *me*," he goes on, a small laugh in his voice. "*Now*."

"Really?" My brows shoot up toward my bangs as I turn to look at him, my gaze steady. "With what mask?"

"With one of my spares."

"And I don't have my laptop."

"I *literally* have two laptops, Blair," he snorts. "Come on, don't treat me like an idiot who can't think things through. I know what I'm talking about. It would be the easiest stream of your life. And the second most fun of mine."

"You want to fuck me on my stream again?" I assume, wondering if it's the best idea after what happened before. "Aren't you worried about another Rob of the fuck Rob clan?"

"I'm not worried about anyone," Oliver dismisses with a quick kiss on my cheek. "You'll have your mask on. You'll have me. Hell, you'll always have me."

Until I push him away.

I try not to jerk away from him, hating the thought as soon as it occurs. But it's also the thing that makes me give in, and I lean back against him with a sigh. "Maybe I don't like streaming with you," I tease, though the words are unbelievable the moment they leave my mouth. "Especially since you're going to fuck me again."

"I never said I was going to fuck you, wonder girl." His voice is a soft, amused purr in my ear. "I want to edge you for your viewers. You can't tell me you don't think they'll fucking *love it.*"

I can't help but tense under him, and Oliver leans forward to drape himself over me, arms wrapped around my body. "What's wrong?" he inquires, delight dancing in his voice. "Not what you expected?"

"Maybe I don't like being edged," I point out dryly, after a moment of thought. He's not wrong that my particular brand of viewers would probably get off on it and come back for more. It would be an excellent welcome back stream, and Oliver knows it. Sometimes it's disgusting how skilled he is at marketing himself and helping me market myself on *funxcams*. But that's what makes it even harder to tell him no.

"No one likes being edged." He's laughing, shoulders shaking. "Well, not in the moment. But I'll certainly enjoy it. And I promise to get you off so well, wonder girl. I won't leave you wanting for me. I'm not cruel."

He glances up at Rook, who's walking to the closet in his bedroom, causing our professor to stop and roll his eyes in our direction. "Shall I assume that's directed at me?" he asks, voice deadpan. "If you're trying to offend me, you're not doing a very good job." When he looks at me, I raise my hands as much as I can in surrender.

"Wasn't me this time," I tell him, garnering a snort from Oliver. "Can't punish me for something Oliver said. Well, you can," I amend, looking up at the ceiling with narrowed eyes. "You can do whatever you want. But I would like to implore your sense of fairness—"

"Oh, just let him stream with you." Rook's sigh is loud, and instead of going to the closet, he comes over to lean over the bed, reaching out to cup my jaw in one long-fingered hand as he stares at me. "You know you'll love it, and he's been thinking of asking you for a week." Oliver stirs, offended, behind me until Rook's fingers slip from my face to hold his as well. "Don't pout, my love," he coos, half affectionate and half teasing as he kisses him. I watch the sweet, chaste kiss, but before I can even consider becoming envious, he moves to kiss me on the cheek, his stubble brushing my skin and sending a shiver down my spine.

"Are you going to watch?" The question is out of my mouth before I can help myself, and earns me Rook's fingers in my hair, nails scratching lightly, deliciously, against my scalp.

"Of course I will. I watch both of yours separately, don't I? You had better believe I'll always watch you together as well." His gaze tells me he's almost offended by my question, and I consider making a joke out of the moment; before I choose instead to settle back into Oliver's hold.

"I'll have to get up," he admits unhappily. "If you're going to stream, you should do it now. It's close to your normal time, and your fans are more likely to be online right now, we're going to hope. They'll see you, tune in... and bam!" His arms fall to the bed, and when he slides away from me, I flop down to the pillows with a sigh, eyes fluttering shut.

The mattress sinking on either side of me isn't exactly a surprise. Neither is Rook's weight when he settles over my hips, his stomach splayed against mine. "What do you want to eat?" he asks, his tone shockingly polite. "I don't feel like cooking tonight, so I thought I'd order in."

"Do you want me to cook?" The question is out of my mouth before I can think better of it, but Rook's smile is... *sweet*.

"No, Love," he all but admonishes. "I know what you've been doing for the past day. You're not cooking. I just want to know what kind of food you like." He strides away when I finally manage to mumble out a few options, disappearing into the hallway as Oliver drags me back down to the nest of blankets.

Why is he so good at this?

The thought has been going through my head for at least twenty minutes. And every time Oliver's fingers thrust into me harder, pushing me back to the edge of my release, I want to *scream*.

I do, though not as loudly as I want to. Even now, I want to look appealing to the seventy-four viewers on my stream. Plus, Oliver's is pulled up as well, with both laptops facing us from two very slightly different angles. With my mouth open in a gasping pant, I can barely see the latest comment to flit across my screen, let alone hear Oliver's purring words in my ear.

"You're doing so good, wonder girl," he murmurs, the words all for me. "You're so close, aren't you? Should we let her come? We've been torturing poor, *sweet* Envy for thirty minutes now. I think we're sort of cruel," he pauses, then chuckles at something someone says on one of our streams. "I'm not going to fuck her tonight. Not like how you want. I think that's something our viewers should *earn*. She'd agree if, well, she could talk." He wipes his fingers across the mask I wear as if it's my face, and shoves it up just enough to press his fingers into my mouth. "Lick them clean, gorgeous girl," Oliver, or *letsplayjay* in this case, growls against my ear, just loud enough for them to hear.

I open my mouth without needing to be told twice, closing my lips around his fingers and hollowing my cheeks as he repeats the in and out motion with his fingers.

"*User234*, I just got lucky," he laughs, still taking over the job of talking to our viewers while I try not to kill him for edging me this long. My thighs tremble, and I'm sure by now everyone watching has noticed.

Including Rook.

"Envy just happens to live near me, so sometimes we meet up. Seriously, I'm delighted she gives me this much attention once in a while. We all know she could do way better than me. Plus, I don't hear any of you complaining." He tilts his head to the side as both chats move faster, most of the people thrilled by his words and promising that they're the opposite of disappointed.

I'm definitely relieved by that. One of my worries was that people wouldn't be happy, like Rob hadn't been last year, or would say something kind of shitty about us doing another partner stream. Or, worse, ask why I'm not wearing my mask. The question had come up a few times, until I'd explained that I'd left it at home, so Oliver had let me borrow one of his. It's one of the few parts of this that isn't a lie, but we're the only ones who know it.

"He won't be partner-streaming with anyone else if he doesn't let me come soon." I laugh, my tone breathy as my chest heaves with my panting breaths. He wipes his fingers on my mask again, making a show of it for the camera, before he moves both hands down to cup my breasts, thumbs teasing at my nipples.

"So needy, aren't you?" He laughs sweetly, dragging me further against him. He's naked as well, having stripped out of his clothes within minutes of our streams starting, before tackling me and ripping mine off as well.

It was hotter than I'd like to admit, and I love the rough side of him that he shows in a playful, light way to his viewers.

In my lapse of paying attention, I realize I haven't been keeping track of his hands. When two fingers enter me again, however, I cry out in both relief and surprise, back arching against him as my hand snakes up to grip his hair between my fingers. I'm sure I look desperate and more than a little wrecked, but that's the point. My viewers love this, or so they say. They love when I look fucked out and appear to be a mess.

Though at the moment it's definitely not just an act. My head spins as Oliver fingers me once more, his other hand wrapped around my waist so he can tease my clit. "Should we let her come this time, chat?" he hums. "It is almost time to end the stream... I think she deserves it." A few tips filter through on both of our screens, and I drag myself up just enough to press the line of my body against his, my hips grinding back against his cock.

It drags a low laugh from him, and he clamps down harder on my waist. "Don't play games you can't win, *Envy*," Oliver purrs. "I'm trying to give you a break. Don't distract me into breeding this cunt like you deserve."

A flurry of messages come through, all of them begging for him to do just that. He laughs ruefully, shaking his head. "Nah, I'm sorry, guys. Next time, though. If all of you really want us to do it. I'd love to fuck her again while all of you watch. She's just so sweet when she's being watched." He nips my ear, his fingers picking up until he's slamming into me. His other hand finds my clit again, and he forces my thighs wide with his knee to show the viewers exactly what I look like, while a slight hint of embarrassment rises in my chest.

It isn't all bad. I almost like the feeling, especially as he takes me closer and closer to my peak. I cry out for him, begging over and over for *Jay* to let me come. He takes pity on me, telling our viewers they should learn to be nicer to their favorite streamers just as his fingers push me over the edge and into a screaming, shaking mess as I come apart. He drags it out, though I can do little more than hold on to him, pleasure wracking through my body like shivers.

By the time I'm back in a normal state of mind, he's wrapping up. Moving the mask just enough to show my viewers a grin; I then lean up to kiss the side of his mask, on my knees now with him. "I appreciate all of you sticking around for me," I tell my viewers specifically. "I won't go that long again without streaming, I promise." Oliver is already shutting down his stream, so I crawl forward to the other laptop, not trying to be modest by anyone's definition. "Have a good night, my friends. Or day." With a small wave, I turn off the camera, then fall down on the bed with a groan as Oliver rubs my thighs with his thumbs.

"Are you okay?" he asks, rolling me over so he can pull off my mask, then his own.

"Ask me later," I groan, throwing a hand over my face. "After I drink seven bottles of water to feel alive again." Oliver laughs at my words and leans over me to kiss me, the sweetest grin on his face that makes my heart twist in my chest as he gets up and puts on his sweatpants.

"I'll go get you some," he promises, leaving the room just as Rook leans against the doorframe. I don't say anything as I watch him, but my eyes do fall on Rook's and I'm surprised to see that he isn't particularly pleased or bored.

In fact, he almost looks *worried.*

CHAPTER 9

T here's nothing worse than watching the clock.

Except, maybe when I'm watching the clock and dreaming of my two serial killer not-boyfriends. It had taken a day of sleep and probably six gallons of water for me to feel like myself after the weekend. When I'd stumbled home to see Juniper there, she'd been out of her mind with concern before I'd given a Cliff's Notes version of what had happened.

Not with who, exactly. But it would have been dumb of her not to know. After all, there's no one apart from Oliver I care enough to even give the time of day, in a romantic sense. No, there's no way that she wouldn't know who I'd been with, even if I have no intention of telling her all my weekend's details.

There's a knock on the door, startling me from my thoughts. A freshman with the terrified look on her face that I know well, waits for me to notice her before she slinks inside. Her backpack is over one arm as she looks around like she's expecting Professor Carmine to pounce out of a file cabinet at her.

"You're our TA, right?" she asks, her voice soft. "Is it too soon to come see you?" Not exactly, but I won't tell her the fact that she's here after two classes either shows her dedication or is a pretty concerning indicator of where she's at so far.

"It's not too soon," I promise, sweeping my phone and iPad to the side of the desk. It's weird sitting here, *in* Professor Carmine's office, but I get around it by staying clear of anything that's hers and keeping all of my belongings at the desk under my feet. "What can I help you with?" I don't know her name. There's no way it's been long enough in the semester that I could know. The only thing I remember about the blonde is that she sits near the back, though not completely against the back wall. That's what I like to call the *safety row*. Where students don't get in trouble with our professor for trying to meld with the wall and leave, but don't get called on, either. It's the invisible row, and the safest in the room.

It's also the space with the least chance of a reward, to go with its absolute lack of risk.

"There's a quiz next week," she whispers, eyes wide like Professor Carmine might somehow hear, even though I'm not sure if she's even still on campus. If she is, then she's teaching, and I doubt she'll show up here while I'm having my 'office hours' for the students of her freshman class. "I'm terrified. I'm here on a scholarship. So, I can't *fail*." Horror edges her words and I fight not to grin. I don't think she's funny, exactly. But she reminds me somewhat of me, though I hadn't gotten this way until I'd been smacked in the face by a failing grade on a test that counted for way more of the semester than I could really deal with.

But I'd worked hard to make it better. I'd done the extra

credit, improved my grades, and showed that I could cut it for Professor Carmine not to write me off as a failure. "Have you read the chapters she assigned? Not the extra ones. She doesn't give quizzes on those." The girl is nodding before I've finished speaking, but she still looks petrified. Does she know I can't just wave my magic Apple pen and make it so she won't get a bad grade?

"If you've done that, then you're going to be fine. Give them a quick reread before the quiz next week, and seriously. You'll be fine. It'll be a good indicator for how much you'll need to study, and even if the worst happens and you don't do well, it'll be okay. It's a *small* quiz." I smile slightly, hoping to give her some kind of faith in herself. It's not like I can give her the answers. I can't make her flash cards or run her through study guides.

I can't do much until Professor Carmine has handed back the essays that show up on her infamous exams. The girl nods jerkily and gets to her feet, forlorn, like I've sealed her fate. I predict that she'll do better than she thinks she will, and I tell her that, but she only nods and looks like she's about to cry.

Maybe I'm just a shitty teaching assistant. It's a strong possibility, given my inability to make good decisions or deal with the mess that is my life right now. But I choose to believe she's just more nervous than she needs to be, and that she'll be fine after she takes the quiz and learns it isn't impossible.

"See you later," I call, as she picks up her backpack and heads for the door.

She pauses there and turns to look at me, suddenly shyer than she had been when she came in. "Were you ever afraid of her?" the girl asks, barely making eye contact. "I know she's amazing, and the papers she's published are astounding, but..."

I can't help but grin, and I'm finally able to give her an

honest, helpful answer. "I was *terrified* of her as a freshman," I promise the girl. "Literally petrified. She almost failed me." That gets me a wide-eyed look of shock. "So trust me when I say it'll be okay. If I can get myself through, you absolutely can. You're already doing better than me by actually completing the reading."

She stands there, looking thoughtful, before the girl rewards me with a last, bright smile and flees out the door, not quite closing it behind her. I endeavor to learn her name by the end of the next class, at the very least, because I'm sure she'll be back.

I wonder if anyone else will ever show up, or if this is going to be more or less a study-hall type session where I stare across the empty art department into Professor Solomon's office.

Will he mind if I do? It would be *so* weird, but I'm pretty sure we're past that by now.

This isn't the mindset of someone preparing for a breakup, an unhelpful part of my brain that sounds a lot like Juniper informs me snidely. *Weren't you going to tell them you can't do this anymore?*

Yeah, I've definitely thought about it. I've been thinking about it for weeks. And now, a few days after spending a day at their house and having the best sex of my life, the thought is more painful than it ever has been before.

Because, like it or not, it's not just the sex. It's Rook's soft touches and his sternness. His sweet, affectionate tone when I've done something so good and how well he takes care of us. It's Oliver's golden retriever attitude. The way he throws himself into whatever he's doing and his smile when he stares at me like he's soaked up the sun and decided to reflect it for us mere mortals.

It's *them.*

And that's the problem.

A knock on the door gets my attention, but I don't look up from my iPad this time as I say, "I'm still here. Come in."

There is no reply. The door creaks open before closing, and I glance up to see whatever student has darkened my doorstep twenty minutes before I'm going to get out of here.

But... it isn't a student.

Professor Langhorn stands inside the door, examining one of the more minimalistic paintings that hang on the wall. They match Professor Carmine's personality, in my opinion, though minimalism isn't my favorite thing in the world.

"I would've expected O'Keefe," he remarks, eyes sliding to mine. I fidget at the desk, suddenly wanting to get to my feet and kick him back out the door. "You certainly don't look like Professor Carmine."

"I'm her teaching assistant this semester," I say, sitting back in my chair. My heart pounds in my chest as he looks me over, gaze sliding down my face and going until it hits the table that hides my lower body from him. He makes me feel *dirty* for wearing a skirt and hoodie. He makes me want to cover up and crawl under my blankets until he's dead.

By the way he wheezes and from the gray in his hair, it can't exactly be long. Or so I'd hope. "Do you need something, professor?" I keep my voice polite. Professional, in a way that still rings as innocent and appropriate. "Umm. These are my office hours for Professor Carmine." He doesn't look away at the sound of her name, though I'd kind of hoped he would. "I have to keep the office empty in case any students need me."

"Why would they need you?" He huffs a dirty chuckle and grins at me, showing teeth in a grimace. "It's the second week of school. That little blonde that came in here didn't need help, did she? I bet she just came in to talk to the pretty assistant." He wiggles his brows, and I want to vomit. Dryness coats my throat and I glance back at my iPad, wondering if I can ignore him. I want him to go away. I *need* him to stop looking at me while he breathes heavily, his mouth open so he can pant through the heart failure that I imagine is killing his body.

What are my chances of him just dropping dead right here and now? That clearly would be too good to be true. He strays closer to me, his eyes on mine, and finally leans against one of the file cabinets, making it groan softly.

"You're too pretty to be a teaching assistant." He laughs at last, the unpleasant and greasy look still covering his face. "You're too *nice.* Hasn't anyone ever told you that? You don't belong in Carmine's office." My fingers drum on the desk under me as I fight not to reply, and my lips purse, throat still as dry as the Sahara desert.

"Well, that's nice and I appreciate your opinion," I lie, tilting my head to the side. "But umm. I need to get some work done. And I really need to make sure I'm available for my students." He doesn't move. The smile slides off his lips like oil, and he glances at me again, still not bothering to look at my face. In fact, if I didn't know better, I'd think he was trying to edge around the desk to see under it.

But surely I'm just making things up.

"Sure," Professor Langhorn says at last, his voice unpleasantly flat. "I'll check on you again, Miss Teaching Assistant. Since Professor Carmine thinks that you're fit to be left here *alone.*" I can't tell if he's implying I'm unsafe to be here, or if there's something unsafe here for me.

I don't want to know, either way.

He opens the door and steps back, but when he turns I see a flash of dark brown, and when Professor Langhorn has finally levered himself out the door, I see Rook standing there, looking more than a little confused.

"Professor," Rook greets, nodding his head at Langhorn. "I didn't know you were on a chatting basis with Professor

Carmine's assistant." His gaze flicks to mine, bored and disdainful, like I'm just another student. "Doesn't she have work to do?"

"I was just checking on her." Langhorn chuckles, his good humor back in place. "Lighten up, Professor Solomon." He claps Rook on the arm, getting a look so full of irritation that I hope his hand bursts into flames. It doesn't, though. Instead, both of them turn when Professor Carmine approaches, confusion on her pinched and ancient face.

"Is there a problem with my office?" she asks, her gaze going between them. "Or with my TA?"

"Neither," Langhorn promises, fidgeting under both of their scrutiny. "I was just leaving. Goodbye, professors." He nods at both of them, not bothering to look back at me. I'm glad for it, and I watch him stagger off, his stature not doing much for his balance.

Rook hesitates, waiting at the door as Professor Carmine strides in with a shake of her head. "Is everything okay, Blair?" she asks, her gaze flicking over mine.

I hesitate before nodding, gathering my things. "Yeah, it's just... he says things. You know? He's—"

"You just have to ignore him." Professor Carmine is obviously in a hurry, and I wonder if she's really listening to me. "He's a harmless, ancient idiot who needs to retire, whether by choice or by force. Just ignore whatever he says and shrug it off. It's not worth caring about."

That's easy enough for her to say, when she wasn't the one trapped in her office by him. Or at least, that's what it had felt like. She gathers what she needs and glances my way again, her light eyes sharp. "I'll see you tomorrow morning, yes?"

"Yeah," I agree automatically, trying to do what she'd said and shove his words to the back of my mind. I see Rook amble back to his own office, and I get to my feet with my things shoved haphazardly in my bag. He won't blow me off. He'll make this better, even if it just means soothing my nervous senses. My fingers curl around the strap of my bag as I try not to fidget, needing to exit the closet-sized office before I can.

They really should've given her a bigger, better space to do her work. When she does finally leave, I try not to make it obvious that I've been waiting for just that. I try not to book it across the wide open hallway with its small lounge and multiple classrooms. I need to be subtle, or at least somewhat ambiguous with what I'm doing.

But I don't do any of what I *should*. Instead, I bolt into Rook's office, only realizing belatedly that he could have another student or professor in here. Hell, he could just be *busy* and not want me in here, but none of that stops me.

I don't expect him to be standing at the cabinets by the door. He turns as I come in, hands raised to stop my forward momentum that takes me straight into his chest. "I'm sorry," I mutter, but I don't pull away as I fall into him. "I'm sorry, I'm—"

"Don't be sorry." He pulls me back a little, just enough to look at my face. "He freaked you out," he correctly deduces, his eyes narrowing ever so slightly. "Didn't he?"

Sudden fear rises in my throat, nearly choking me even as my lips part to give him the answer he's asking for. What if he tries to murder him? Or, more accurately, *succeeds*? I can't let someone get murdered for the crime of making me feel slightly uncomfortable during my office hours.

I stand there, staring up at him, with my mouth open and my throat sealed shut. My fingers slide against his shirt, finally gripping the thin material harder than I should. As if he can read my mind, Rook's face softens, becoming less severe. "I'm not Oliver, Love," he promises, voice quiet. "I know he freaked you out, but I'm not going to kill him for it. Or hunt him down to do something stupid. I know how to control myself." One hand leaves my upper arm, and he tucks my hair back behind my ear before tapping two fingers against my forehead. "You can talk to me."

So I do. I tell him exactly what Langhorn said and how he'd blocked the door. I tell him how I'd felt, how the older man makes me think of flies and rotted meat, and Rook doesn't interrupt me. He does steer me to the chair in front of his desk, arms around my shoulders as I get it all out.

"He's a creep. But I also agree with Professor Carmine," Rook says at last, when I've told him everything. "He needs to retire. *Fired*, if it comes to that. He says shit that he shouldn't be allowed to. But Blair?" Rook kneels beside the chair, his face earnest. "They're just words from a creepy, *lonely* old man. He's not going to hurt you. I'd never let him."

That thought opens something up in me, and I feel like the vice grip around my heart and lungs releases when he says it. I can't help myself. I lean forward and wrap my arms around his shoulders, dragging him close so I can bury my face in his neck and inhale his uniquely spicy but comforting scent.

It's too long before I pull away, and I glance up to see the door is closed. Thank God. "I'm sorry," I mutter quickly, looking away from him as my heart pounds in my throat. "I am *so* sorry, Professor, I—"

"You don't have anything to be sorry for, Love," Rook purrs, pulling me back in against him. He hesitates, looking thoughtful, then glances toward the door like I had. "Do you want to get dinner?" he asks at last. "I understand, if you don't. Spending time with me isn't like spending time with Oliver." His smile is both exasperated, and dry, but already I'm nodding my head, finding that I'm thrilled he's asked.

"Yes, please *yes*. Juniper has class late tonight, too. I'm not *afraid* or anything," I assure him, in case he thinks this is only to get away from the ick that Langhorn has left me with. "I *want* to get dinner with you."

"I wouldn't have minded it if it's just to get you away from some stress." He stands with a grimace, massaging his knee as he does. "Okay, Love. Give me just a minute and we can leave, all right? I just need to pack up."

CHAPTER 10

I expect him to take me to a casual diner, like Oliver would. Both of them know by now that I'm obsessed with breakfast, so any place will do as long as they serve eggs and toast. It's easy, inexpensive, and St. Augustine is littered with inexpensive breakfast restaurants.

But when Rook's dark silver SUV slides to a stop in a well-kept parking lot outside of a stone building, I realize we aren't at any of the cheap diners in town I'm very acquainted with. I lean to the side, looking up and out, but I can't see the sign. I should've been paying attention, instead of half-dozing off and half-listening to Rook talk.

It's nice just to listen to him talk. When I'm not afraid of imminent failure or a bad grade, his voice is relaxing, calming, and definitely on the good side of soothing.

"Was I boring you, Love?" The controlled serial killer hums as I grind my palms against my eyelids. Immediately, I shake my head, not wanting to offend him. "No. Sorry, I..." I dart my tongue out to lick my dry lips. "I like your voice. It's nice to listen to," I admit truthfully, not missing the small arch of one brow before he drops back into neutrality. "Did you invite Oliver?" I add, unbuckling my seatbelt and hoping to change the subject.

"No. Would you like me to?" The way he asks is so carefully neutral, so empty, that I can't help but look up at him, eyes narrowed.

"You don't want to. Even though I'm pretty boring and sort of afraid of you, so conversation is either going to be traumatizing or real rough." My voice is flat as I say it, and I don't look away from him during my educated hypothesis.

Now his lips hitch into a small smirk, and he shakes his head. "I'll invite him if you want me to."

"That's so disappointed parent of you. So... passive aggressive friend who doesn't want confrontation." It's easier to ramble when I'm still on the verge of being drowsy. It helps chase away the discomfort that's crawled over my skin since Professor Langhorn came into my borrowed office. But I also wish he'd grab me in a rough hug to help completely get rid of the smell of rot and imaginary buzz of flies.

But I'm not needy or weak. And I don't want Rook thinking I'm either of those, even if I have to fake it.

"Love." I adore the way he sighs my name in exasperation, even though I shouldn't. The implicit threat in the word should make me shiver in fear, not try to ignore the jolt of excitement that zips down my spine. Thoughts of how hard it'll be to end this try to invade my brain, but I push them away and stare up at Rook, my own brows climbing towards my bangs.

"Yeah?"

"I'm neither disappointed, nor passive aggressive," he points out. "If you want Oliver—"

"I don't get why you want to spend non-sex time with me."

I don't mean to interrupt him, and my fingers dig into the hem of my sweatshirt. "It's just... I'm not that interesting."

"You're incredibly interesting." He reaches out to snag his fingers into my sleeve, tugging me closer to him over the console. "Maybe you just need to spend more time with us with your clothes on so we can help you see it." The kiss he slants against my lips is too sweet, too gentle, too *chaste* for me, but it gets his point across. "I'd like to spend time with just you," Rook admits when he pulls away, fingertips grazing my face.

"Will you tell me something interesting? A secret?" I wonder, eyes widening in curiosity. "Oliver told me, vaguely, about people being cruel to him and you know. Murder. What've you got for me?"

Rook blinks, clearly unamused. "I have a passing grade that I'm willing to take away," he tells me evenly, and I snort.

"I still have two weeks to drop, *Professor*," I remind him, opening the passenger door to get out, just as he leans forward to grab my upper arm through my hoodie.

"You won't," he promises, his eyes on mine. There's no question in them. No request or plea. There's just his dark, arrogant certainty that everything will go the way he says it will. And while there's definitely something hot about it, especially when he's taking my clothes off or I'm this close to him in a small vehicle...

I won't let him make decisions for me.

My hand curls into a loose fist as I look at him, and a reckless grin curls over my features. "Watch me," I challenge, my eyes locked with his. "I know that you've known Oliver long enough that you can predict everything he does before he does it. But I'm not like Oliver." Not in a few ways, though most of them are obvious. "You don't know what I'll do if I'm pushed."

Rook's gaze turns calculating and almost cold. He looks me

over, eyes flitting from my hand to my hoodie, then finally resting back on my face once more. He's impossible to read, though I don't think he's exactly thrilled by my words. "We'll see if you surprise me," he murmurs finally, cracking a small grin. "I haven't been surprised in a long time."

"Not even when I held a gun to Oliver's head last semester?" I ask, heart pounding against my ribs as I do.

He releases me and sits up with a snort. "No. I was more surprised you didn't try to shoot him. But I didn't actually think you would. You *do* like him, you know."

"Do you think I like you, too?" I don't know why I ask it. I don't know why I confirm to him through those words that he's right and I *do* like Oliver.

But I don't know why I care, or why I ask. Because if he knows everything about what I'll do, he has to know I'm just waiting for a reason for this to come to an end. I've had the talk in my head over and over by now. So I know what's coming. I just don't know how to do it, or how to make myself okay with losing both of them from my life.

But you have to, that small Juniper-like voice whispers in my mind. *You can never be like them. Only a killer could be with them, and you're as harmless as a mouse.*

The insult, even though it's coming from my own brain, makes me cringe a little, though I don't let it show on my face as Rook starts to speak again.

"I think you're complicated. I think you're afraid of me." He's not wrong about those things, though I'm not sure if he means complicated as an insult or something else. "That you aren't sure what you want, and you've been trying to push Oliver and me into a box that you can close up and label for your own peace of mind." His attention remains fixed on my face, but I can't help it when I look away from his words.

Suddenly, I don't like this game as much anymore.

"As for you liking me? I think you'll like me more if I don't fail you, and after I feed you." He chuckles, releasing my arm. "I know you're addicted to breakfast, but I thought I'd help expand your horizons. If you'd get out of my car so we can actually eat." That mocking edge that I do so love is back in his voice, and Rook doesn't wait for me to move. He gets out of the car, gently closing the door behind him as I scramble to do the same.

Almost immediately he's beside me, holding out his hand for me like a Jane Austin love interest. He's certainly got the charm to be one, and I bet he'd look great in a fluffy, ruffled shirt. I drop my hand into his and don't miss the small smile on his lips as he tugs me up the sidewalk.

"Aren't you afraid someone from Wickett will see?" I ask as he laces his fingers with mine.

"No," he replies breezily, pushing open one of the large, heavy doors. They look to be made of wood, but when I press my fingers to them, I find the grain is smooth and fake, though it is a convincing illusion.

The restaurant itself is full of charm. Vaulted ceilings house chandeliers and stone climbs up the inner walls, just like it does on the outside. The sections are separated by half walls capped in a panel of stained glass, and greenery blossoms throughout nooks and crannies, over the half walls, and in centerpieces placed on small columns.

My nose tells me instantly we're at an Italian restaurant, and something better than the Americanized variety. In response to that, my stomach clenches, excited to load up on carbs as I chow down on my favorite food group. *Bread.*

"Good afternoon." A short, dark-haired woman stands behind the hostess stand and beams at us, her eyes flicking from mine to Rook's. "Just the two of you?" From what I can tell, the restaurant isn't full, and when I check my phone, I see that we've made it in before any kind of dinner rush can start.

Rook nods and the woman picks up two menus, leading us down the hallway that twines between sections until we're finally in a room that faces a nearby park. Windows line the outer wall to show off the view, and through one I can see a nearby fountain currently playing host to a couple of dogs. I slide into the booth across from Rook, glancing down at the small menu the lady gives me. As long as there's something without fish, I'm fine.

"Drinks?" the woman asks, glancing between us. "Dana is your server, but I'll go on and put them in with her."

"Sprite?" I ask hopefully, looking up at the woman. She nods and writes it down, along with Rook's order of unsweetened tea.

"That's very adult of you," I remark, looking at the menu and letting my eyes flick over the pasta selections.

"It's just tea, Love." He taps the back of my hand with one long finger. "Don't be so *nervous*. What do you think I'm going to do, murder you in a public place?"

I don't, exactly. "I hope you're not going to murder me at all," I mutter, rolling my eyes up towards him.

"We'll see how the semester goes." His voice is careful when he makes the joke, but he doesn't need to worry. It doesn't bother me to hear him talk like this. But that's part of the problem. The biggest part, actually, and something I can't get my brain to ignore or accept.

I should be much less okay with them.

"You're not going to tell Oliver, right?" I find myself asking, mouth betraying my thoughts I'd been too afraid to let loose.

Rook doesn't answer, but does pull his hand back so he can lean on his arms on the table. "About?" he asks, hesitant. "This? Why wouldn't I—"

"About Professor Langhorn." Now that it's done and over with, it's easy enough to shrink the severity of the incident in my mind. Professor Carmine is right, after all. He's just an old man who needs to retire and probably get checked for dementia. If he were dangerous, the school wouldn't let him continue working. The other professors wouldn't be telling me to just let it go. "I just..." I don't know how to *politely* say I'm worried about what Oliver would do.

"You just don't want him murdering some old man?" Rook supplies helpfully, though keeps his voice soft. "No, I'm not going to tell him. I was trying to figure out if *you* wanted to tell him. Oliver cares a lot about you, Blair. He wouldn't do it out of jealousy or from being possessive. He's not either of those things, unless you're ignoring him or with Juniper." There's a dry twist of his voice that I don't miss, but I snort anyway.

"He'd do it because he would want to protect you from any future harassment. He just doesn't think things through sometimes, and I'm already thinking we're going to have to move after the two of you graduate." There's a sigh in his voice, irritation on his lips, and he quirks his mouth into a frown.

I look up, surprised. "You're moving? Where will you go?" The words are out of my mouth before I can remember that I won't care, because I'll be long gone.

He just shrugs. "I don't know yet. Hopefully, somewhere with *seasons*. But Oliver has done too much down here, and I don't want to wait until something worse happens and we *have* to move. I'd rather remain as inconspicuous as possible." He grins crookedly in my direction, still drumming his fingers on the table.

So many things come to mind. There are so many things I want to say or ask. *What about me?* Is the top among them, but I definitely won't ask that. *I'll be gone*, I remind myself forcefully, yet again.

I'll.

Be.

Gone.

"Canada is nice anytime of year," I finally remark casually. "Have you considered going international? I bet the Canadian colleges would just *love you.*"

"Oliver actually has dual citizenship there. So yes, I have considered it," Rook replies offhandedly. "I could probably get it, though it would take a little while. I think we're going to need to move more quickly than I would get my visa. But we'll see. What about you, Blair?" The question causes my stomach to twist, and for one wild moment I'm sure he's going to ask me to move *with* them.

"What?" I ask, blinking rapidly to recover my thoughts. "What do you mean?"

"You aren't going to stay in St. Augustine, are you? Will you go home to Indiana? Or somewhere else, maybe with Juniper?" The way he speaks, it's as if he already knows my intention to leave them. But that can't be right, can it? When he's trying so hard to win me over and help me fall in love with both of them?

"I don't know," I admit truthfully. "There aren't a lot of places clamoring for an art history major. I probably should've thought of that three years ago, but..." I shrug my shoulders. "Well, it's too late now. While I have no idea what I'll do, I know I don't *want* to go home." My own lips twist into a frown. "I love my parents to death, but they're more conservative than I'd like to deal with for the rest of my life, and I *like* being on my own, making my own decisions. Maybe I'll... Uh, become a famous streamer-turned-director, huh? Make the spiciest movies ever and become famous for it. That's totally an option, right?"

"It is if you want it to be. But you'd better start taking

photography seriously, since you'll want to know what your cinematographers are talking about." He cracks a smile at his own words, just as our drinks are brought out and our waitress, Dana, introduces herself.

"Do you two know what you'd like?" she asks, looking between us without an ounce of unfriendliness. She seems like she has all the time in the world for the two of us to order, and I can't help but return her infectious smile.

"Can I get the cheese-stuffed ravioli?" I ask, brushing my fingers over the menu. "With just marinara? No meat sauce?" She nods as I talk, jotting down my order on the small pad she holds.

"I'll do the lasagna," Rook orders smoothly, handing her both of our menus. "Thank you." She nods enthusiastically before walking away, presumably toward the kitchen to give them our order.

"So..." I lean back in my booth, arms folded. "This is where you tell me a really cool story about why you became a, you know." I wiggle my brows at him pointedly. "*You know.*"

"A photographer?" He leans back as well, gaze catching and holding mine. "You got it, Love. Though I have to tell you, it isn't that interesting."

"I meant—"

"You meant why didn't I become a nature photographer and instead, I picked to do what I do? No problem. I'll tell you that too." He launches into a story about being a boy full of longing, though the goading look on his face tells me all I need to know while he weaves the details around a troubled, inspired childhood and a miracle of *deus ex machina* level that presented him with his first camera, and therefore awakened his passion.

It's a lie. All of it. I can see that easily enough. Though the entertainment value is high, I remark twice on inconsistencies, which he shrugs off without any real explanations.

"This is my childhood tale, not yours," my asshole of a professor informs me when I tell him he's changed his mother's age again. He sniffs in disdain and looks away, his nose up in the air. "When it's your turn to tell of your harrowing, eventful life, then you can tell me what age my mother was supposed to have been."

I mumble my agreement, and nod along with the *of course* that spills from my lips to agree with him. It stops mattering if the story is true, when he starts joking about it. And by the time our food appears, I'm surprised he's been talking for almost twenty minutes.

"Will you really not tell me the truth?" I ask curiously, poking a fork into my ravioli. "Seriously?"

"Of course I will," he tells me, head tilted to the side. "When I think you can handle it." I don't get what he means. I don't understand why it's such a secret, when I know so much about him already. But I go along with it, and let him draw me into a conversation about my life, giving him details I tend not to share with anyone. I can't help it when he asks nicely and gives me the kind of wide-eyed, curious look that before today, I would've only associated with Oliver.

It's...*nice*, I think, as I get back into the SUV so he can drive me back to my apartment. He's nice when he wants to be. Even if I never would've thought he was capable of it unless he was trying to get something from the exchange.

He's given me something to think about as he takes me home, and it only makes my stomach twist up in tighter knots, hating the confusion that he so easily dishes out. I can't let him shake my conviction, but it's so hard not to come clean about my intentions, or my thoughts.

But I keep my mouth shut about them and reply to his easy conversation, leaning into his kiss once he pulls up to my apartment and tells me to have a goodnight.

I even manage not to invite him up or tell him to take me back to his place instead, though it's definitely a near thing.

CHAPTER 11

"**A**re you sure this isn't *B minus* work?" I ask shrewdly, brushing my hand over the photos we printed to turn in with our project.

Oliver snorts and tweaks my fingers with his, giving a quick shake of his head. Stretched out on my bed, he looks so at ease. Like he could fall asleep here without an issue. It's hard to believe he hates my roommate enough to want to murder anyone that looks like her, but maybe that's because she isn't here right now.

Are you sure you're okay coming over? I'd asked, hesitating beside Oliver's Mustang. He'd promised me, rather enthusiastically, that he was. And that had been that. He'd driven me home and stretched out on my bed, his shoes on the floor, and now I can barely take my eyes off of him.

God, why does he have to be so gorgeous?

"It's going to be fine. There's no way he doesn't give you something better than a B," Oliver assures me, sitting up just enough that he can lean into me. When he lays back down, I realize that he'd moved enough that he's draped across my lap, and I shake my head as he curls closer to me, face against my thighs.

"Are you tired?" My fingers seem to move automatically, trailing through his sun-soaked auburn hair. "Do you want to take a break?"

"What I want is to take you home and keep you," Oliver purrs, one arm around my waist. "I want you to stay with me and Rook. I want..." He trails off with a lazy sigh. "There are a lot of things I want," he admits at last, not looking up at me. "But more than anything, I want you to *please* keep running your fingers through my hair."

I smirk, though he can't see it, fingers picking up their movements as I comb through his hair. My attention is fully off of the photos for now, and I watch his shoulders rise and fall as he breathes evenly, as if he might fall asleep.

"You think I'm pretty." The purred statement isn't even close to a question, but I snort anyway. "You're staring at me."

"How do you know?"

"Because I can feel it, wonder girl." He rolls over onto his back, carefully moving the photos and the report I'd written up for them, until he can lie in my lap and stare up at me. His green eyes glitter, without any malice or ulterior motives in his features. Just... *Oliver.* Every bit of Oliver that I've come to enjoy being around. "See?" he murmurs, reaching up to touch my face. "Knew it. I—"

The front door opens and closes, and I can immediately feel the difference in the psycho serial killer in my lap. He goes to move, but I don't let him. I move instead, straddling him on my bed, my hands on either side of his face.

"It's Juniper, huh?" he asks, tilting his face cutely to the side. His gaze is bright. Too bright, in my opinion, and he slants a look at the door. "You're afraid I'll do something."

"I think I'd like you to tell me that you won't," I breathe. I still haven't told him about Professor Langhorn, and the look on his face reminds me exactly why that is. Oliver is unpredictable and wild. He's not controlled and cool, like Rook. Bringing him here may have been a mistake, but I *need* to know if he can be around Juniper without doing something awful.

Though, maybe a trial by fire wasn't the best thing I could've done.

"Blair?" Juniper's voice is half-distracted as she puts her things away, walking back into the kitchen past my closed door. "You home?"

I don't take my eyes off of Oliver to call, "Yeah, I'm home. We'll be out in a minute."

"Okay." She doesn't remark on the *we*. She doesn't even hesitate to answer, like she heard me. But then again, maybe it just didn't click for her.

"You can get off of me, wonder girl," Oliver promises softly, and leans up to kiss my nose. "I'm not going to do something that will hurt you. You should know that by now." He pushes up against me gently, prompting me to get to my feet and hold a hand out to him with my heart pounding in my chest.

He takes it, sliding on his shoes, and grabs his backpack from the bed as he does.

"You're leaving?" I asked, not exactly surprised but still a little disappointed.

"Yeah," he confirms. "I'll do anything for you, but I know my own limits. I can't help how I feel, or what that makes me want to do." His eyes pin mine, making it clear what he means. Not that I needed the clarification. Nerves tingle in my chest, and I take a step back to watch him get his things. I want to argue. I want to tell him he's fine, that I want him here.

But...

Well, I don't exactly want a dead roommate slash best friend.

Opening the door, I walk out first, heading for the kitchen with Oliver behind me. When Juniper glances up, her attention immediately goes straight to him, and her hands still on her phone and planner.

"Hey, Oliver," she greets, her tone somewhat strained. "Sorry, I didn't know you were here."

"I'm just leaving," Oliver promises, wrapping his arms around me from behind. "We were doing some work on our photography project." He nuzzles his face against my hair, but I don't pull away or lean into him. I'm too busy staring Juniper down, trying to predict her next move.

"Do you want to stay?" she asks, still the epitome of politeness and courtesy. "We could order something. I don't want to cook and I think we're out of food, anyway." Even before she's done talking, Oliver is shaking his head against my cheek, gazing up at her with wide, earnest eyes.

"Not tonight," he tells my roommate sweetly. "I have to get home. Sorry, Juniper. Maybe next time?" It's hard to doubt his sincerity when he's like this, and Juniper readily agrees with him.

But of course she does. She may not like him, but she has no idea how much he hates her.

"I'll walk to your car with you," I offer, firmly lacing my fingers with Oliver's, so he knows I'm not willing to argue about it. His smile turns bemused, and he leans in to kiss my cheek.

"It was good to see you again, Jun," he tells my roommate enthusiastically, the golden-retriever-ride-or-die act back in full force. It's more genuine than I've ever seen him with her, but that makes it even more obvious to me that it's just an act he's putting on so that she doesn't bother him or push him away from me anymore.

Well, I can't say he isn't *trying*, now can I? He's giving it his level best, and there's definitely something impressive about that.

"You too. Let me know next time, and I'll bring something home?" Juniper looks between us, and it's so painfully obvious how hard she's trying that I do my civil duty and *drag* Oliver to the door. It's that, or this gets worse and worse by the moment. I give Juniper a quick smile over my shoulder, noticing her bewildered look, and then Oliver closes the door behind us, cutting off my view.

"I told you I wouldn't do anything," he reminds me with a dark, rolling chuckle. His arm snugs up over my shoulders, pulling me closer until I have to fall in step with him.

"I know," I mutter, tucking my hair behind my ear as he leads me towards the elevator. "And I'm super grateful that you're making the effort. But..." I don't know how to put into words what I'm thinking in a way that won't irritate him. The old, familiar fear rises in my stomach when I'm confronted with what he is up close, and I hope he doesn't feel the shudder that drags up my spine.

"But you still don't trust me." He seems too cheerful when he says it, and his ensuing grin is just a little too wolfish and over-enthusiastic. "I get it. Sort of. Even though I did give you my word, and I haven't, uh, looked for an outlet since the last time that you know about."

I don't tell him that I can't just believe that so easily. After all, I have no way of knowing if he's lying or not. Instead, I just look at him, not sure how my face reads or what he'll see there. Whatever it is, it brings a smile to his face, and he leans forward to kiss my temple. "You're adorable," he murmurs against my skin, punching the button for the elevator.

"You're... certainly you," I reply, my smile too wide and overly happy. Not that it bothers him. He just laughs as the elevator opens, and yanks me through the doors until my back is pressed against the wall.

With a quick press, he lights up the button for the underground parking level, and then crowds me against the wall once more, his hands on my hips as he keeps me there. "Oh, wonder girl," Oliver sighs, pressing his forehead against mine. "What am I going to do with you and how little you trust me? This will never work unless you do, you know. You have to trust me enough not to do something stupid, or put me on a leash for the rest of our lives." He wiggles his brows, but I can't help the scoff that morphs into a grin on my lips.

"Putting you on a leash is on my bucket list." I snicker, reaching up to curl my fingers in his jacket. "But I'm looking for a cute pair of ears to clip in your gorgeous hair first. I expect you to practice being a *dog* for me, Oliver, until then." When I wiggle my brows, he laughs outright.

The elevator dings open and he pulls me out into the parking garage to seal his lips against mine. "It's always so hard to leave you," he hums, nipping at my bottom lip when he finally pulls away. My breath comes fast and my heart flutters in my chest as I look at him, my fingers digging deep into the fabric of his jacket.

Shit. I can't do this. I can't push him away.

I have to.

"Go away," I tell him, thumping my hand against his arm. "I'm going to *starve* soon, okay? If you aren't staying for food, I still need to figure something out."

"You could just come have dinner with us," Oliver suggests. "Hell, you can just come *live* with us. Your wing hasn't been finished, but you could sleep in my room until it is. Hell, we could stage a coup and take over Rook's room. I like his room."

"You only like it because it doesn't look like a tornado hit it," I point out dryly. "No, I'm eating dinner with Juniper.

Pancakes, maybe, or I guess I could suffer through pizza as long as there's pineapple on it for me. I'll talk to you later?"

It's as much of a dismissal as I can muster, but Oliver certainly doesn't seem put out about it. He nods his head a couple times, then steps forward to kiss me once more, as if he can't keep his hands or his mouth off of me.

It's definitely a fun thought, imagining him *needing* to touch me. But one that I force out of my mind for the time being. "Bye," I say again, wrapping my arms around myself. "Oliver?" He stops, almost halfway to his car.

"What's wrong, Blair?" he asks, when I don't continue.

But I just shake my head, a crooked smile on my face. "Nothing. Sorry. Have a good night." He holds my gaze for a moment, causing my breath to go stale in my chest and my lungs to squeeze in protest. I think he'll say something or ask me what's really wrong.

I even think that I'll tell him, so maybe he can find a way to convince me that I'm wrong and that I can't live without them.

But he doesn't. He gives me one last, tiny wave before he gets to his car and unlocks it, sliding into the driver's seat without another word and starting the engine as he does. He doesn't wait around. Oliver leaves, and though I try, I can't tell if he waves through his window as his Mustang creeps up from the parking garage and out to the street beyond.

And once he's gone, my resolve crumbles. I step back into the elevator and realize that if I don't tell both of them now that I'm done, then I never will.

Tomorrow, I tell myself, fighting the urge to cry. *I have to do it tomorrow.*

CHAPTER 12

Readjusting my hand on my backpack strap reminds me of how painfully tight my grip is on the black material. But I barely notice, even when my knuckles creak in protest. Instead, my eyes are glued to Rook's office, and even though I need to talk to him *today*, I pray to God he isn't there.

If he isn't there, then I can put this off just for a little while. I haven't cried, but my eyes feel gritty and dry. Like I'm holding something back and punishing myself for what I'm about to do.

But honestly... aren't I?

I can't believe I'm going to do this, but there's nothing else *to* do. Sure, I haven't asked Juniper her opinion, or told her about them for her safety, but I know what she'd say.

I know what everyone in my life would say.

Get away from them.

They're dangerous.

They'll kill you too in the end, because you aren't a killer like them.

The last thought is the one that hurts the worst. That they

can never really love me because I'm not like them. In the end, I can't help but think, it'll just end in tragedy for me. Unless I was *different*. Unless I—

I close my eyes hard against that thought. I'm not a killer, and I don't think I ever could be.

Still, I can't help but let out a sigh of relief as I see that Rook's light is off and the door to his office is firmly closed. Just for good measure, I check the small window by the door, but all I see is the empty office chair turned to the side, and a desk littered with papers in haphazard piles.

Yeah, there's no chance he's in here. Something in me relaxes, like a fist around my heart has loosened its grip enough for the blood to finally flow to my extremities. Maybe my fingers will even stop tingling soon, though I'm not holding out hope.

Quickly I leave, not wanting to look like I'm spying on a professor like some weirdo. I cross the hall, surprised to see that Professor Carmine is already gone. It's ten minutes before my office hours technically start, but since she's already gone, I fall into her chair with a sigh, leaning back to listen to the thunder that rumbles through the concrete walls of the art department.

According to my phone, it's supposed to rain on and off throughout the weekend. These storms are supposed to be mild compared to the worse ones coming in later in the week. By now, I'm sure conspiracy theorists are thinking that St. Augustine is cursed, since rain isn't common this time of year. More than that, the average rainfall for February is so low that we're using up our entire allotment in the first week.

Not that I mind. As someone from the Midwest, I adore storms. Florida doesn't have enough good thunderstorms this time of year for my blood.

I wonder if St. Augustine has ever *seen* snow, and if the city would survive if it did.

The light above me flickers, and I cross my fingers for a power outage while knowing that, in reality, it's simply the shitty old bulb that needs to be replaced. This isn't the first time that it's flickered or gone dim. And it happens enough that I can't believe Professor Carmine hasn't gone up in arms against the department for not fixing it yet.

Kicking back in the less-than-comfortable desk chair, I close my eyes and listen to the rain. It's hard enough that I can hear it, even without windows in the room, and I can't help but think that no one is going to show up today. Especially since the school is closed this Friday, and I'm sure that since it's Thursday, a lot of students have already taken off for a long weekend. I would, if I had anywhere to go.

But all I have to do this weekend is to break Oliver's heart, disappoint Rook, and ruin myself in the process. My insides twist at the callous thought, and I squeeze my eyelids together hard enough that my eyes burn. I know how much I'll hate this, but I know that it's necessary.

And I won't keep rehashing it in my head, looking for a loophole. I'm old enough to know by now there isn't one. So I'll keep an eye on Rook's office that I can see across the hall. With my door open, it's easy to see his closed door, and I'll be able to tell if he shows up so I can sneak across and maybe mitigate Oliver's heartbreak by talking to our professor first.

After all, he's the more level-headed one, and hopefully he'll know what to do about *Oliver*.

A knocking causes me to flick my eyes open, and as the office door closes, I think for a moment that my thoughts have summoned my photography professor.

But it isn't Professor Solomon, or Oliver, or one of my students.

Professor Langhorn is here; the light from the hallway is blocked by the now-closed door that he stands in front of. Once again, he examines the paintings on the wall, and I resign myself to another awkward, creepy conversation with this professor.

God, I wish someone would offer him retirement. Or force it on him. But if I keep pretending that he's basically ninety years old and losing it, then he doesn't seem so scary. Even if the reality is he's closer to sixty, stinks like rotten meat, and seems to know exactly what he's saying. From what I know, he's married, but clearly his wife either doesn't know or hasn't tried to stop his weird behavior.

His mouth opens as he breathes, the whistling noise filling the small space. I don't know what he wants or why he's here, but my eyes keep flicking to the closed door as I cross my legs under the desk, muscles tense.

"Can I help you, professor?" I ask, unable to keep my voice from being tight and unamused.

"Still just wondering why Professor Carmine doesn't get art that fits you better." He laughs hoarsely, tongue darting out to lick his bottom lip. His dark eyes slide over mine, and he looks over as much of me as he can before finally meeting my gaze. "You don't mind me coming in for an appointment with you, right, Blair?" While I know he's only aware of my name thanks to Professor Carmine, that doesn't make it any better. I hate the way my name sounds on his lips. "I know I'm not one of your students, but you can spare some time for me, I'm sure."

"Oh, no, actually. Professor Carmine was really clear about what she expects." I smile nervously, tapping my fingers on the laminate of the desk. "I have to keep the office door open so her students know they can come for help. And I can't close it or have anyone else in here until my office hours are done."

Really, it's just *one* hour, so it's not a big deal. And it's not just because of Professor Carmine that I don't want him here.

"Could you leave, please?" I ask nicely, getting to my feet like I'm going to escort him out the door. In reality, I don't know if I could even get past him, but I'm more than willing to try. "I have a couple of students coming in. If you need something, we can talk about it later." There's nothing he should need from me, and I keep my eyes off of him in order to keep a polite smile on my face. Somehow I manage to reach past him, my hand going for the door handle as the too-sweet smell of sour breath and body odor falls over me.

"Don't be so rude, Blair." He laughs as suddenly his hand finds my wrist, pudgy fingers curling around my arm. I automatically try to pull away, jerking back, but his grip is stronger than it has any right to be, and he steps closer into my space.

"Let go," I breathe, my heart choking me as it jumps to my throat. "Let *go*, please." His hand is sweaty and slides against my skin like it's covered in oil, but he doesn't release me.

"Blair, I'm trying to have a conversation with you," Professor Langhorn goes on, following me to the desk. He pushes me back until my legs bump against it, Professor Carmine's stapler toppling to the ground.

"Oops," he tells me, eyes on mine. "Look what you did. You should be more respectful of your professor's property. You're terrible at this."

"No, I..." I look down, my mouth open, at his hand on my arm. I want to scream. To yell for him to stop, so that someone else will come in and *stop him*. But I can barely gasp in a breath into my paralyzed lungs. "Let go of me." I'm sure I've said it before, but it has no effect this time, either.

Instead, his other hand comes up to rest on my thigh, pushing up under my skirt and keeping my leg pressed against the desk. His hand is cold and harsh against my skin, nothing like Rook or Oliver's, and I jerk away from him, just for him to dig his fingers so hard into my skin I almost do scream.

"Shh, *shhh*!" Professor Langhorn's gaze doesn't leave my face. There's something different in his expression today. Something broken and gone. Like he really doesn't know or care what he's doing.

"Professor, *stop*. Please," I say, my hands coming up to try to push at him. Our size difference becomes evident quickly, and the fact is that no matter how I push at him, he doesn't move.

"Don't scream, Blair. You don't need to make any noise." His fingers tighten even more on my thigh, nails digging into me hard enough to make my head spin. "Think of what someone would say if you *did* scream. They'd call you a whore. A stupid *slut* for her professors. Is that what you are?"

"There's something wrong with you," I tell him, not quite meaning it as an insult but more of a plea. "There's something *wrong*. Please don't do this. Please *stop*." My voice climbs in octave but not volume, and when I try to drag in a breath to scream, I still just can't.

Why can't I scream? No matter how I push at him, he doesn't move, and every inch that his hand climbs up my leg feels like a searing, burning pain in my flesh.

"Something wrong with *me*?" Langhorn's brows climb. "No, no, there's nothing wrong with me. You're the fucked up bitch who comes in here in those skirts trying to show off. You've been asking for this all semester. And I see the way you talk to Professor Carmine. She knows, doesn't she?" His voice gains a hysterical, accusatory edge.

"No. No, there's nothing to know." I grab his wrist in my hand, pressing down hard with my nails. "I'll scream," I threaten again, just as I catch sight of my phone. While I may not be able to convince my lungs to let me scream, I can text someone. Maybe I can tell Rook. He has to be coming to his office soon. If I could text him *something*, he could come over here and help me.

My hand darts across the desk, my whole body turning as I go for my phone. But I'm too slow. Too stupid, too *fucking dumb* to hide what I'm doing or even *scream*. Professor Langhorn sees what I'm going for as well and his hand leaves my arm, knocking my phone to the floor in one movement and, in the next, turning back on me again, his fingers gripping my hoodie.

"No," he tells me, eyes glittering. "No, stupid girl. You're not going to call *anyone*."

"I'll scream if you don't—" I hope the threat is enough, and I barely see his hand move. I only catch sight of a blur, then pain blooms in my cheek, sending tears to my eyes and dazing me before I can make good on my threat.

I stare at him, my chest heaving. His touch still burns on my leg, and I'm just so *frozen*. I can't move. I can barely breathe. The only things I know are how badly my face hurts and how much I hate him massaging my leg like he's trying to comfort me.

When he moves it further upward, I start to say something again. I don't know what—I don't know whether I'll scream or cry or beg or threaten—but I don't get the chance.

He hits me again, in the same place, drawing a soft cry from my throat and causing my knees to buckle against the desk so that I'm only held up by it and his hands.

"Shh, *shh*," he murmurs soothingly, hand sliding my skirt all the way up. He grabs it suddenly, jerking the material away from my body until it rips enough to not be in his way.

But all I can do is whimper. Screams wail against my insides, hitting my ribs and thrumming in my head. There's a stapler on the floor that could be a weapon, and surely I should be able to *do something—*

He grabs my underwear in his other hand, and I can't tell what he's saying. There's only the low buzz of his words like flies in my ear as he tears through the thin material, pushing them down my thigh.

All I need to do is scream—

I tell myself that as tears run down my face, and my mouth opens in what I pray-hope-*beg* will be something more than a soft whimper. Then he shoves his two fingers into me hard enough that it *burns* so badly that my breathing picks up and the tears on my face fall to my lap.

Help me, I want to yell. I imagine my gaze burning a hole through the door as Langhorn's sour-sweet breath curls through my nostrils.

Help me, I imagine screaming when Rook can see me. He'd run toward me with some hidden knife, ready to do all the things I wish he would.

Help. Me. I think, clenching my eyes shut hard as Professor Langhorn thrusts his fingers in and out of me, oblivious to or uncaring of my pain. His other hand gropes my breasts, digging under my hoodie until he can push my bra up and get the access he wants. His words are wrong, wrong, *wrong* as he moves to grip my arms, giving up groping me so he can hold me when I suddenly find the will to struggle.

When he finally steps back and wipes his fingers on my shirt, I can barely see him through the veil of tears that fills my eyes. My body is numb, save for the pain, and the moment he steps away I slide to the floor, knees crumpled under me, unable to hold myself up.

"Might as well just stay down there," he sneers, shoving his hands in his pockets. "And don't look at me like that, Blair. You've been asking for this all semester. You've been begging me to do something about you. Don't pretend you haven't." He kneels down, and a flash of fear goes through me, only for him to throw my phone at my face.

I don't even move to catch it. I wince when it hits my nose; it hurts, then goes numb. There's more pain in my mouth, then a trickle of blood heats my skin as I watch Professor Langhorn walk for the door, like nothing has happened and he didn't leave me full of bruises and more hurt than I've ever been in my life.

"And tell her to get better fucking art," he mutters, throwing one of the paintings to the floor and stomping on the glass to shatter it.

He doesn't look at me again, though. Not when he opens the door to jovially greet another professor across the hallway, or before he shuts the office door gently, his conversational tone fading as he goes about his day like he didn't just come in here and hurt me.

Like this man didn't walk in and, in the span of five minutes, ruin everything and destroy me so completely, that I can't bring myself to move.

CHAPTER 13

There's no way to know how much time goes by. At some point the rest of me goes limp, and I fall onto my side on the rough carpet, eyes fixed on the fibers I can see unraveling from it.

I need to move. I need to do something, or at least fix my clothes.

But everything hurts too much.

My gaze falls on my phone as tears slip from under my eyelids. Why couldn't I have yelled? Or called them? I could've fought him for my phone, but I'd let him throw it to the ground.

I'd let him do this to me.

A full body shudder goes through me, and I clench my eyes shut hard against the roughness of the carpet and the pain in my body. Between my thighs hurts the worst. A burning, aching feeling that makes me grit my teeth until I hear them creak. Second to that is my thigh, but I'm too afraid to look down and see the bruises I'm afraid mark me as the failure I am.

I should've stopped him from doing this to me.

The door handle turns, and as much as I want to roll away, as much as I want to make sure my skirt is still covering me, all I can do is watch, with my heart in my throat and wait for the telltale signs of a student or, worse, Professor Langhorn.

But it's Professor Carmine that appears in the door, her mouth moving as she talks. She doesn't look at me right away, and I want to beg for her to close the door as she lays her briefcase on the file cabinet with a *thump*.

Then, finally, she turns and sees me.

Professor Carmine freezes. Her face falls with shock, with surprise, and finally contorts with horror. She slams the door behind her as she comes forward, only stopping when I flinch away from her questing hands. "Blair," she whispers, fingers shaking as they hover over me. "What... Who did this? Blair, can you hear me?"

I nod, though I close my eyes tight. Her words have pushed some life into me, and I lift one trembling hand to adjust my skirt, though quickly learn that it's torn too badly to do an effective job of covering me.

"God. Blair..." She stares at me with all the horror that I feel, and when I open my eyes, I see that reflected in her gaze. It's too much. I close my eyes again, burying my face against the rough, dirty carpet that rubs my skin raw with every movement. "Okay. Can I help you sit up, please? I need to..." She looks around, clearly out of her depth. "Blair, I need to call 9-1-1."

Immediately I'm shaking my head, even though I don't know why. I should *want* her to call them. I need to tell them what happened, and who did it.

"But I'm going to have to get someone to help me get you up." She goes to touch my shoulder, but pulls away quickly, as if contact with me is painful or forbidden. "Is there a professor who—"

"Professor Solomon." I whisper his name with a shaking, trembling breath. For a second I don't even realize I'd said it, but when I do, I say it again. "Can you get... Professor Solomon? Is he here?"

She hesitates, her eyes going from her desk back down to me. "Are you sure that's who you want to help?" my professor asks so gently that it hurts. I nod fervently, eyes still closed, unable to look her in the eye.

"Okay. He's here, Blair. Jus-just wait for me." She doesn't hesitate again. My professor is out of the office before I can even blink and pulls the door closed behind her quickly enough that no one can see me.

I imagine I can see her, and through the sound of the rain on concrete, I create the sound of her rushed steps in my head. I can almost hear her knocking on Rook's door, and I can see the scowl on his face when he opens it.

But I can't imagine how he'll react. Will he be upset? Angry, maybe, to the point he won't come help me but instead want to get Oliver and hunt down Professor Langhorn?

Or will he be disappointed in me for not doing more to stop it?

The door bangs open on its hinges, causing me to flinch, and my eyes open to slits to see Rook in the doorway, his face showing none of the emotions I'd expected. He's... calm. There's no expression at all as he looks around the room, but when his gaze finally falls onto mine, I feel tears welling up in my eyes all over again, and I shiver.

"Andrea?" He turns, using Professor Carmine's first name. "You have your phone, don't you?" I can't hear her answer, but he goes on a moment later. "Call from the art department office. Let me see what I can do in here, all right?"

This time I hear her argue, but I just can't seem to focus on it. My eyes drift shut again, and the next thing I know, a hand is smoothing down my arm.

I jump. A half-cry leaves me as I nearly come up off the ground, but when my eyes fly upward, I realize it's only Rook. Only Rook, but I'd thought for a moment—

"I'm sorry," I whisper, falling back to the floor. "I'm sorry, *I'm sorry.* I tried to get away from him. I wanted to yell for you, or call you, or..." I wave my hand dismissively, unsure even of what I'm trying to say. "I didn't *mean to*—"

"Blair. Listen to me. Please, just listen." I think I can hear his voice shaking, but at the still neutral look on his face, I can't imagine this calm professor losing control of anything. So I must be imagining it. Just making up things in my fuzzy head. I can barely hear anyway, with my heart pounding in my ears and the rushing that hasn't completely gone away since Professor Langhorn hit me.

"You didn't do anything wrong," he tells me, eyes fixed on mine. "I just—" He closes his eyes hard, and as I watch, he takes a deep, steadying breath. "I just need you to work with me. Let me help you." I'm not imagining it this time. There's a tremor in his tone, like he's barely holding it together.

"I should've—" But he waves me quiet.

"No. Don't say that. Can you stand up for me?" I think about it, and the confusion must show on my face, because he reaches his hands out to me and asks, "Can you take my hands and let me help you sit up?"

That seems... slightly more reasonable. I reach one hand up, clasping it with his, then let him tug me into a sitting position and grip my other hand. "Good girl," he murmurs, eyes never leaving mine. "You're going to be okay. I've got you."

"I—" The gentleness in his words *hurts.* Tears sting my eyes, and though I try to blink them away, they fall like a downpour across my cheeks, burning hot lines where the rug had rubbed my skin. "Rook, I'm sorry. I'm *sorry*." He drags me forward into a hug and I let him, finally breaking down into sobs against the warmth and safety of his chest.

"Professor Carmine is calling an ambulance," he tells me soothingly, one hand tucking my hair back from my ear. "But I need you to do a couple things for me. Can you please listen for a moment, Love? Please?"

I nod without moving, arms clamped around him like I'll never be able to let go.

"I need you to be okay with the paramedics when they get here. They're not going to let me go to the hospital with you, Blair." My grip tightens on him and I shake my head against his chest, but he gentles me with a fierce hug. "I'll be there," he promises me. "I'll be there with Oliver, I *swear*. But I'm not family, and it won't look right to anyone else if you beg for me to come. I need you to remember, darling, that I'm your professor. Can you do that for me, Blair?"

I don't know if I can. I don't see myself peeling my arms away from him, walking by myself, or going with other people–other *men*–to the hospital without him. But the sureness in his voice and the steadiness of him makes me nod. I'll try, because he wants me to. Because it's what he needs me to do and some part of me can still comprehend that much.

"And second, Blair." I can hear other voices, and he pulls away just enough to look me in the eye as the sound of campus security officers coming down the hallway fills my ears with yells and quick steps.

I almost don't hear him when his lips move. I have to lean close, but when I do hear him say, with absolute clarity, "*I need you to tell me who did this to you.*"

For a moment, I don't think I've heard him right. I blink

owlishly at him as his grip tightens on my shoulders, only to loosen when there's a knock on the door.

"Can we come in?" a woman asks, her voice tight. "It's campus security. The police and paramedics are on the way."

I stare at Rook who doesn't move, still wide-eyed with confusion and paralysis. He searches my gaze for a few moments before he frowns, and that simple twist of his lips is enough for me to lunge forward, my mouth close to his ear.

"Professor Langhorn," I whisper shakily, the words broken and unsteady. Fear rises in me at the mention of his name, as if somehow that will summon him back here to do something worse. "*Professor Langhorn*," I tell him again, a little more strongly.

He nods and grips my hand, kissing my fingers. "Thank you. Can you stand up?" He still hasn't answered the campus security officer, and when she bangs again and repeats her question, he finally snaps, "Just give her a minute."

Almost forcefully, Rook helps me to my feet. I don't need to look at myself to know that I'm a mess, with my underwear around one ankle and my skirt ripped up the seam. He notices my thighs press together in an attempt to hide myself and without a word, my professor removes his jacket, tying it around my waist a second later to give me some kind of modesty. "Let me help you," he offers, sinking to his knees again.

I stare at him, unable to move, as his hands skim my legs, straightening what he can and putting my clothes back into place as much as they're able to go. At first my mind tries to scream not to let him. That his touch feels the same as Langhorn's on my thigh.

But that thought diminishes, disintegrates on the wind as he gazes up at me with trust and kindness on his face. There's nothing similar between them at all, and for a moment, I want to beg him to cover the large bruise on my thigh that's still somewhat covered by his hoodie. I even reach down and touch it, my fingers nowhere near long enough to cover the darkening purple marks.

At my movement, Rook looks down as well, and stills when he sees the marks. One hand comes up, trembling, and I grab his fingers at the last second, bringing his palm to my skin to cover up the searing, burning bruise that somehow hurts more when he looks at it.

"Rook, I'm sorry," I tell him again, when I don't know what else to say. "I wanted to do something. I wanted to yell for you."

"No, Blair." God, he's so gentle that he might *break* me. "You have nothing to be sorry for." His words almost shatter me. It's a good thing the security officer comes in a second later, glancing between us with worry in her eyes.

"I was helping her stand," Rook tells the officer, irritation glittering in her eyes. He's no longer touching me. No longer holding me upright with his hands or by his words. I sag against the desk, gripping it hard with knuckles that ache from the pressure. "She deserves a minute to get herself under control."

"I understand that, professor," the woman, who looks to be in her mid-thirties with curly red hair, says slowly. "But until the paramedics get here, I need to stay with her and the door needs to be open. Understand?"

He nods his head; the frustration oozing out of him to sink into the offensive carpet below. "I need to go," he tells her, all of his kindness and caring from minutes ago gone. "The paramedics are close, I take it?"

"They just got here. They're coming in now."

He nods and turns to look at me one more time, lips parting as if he wants to say something. I want to beg him to stay. To ride in the ambulance with me and let me just cry. But I just nod at him, shaky and slow, and my professor leaves, going back to his office to where Professor Carmine waits at the door and falling into conversation with her.

"You'll be okay, hon," the campus security officer tells me, not noticing how my attention is riveted on Professor Solomon. "You just stay with me, and you'll be okay."

CHAPTER 14

Time seems unsure of itself after Rook leaves. It's grindingly slow as the paramedics wheel a stretcher through the art department, and it seems to take them forever to get to Professor Carmine's office. At the same time, I see flashes of sped up movement when students are shepherded away from the lounge and the department itself. Students leave too quickly for them to be moving at a real pace, and their movements seem off. Like stop-motion animation, instead of real life.

"What's your name?" The female paramedic is nothing if not kind, and as the man sets the stretcher up outside the office, all I can do is stare. "Can you tell me your name?"

"Umm. I'm Blair," I mumble, barely hearing her question or what I'm saying. "Blair," I say again, needing to hear what my voice sounds like, when nothing about me seems the same anymore.

And yet, somehow, that's the one constant. My voice sounds the same as always to my ears, even through the tremors. For some reason, that hurts more than the bruises, a fresh slice of pain going straight into my chest as I close my eyes against the tears that well in them.

"Blair. Can you give me a last name?"

"Love," I whisper, eyes still closed and fists clenched at my sides, so I don't shake as badly as I have been. "Blair Love."

"Good job, Blair." I want to bristle at the condescending tone. Because I'm not a *child* who's forgotten where she lives or her parents' number. I'm twenty-two. I'm an adult. She can talk to me like one.

But those thoughts, those words, never leave my throat. Instead, I'm quiet as both she and the campus security officer help me onto the stretcher, gently pushing me until I'm reclined with my back pressed flush against the sheet.

I don't want to be here. I don't want to go to the hospital, and I think I ask if I really have to go. If I do, then no one answers. Or maybe I just don't notice.

The world is a blur as I'm wheeled through the art department and out into the rain. It never touches me, however. The ambulance is backed up to the double doors, secure under a large overhang that reaches out a good eight feet.

As the paramedics and the security guard whisper with each other, I turn to look out at the parking lot, eyes roving over empty cars and small groups of students that stare and openly wonder at what in the world is going on.

Faces blend, becoming featureless, and I wouldn't be able to provide any details of the cars in the parking lot as I stare out at them. That is, until my eyes come to a familiar black Mustang and the two people standing beside it that decidedly *aren't* confused.

I blink once. Twice. Again, to sharpen my vision as the two faces swim into focus. One of them is Rook, but he's not nearly so calm and collected now. He's pale, and one of his hands grips Oliver's shoulder as the latter says something quickly, hands balled into fists.

They're angry.

With me? I can't help but think belatedly, just as the stretcher starts to move again. They turn, Oliver's eyes finding mine unerringly, and the anger falls from his face, replaced with something I can't and won't name.

He looks... sad. So fucking sad and guilty. Lost, like he doesn't know what to do, even though he has Rook *right there*. I can't stand the way he looks at me, so I close my eyes and let myself be jostled into the ambulance, not seeing anything else as I'm swallowed up into the back of it and reclined a little bit further by the paramedic at my side.

"Hello, Blair," the woman tells me, reaching out to grip my hand. "I'm Melody. Can you tell me what hurts?" The other paramedic, a man, silently and slowly wraps a blood pressure cuff around my upper arm. The ambulance jolts into motion and I stare up at the ceiling, feeling sluggish in understanding her words.

"Everything," I whisper hoarsely. "Everything hurts." There's no beginning or end to the pain. It's like a never-ending cycle that moves up and down my body, starting and ending between my thighs with bright points above my knee and across my face. I turn to look at her, unable to do more than keep my eyes open. "Can you please, please make it stop hurting?"

Her calm expression falters. Emotions war over her features but I'm too tired, too far gone, to tell what they are. "Yeah, Blair," she tells me, gripping my hand a little tighter. "We're going to help you with the pain."

It's hard to remember the ambulance ride. Lights stream

through the back windows once in a while, even though I stare at the ceiling as the vehicle jostles along the highway, sirens wailing. The female paramedic—Melody?—holds my hands, and she's the one who puts an IV into my arm that she promises will help me feel better.

Whether or not she's lying, I have no idea. By the time the ambulance stops and the man hops out to push the doors open wide, I still hurt just as much as I had when we'd left campus.

"Thank you," I whisper, just as she gets up as well. The paramedic turns and looks at me, a slow smile slipping over her lips until she looks almost pained.

"I didn't do anything for you to thank me for, Blair," she tells me, and hops out of the ambulance to help pull the stretcher out onto the ground. The jolt sets my teeth on edge and I close my eyes again, not wanting to see the faces of anyone here who might know what has happened to me.

I can't stand to see their judgment. Their pity. Their horror. Do they think I don't feel all of that too? Do they think it isn't made *worse* in my mind when they look at me with their own versions of what I already feel?

My hands twist in the sheet that covers me, and finally I force myself to open my eyes just in time to be wheeled into a large, private room with a curtain across the door that's drawn the moment I'm inside.

It's *bright,* is my first thought. I nearly squint in the brightness, until a nurse notices and turns down the lights just enough that it's no longer so offensive.

"Can you verify your information for me, Blair?" another nurse asks, dragging a computer stand closer to the bed. She recites my information, probably shared by my PCP that I've been seeing in St. Augustine since I got the flu during freshman year. I correct the address with a flat voice, fingers twisting together and apart in the sheets.

I can't do this. Everything in the room feels strange. I don't know these people, and terror courses through me.

I can't do this. Can't they see that I'm falling apart again? Even as I answer questions through numb lips and watch my IV get hooked up to a different bag, I know I won't be able to stay in one piece for much longer. I'm falling apart, and none of them notice.

"There are two men here to see you," the nurse adds, finally getting my attention. "Are you expecting—"

"Yes," I gasp, eyes widening. "Yes. *Yes*, please let them in. Please." She hesitates, looking me over, then gets to her feet without an affirmative answer.

She's not going to let them in. The thought clouds up my brain, taking up valuable space inside my skull as I thump my head back against the bed and close my eyes. She doesn't trust them. She thinks I don't need them, or that I don't deserve them.

She doesn't see how much I *hurt*—

"Blair." The voice is almost feral in its panic, and my eyes fly open just as Oliver nearly tackles me. He restrains himself just in time, earning a glare from the nurses as he grabs my shoulders gently and leans in close. "God, Blair. I'm sorry it took us extra time to get here. Are you okay, are you..." he trails off, touching the store spots on my face as he does. I can see the change in him, the way he goes completely still and looks like a completely different person as the humanity drains out of him.

This is the Oliver from the alleyway. The one that I'd been so afraid of before.

But this time, I don't feel anything at all.

Rook looms behind him, worry on his face, and grips Oliver's shoulder hard. "Don't grab her so tightly, Oliver," he warns, the meaning clear in his voice. He's not warning Oliver about his grip. That much is obvious. And the words cause Oliver to blink a few times as he slides back on the mask that he wears so well.

"Yeah," he agrees, his eyes never leaving mine. "I'm sorry, Rook. Sorry, Blair."

"Don't be," I whisper, meaning it. I'd felt something right before his mask came back on. Right when I'd realized who that look is for, I'd felt something that's the exact opposite of fear. It had felt like—

"Are you sure you're all right with them staying, Miss Love?" the same nurse from earlier asks, reappearing at my opposite elbow. "Would you like us to call your family? Your parents?"

"Call..." I trail off, my eyes widening. "I left my phone behind. Did you—" The moment I turn, Rook slides my phone into my hand, closing my fingers around it.

"I didn't forget it," he tells me, and walks away to sit in an uncomfortable-looking chair against the wall.

I stare at him as Oliver sinks down on the side of my bed, his eyes on the nurse that still doesn't seem to want him here. Whether it's because he's a man and I'm, well, the obvious, or if it's something about Oliver himself, I'm not sure.

I'm too tired to be sure of anything.

Though, when I think about it, tired isn't exactly the right word. There's something wrong with my brain. Thoughts process slowly, instead of at their normal rate, and I feel like I'm trying to move through a bog when I push myself to focus on what's going on around me.

But no matter what I do, I can't seem to shake the feeling or the way I'm just... *here*. It's better than crying, I suppose. The terror and pain have dulled, the knife-sharp edge of it fading. When I glance up at the bag attached to the IV in my arm, the nurse smiles kindly.

"I've given you something for the pain," she tells me gently. "You might feel a little out of it. Is that what's going on, Blair?"

I nod at her, one hand reaching out blindly. Oliver laces his fingers with mine and I sigh, letting my eyes close again. "I'm not tired," I promise them, shaking my head against the pillow. "I promise, I'm not going to sleep."

It's hard to explain that my brain just doesn't want to be here anymore.

"We will need to do a physical exam." The nurse's voice is quiet, as if she thinks I really *am* asleep. "A full physical exam, if she'll consent. You'll both have to leave the room."

My fingers tighten around Oliver's, and the brunette stirs, restless at the nurse's words.

"That's fine," Rook states, before Oliver can do or say anything. "We understand. We're not blood related, but we're the closest she has to family down here."

"Does she have a good relationship with her parents?" the nurse continues, worry in her voice. "Could you ask her if we can call them? Or if you two—"

"No," I murmur, shaking my head without opening my eyes. "I don't want them to know. Please." It twists my heart to say those words, but I can't. I *can't* let them know, or face their looks. Their tears.

Their disappointment.

What if they blame me? I'm lucky so far that Oliver and Rook don't, but I don't know how I'll explain to my parents what happened to me. They'll ask me why I didn't push him away, or scream, or do anything except *let him do it.*

A tear burns down my cheek, slipping from under my eyelid, but Oliver wipes it away gently before it can go far. "Shhh," he murmurs, leaning close to press his forehead to mine. "Don't cry, wonder girl." His nickname for me sends warmth up from our connected fingers, but it's not enough to beat back the cold that cracks and hurts every part of me when I try to move or think.

"I don't want to tell them. They don't live in the area, anyway. They're halfway across the country." My voice sounds dead to my own ears. Flat, like I couldn't care less. But in reality, it's too much effort to do more than that.

"We won't call them without your say so," the nurse promises, her words meant to placate me. "But can these two leave for a few minutes? I promise, the exam won't take long. The doctor is here, and we just want to help you feel better."

"Okay," I whisper, opening my eyes, despite them feeling like they're attached to sandbags. Oliver stares at me, his face a mix of hurt and care, with such anger boiling underneath the surface that it warms more of me than his touch had. I reach up, without thinking, and run my fingers along his jaw, letting him nuzzle into my palm and absorbing some of that heat, some of that anger, before I drop my hand once more and look over at the nurse.

I'm determined to seem like I'm not falling apart, or she's never going to let me out of here. "I'm ready," I tell her, channeling Oliver's unhinged rage and morphing it into something I can work with. "Then I need to talk to the police as well, right?" I glance at Oliver when he squeezes my fingers gently before getting up, and as I watch, he follows Rook to the curtain without a word.

The doctor comes in, nodding at both of them, and waits for them to leave before she turns and gives me a kind smile. "Hello, Blair," she greets, sitting on the edge of the bed where Oliver had perched. She's careful, so *fucking* careful, like I'm about to shatter into a million pieces. "I'm Dr. Torres. I need to examine you, and then there are two officers here who'd like to speak to you. Is that all right?"

"Sure," I tell her, voice flat. I don't want her hands on me, and I realize how *much* that bothers me when she pulls the blankets off of me to reveal I'm still in my clothes and Rook's jacket. She hesitates and looks up at the nurse, who so clearly didn't enjoy Rook or Oliver's presence.

"Can we get Miss Love a hospital gown, please?" she asks gently, getting a nod in return. A gown is offered, and I slide the rough material through my hands, staring at it with trepidation.

"Do I have to?" I ask, flicking my gaze up to hers. "I can't just... wear what I have on?" It isn't my ripped skirt that I'm attached to. Or my hoodie. It's Rook's jacket around my hips that brings me some kind of comfort that I don't want to give up.

The doctor shakes her head with a frown. "I'm sorry, Blair. I need you in a hospital gown, please. We'll give you some privacy, all right?" She and the nurse go on the other side of the curtain in front of the door, but I still hesitate.

I don't want to do this. All I want to do is throw the hospital gown at them, walk out the door, and have Rook and Oliver take me home. Then forget this ever happened. I want to watch both of them—

I shut down the last thought before it can form. It's the panic and the trauma that has me thinking of violence. Nothing more. Quickly, I strip out of my clothes, hands still shaking, and pull on the gown. Immediately, I hate it. *I hate it,* and the way the scratchy fabric makes me feel. I *hate it,* because it settles the feeling of being a victim over me, and the thought nearly punches through me.

When I'm back on the bed and hiding under the thin sheet, Dr. Torres and the nurse come back in, both with helpful, tranquil half-smiles on their faces. I don't want them to smile at me, but I don't say anything. Instead, I ball my hands in the blankets, heart beating in my throat.

"I know this is hard," the doctor murmurs, coming to stand beside me. "But can you tell me where you hurt? What I should be looking for?" She hesitates, then adds, "Do you need a follow up to test for STDs, or the morning after—"

"N-no," I cut her off, squeezing my eyes shut against her words. "He didn't... He hit me and he touched me. He touched me *there*," I say, like a child unable to name the parts of her own body that aren't polite for public conversation. God, I sound pathetic. "But he didn't... go all the way." It's so hard to say what I mean. It's so hard to spell things out, and I hate every word that leaves my mouth.

"Okay. I'm just going to look at your face first. Do you feel like anything is broken?" She touches my bruised and aching cheek, moving her glove-clad fingers over it and down to my busted lip. When I shake my head, she moves up to touch the bruises again, a frown of concentration on her face. "Nothing feels broken. Show me what else hurts?"

I don't give myself the time to hesitate. I push the blanket down my thighs, showing her the large, dark bruise in the shape of a handprint on my thigh. She pauses, hand hovering over it, but ultimately doesn't touch my leg. "I'll give you some medicine for the pain. You won't have to stay overnight, and most of this should be healed in a week or two. This bruise might stay a little longer." She gestures at my leg and then settles back on her heels. "I'd like to give you a full exam," she tells me, eyes on mine. "If you'll consent—"

"No." My voice is flat, level, and I shake my head as I say it. "He didn't...I'm not—" I close my eyes hard. "No," I say again. "I'll talk to the police. I'll tell them, and you, what happened. But please don't touch me anywhere else."

Dr. Torres nods without argument, showing that she's not

exactly shocked by my words. "May I take pictures of the marks?" she asks instead. "The police will want them." At my verbal consent, she does so quickly, taking pictures of the bruise on my thigh, my face, and the ones that have started to bloom around my wrist where he'd grabbed me.

When she's finally done, I pull the blankets back up over me, eyes on the door still covered by a curtain. "Can they come back in now? Please?" I know I sound like I'm begging, but I can't help it.

I *need* them. I can't do this alone anymore.

"The police will want to talk to you alone," she replies, her tone hesitant. "They'll want to know that you aren't being coerced, or you're too afraid to—"

"I'm not afraid of them!" My voice comes out loud and hysterical as I whirl on her, something in me snapping. "Do you think I'd *want them here* if they were going to stop me from talking about what happened? I want them because they make me feel *safe!*" I know I'm yelling, but I can't help it.

The door opens before either the doctor or the nurse can do anything, and the curtain is pulled to the side to admit Rook. He strides across the room without a look at anyone other than me, and reaches out for me, pulling me into his arms and crushing me to his chest.

"It's okay," he murmurs against my hair. "It's okay, I've got you. You don't need to yell, Love. I'm right here."

The tension melts out of me, and I grip his shirt tightly in my fingers, not caring if I stretch or tear the fabric from the force of my grip. "I'm sorry," I whisper, tears rolling down my cheeks and staining his shirt. "I'm *sorry*, I just—"

"You don't have to be sorry." He shifts, looking over my head, and I can *feel* the glare he directs at the doctor. "She told you that she wanted us back in here. You should know we didn't do this to her if she *wants* us here. Why are you trying to keep her isolated, Doctor?"

"I'd just like to make sure of the situation," Dr. Torres replies, her tone less friendly than it had been. "You have to understand the situation. We're bringing down a hospital advocate to discuss her options with her, but—"

"Then they can discuss away, but I'll be right here," Rook interrupts. "Unless she tells me otherwise." The finality of his tone ends the argument, though the nurse reminds me twice that I can be alone if I want to, instead of with Rook.

But I don't want to be alone. I *want* to ask him where Oliver is, as the officers ask me to repeat the details of what happened. I do. Slowly, with guilt and fear eating at my stomach as my mouth forms the words I'm trying so hard not to hear. Around me I can feel Rook's rage pawing at me, washing over me like a flame. While outwardly he remains the calm, dedicated boyfriend and doesn't say a damn word.

It's not until hours later, when the sun has long since set and I'm walking out of the emergency department in a pair of spare sweatpants that probably belong to Oliver, a borrowed tee, and Rook's jacket, that I finally ask, "Where did Oliver go?"

Rook eyes me, brows lifting just enough, that I know the reason he isn't here is something that probably isn't quite legal. "Can I take you home with me, Blair?" he asks, when we get to his SUV. "You look exhausted. And I think Oliver was going to pick up some things for you from your apartment. If you don't want to stay, I'll have him take them back."

"I..." That's a lot of information for my brain to handle. How did Oliver get into my apartment, first of all? Second, how did he get past Juniper? I hope she isn't dead, but the part of my brain that would normally panic over that seems to be out of commission.

And why did he leave the hospital?

"Okay," I whisper finally, closing my eyes against another wave of tears. "Whatever you want to do. I'm just... I'm really tired."

He pulls me close, his arm around my shoulders, and presses a careful, tender kiss to my forehead. "I know," he murmurs, voice low and husky. "I know."

CHAPTER 15

When Rook parks in his driveway, my eyes fall on Oliver. Sitting on the porch, he chews one thumbnail and stares down at the phone in his hand, not once looking up as my feet touch the ground and I close the door behind me.

Rook hadn't told me exactly why he hadn't been allowed to stay at the hospital, but when I trudge up the path to stand in front of him and he finally looks up at me, I ask, deadpan, "Who were you going to kill that Rook sent you home?"

That earns me a quick, surprised smile and a flicker in Oliver's green eyes. "He told you?" he assumes, his own voice full of wry humor. He throws a look Rook's way, just as I shake my head.

"No," I tell him, sounding slightly hoarse. "No, I just... I can make an educated guess." A humorless smile slides across my lips before immediately falling once more. Oliver gets to his feet, hands out, and wraps me up in a hug that cocoons me in safety.

"The doctor," he admits in a whisper as Rook steps past

him to open the door. "She was a bitch, and she kept looking at us like *we* were the ones that had hurt you. I'd never hurt you, wonder girl." He hugs me more tightly, enough that I feel like my bones are creaking.

"Oliver," Rook admonishes. "Don't crush her."

Oliver starts to pull away, but I grip his shirt, dragging him back to me. "Ignore him. Hug me harder," I mutter, startling a snort from him.

"No, he's right. I don't want to hurt you." He disentangles himself from me, though I'm certainly not helping that process along, and takes my hand to lead me into the house. "I went to your apartment, in case he didn't tell you," Oliver informs me, showing me my keys that rest in the bowl beside his own by the door. "Sorry. I wanted to ask, but Rook wouldn't let me in. I thought you might want to stay here, and you'd want your things."

"Don't be sorry," I reply, barely aware of the words as they come out of my mouth. I'm so *tired*. So impossibly exhausted and numb. I want to sleep, yet every time I closed my eyes in the car, the smell of sour-sweet breath and the buzz of Professor Langhorn's voice comes back to haunt me.

What if I *can't* fall asleep? What if I'm stuck like this, in limbo, until my body decides that it's had enough and just turns off like a light switch?

A tugging on my arm has me looking up, and I realize I've stopped just inside the door, making it impossible to close. Oliver looks at me, waiting, not saying anything as he holds onto my arm like he's the only thing keeping me above water.

And maybe they are the only defense I have against drowning. I feel better when they look at me, when they talk to me. When Oliver grips me like this, it reminds me that I don't have to stay lost in my mind.

"Was Juniper there?" I fish my phone out of the pocket of

Oliver's sweatpants, seeing that I have a ton of messages and missed calls from her. Judging by the fact the last was only twenty minutes ago, I have a feeling that she wasn't there, or he somehow managed to avoid her.

"No," Oliver grimaces apologetically. "I thought if she was, I'd tell her *something*. I wouldn't tell her everything. Not when it's your place to do that or decide not to. But she wasn't. Sorry, Blair."

He doesn't need to be sorry. He *never* needs to be sorry. Belatedly I call Juniper, bringing the phone up to my ear and closing the door behind me so that I can lean on it.

She picks up after the second ring, her voice accusing and panicked the moment she speaks. *"What the fuck, Blair?"* she demands angrily. *"You've been gone all day, and I haven't been able to get a hold of you. I thought something had happened."*

"Jun," I sigh, resting my head back against the door. "I'm—"

"Where are you, even? Your laptop is gone, and it looks like someone half-ransacked your room." I open my eyes to look at Oliver, but he's already in the kitchen, away from the danger of my glare as he goes to say something to Rook, one hand sneaking out to grip the edge of his shirt.

"I'm..." I don't know what to say. Or how to say it. She's my best friend, and I've never kept a secret from her. Until last semester, anyway. Oliver and Rook are the first big secrets I've kept from anyone. Oh, and my cam work. "Can you stop for a minute? Let me talk, please?" I don't have the energy to talk over her right now.

Her tone changes. Her angry words die mid-sentence and after a brief hesitation, she asks, *"You're not okay, are you? I saw an ambulance and police cars at the art building today. Tell me it had nothing to do with you?"*

I grin at nothing, head tipped back once more so I can look

at the ceiling. "Man, I really wish I could." My voice wavers, tears falling down my cheeks without anyone to catch them or to stop them from burning lines across my rubbed-raw skin. "I..." I lick my lips, the words dying in my throat, and try again when I've taken a deep breath to steady myself. "I was assaulted. By a professor. It's..." My eyes clench shut harder, more tears seeping past my lashes. "I've been at the hospital."

It takes a moment before she replies. I hear her draw in a breath to hide her shock, then another like I had before she speaks again. "*Oh my god, Blair. Oh, my god. Where are you? Do I need to come get you? Have you told your parents?*"

"I'm with Oliver," I tell her, trying to add a hint of firmness to my words. "He's helping me." I don't include Rook in that statement. I wouldn't know how to explain that can of worms. "Please, just... just give me space, okay? I haven't told my parents. And I don't want them to know. I don't want *anyone* to know right now. But I knew I had to tell you. Don't say anything to anyone, please?"

"*Of course not. I wouldn't do that to you. But...*" I hear the indecision in her voice, along with the worry. "*Are you sure being with Oliver is the best thing right now? I can hear how upset you are. Why don't you let me come get you and—*"

"No." My voice is firmer than I intend it to be. "No, Jun. I *want* to be here. Please." I'm not *asking* her to let me. I'm an adult, same as she is. But I don't want to tell her that the real reason for not wanting to be at home—apart from how safe I feel with Oliver and Rook—is because if she tries to coddle me, or take care of me, or treat me like I'm made of glass that's about to shatter... then I'll fall apart.

I can't be around her right now, no matter how good her intentions are. "I'm going to stay for a couple of days, I think." If they'll let me, is the part I don't add. I don't know if they'll want me around that long, and I definitely need to ask. "The police said—Well, they told me that until they can find Professor Langhorn, I shouldn't be at Wickett. Not for right now, until it's taken care of." Until he can't come back for some sort of revenge, or part two. According to Rook, it's already been taken care of. I'm grateful for him keeping an eye and ear out, since most of my classes are in the art department, and he'd know where to find me, if I did go back.

Though I still can't understand how they haven't found him. He's *ancient*, and he stinks like a rotting corpse. Is it not easy to just stick a dog on his trail who may or may not accidentally maul him to death?

"*Blair?*" Juniper's careful use of my name makes me realize that I haven't been listening to her, and I blink, drawing myself back to reality.

"Sorry. What did you say? I just. I was just thinking." About murder.

"*I asked if you needed anything. Or if you want me to get anything from your classes for you?*" Her voice is so careful that it makes my teeth ache. Why does she think I'll scream at her if she talks to me normally? Or is it that she thinks I'll *break*?

"No." I suddenly want to end this conversation as quickly as I can to get her voice out of my head. "No, but thank you. I'll text you tomorrow. We'll..." Fuck, I can't commit to anything when I don't even know if I'll wake up sane tomorrow. "I'll talk to you tomorrow," I finally say, barely listening to whatever she says before I make my excuses and hang up, sagging back against the door until it takes my full weight.

I don't realize someone is near me until fingers pry my phone out of my hand. That makes my eyes flick open, and I see Rook brandish it in front of my nose. "You can have it back tomorrow," he tells me. "Unless you want to call someone else. Like your parents. Are you *sure* you don't want to call them, Love?" he asks, reverting to his nickname for me.

Nodding, I drop my hand to my side, not willing to fight him for my phone, or really caring to. "I don't want them to know," I tell him sharply. "I can't handle them knowing right now. Please don't push me on this. I'll tell them. Well, I'll *think* about telling them," I amend, not wanting to promise something that I'm not sure of.

He doesn't understand what they'll say. What they'll do. Hell, they'll probably move down here or convince me to move back in with them to finish college. I can't handle that right now. I can't handle their overbearing love, or how they'll try to push everything too far, while remaining entrenched in my life while things get figured out.

I know they love me, and I love them.

But for the sake of that, I can't tell them right now.

"All right. Are you hungry?" When I shake my head, he frowns. "You have to be hungry. It's been hours since you've last eaten. Did you at least have lunch today?"

Again I shake my head, tired eyes on his.

"Then you have to eat."

"I'm *really* not hungry," I protest dryly, pushing away from the door to follow him into the kitchen.

Oliver leans against the bar-style counter, a can of Sprite in one hand and a bottle of chocolate milk in the other. He holds them both up to me, lifting one, making a show of it, then doing the same with the other. The stupidity of it, and how bad of a game show model he would be, brings a wry grin to my lips, and I point at the chocolate milk.

"Thank you." It's cool in my hands, and I watch as he cracks open the can of Sprite, swallowing what has to be half the can before he comes up for air.

"Your stuff is in my room," he tells me, still leaning against the counter. His gaze flicks from Rook to me, and he tilts his head to the side. "Do you want me to get it? You don't have to

sleep in my room with me. Or with him. He's a blanket stealer."
I almost grin because I can feel Rook's eyes rolling behind me
without even looking up. "Or you can just... have my room. I
can sleep with him if you—"

"I don't want to steal your room, Oliver," I tell him,
twisting open the bottle of milk. "Can I just sit? Somewhere?
Anywhere?" There are a thousand places to sit in their house, if
I'm including the floor, and even that feels like a reliable option
right now. I'm tired. I'm *exhausted*, and I don't think I've ever
been this worn out before.

Thankfully, my brain is still doing a lot to block out the
memories of this afternoon. It's hard, but I somehow pretend
that it happened to someone else. That I was just in the room,
watching, instead of the one on that desk, with Professor Langhorn's hands—

I must make some noise of distress, or Rook is just inher-
ently psychic. He hugs me, sweeping me into his arms and
chasing the memories out of my head with the abruptness of it
all. "You can sit," he rumbles against my hair, and picks me up
before I can even register what he's doing. It only takes him a
few steps, twelve to be exact, before he's able to place me on
the long, wide couch that's situated perfectly in their living
room, in front of their tv.

Oliver reappears moments later, his huge, king-sized
comforter in his hands as he sinks onto the sofa beside me.
Without a word, he tosses it over our bodies and hands me the
remote for the smart TV as Rook walks around the room,
moving things or just resettling everything as he sees fit.

It's so quiet in here that the soundlessness pushes on my
ears. Out of necessity, I turn on the television, curling my legs
up under me as I do.

It isn't until I realize I'm staring at the menu that I move again, and notice that Oliver is watching me, his face full of concern.

"Here," I sigh, handing the remote over to him as the beginnings of hunger claw at my stomach. To combat it, I take a drink of chocolate milk, hoping it's a temporary fix. I can't eat right now. I don't think I could keep anything down, truthfully.

To his credit, Oliver doesn't ask me what I'd like to watch. He nods, heads to one of the streaming apps they've got installed, and within a minute or so, a cooking show plays on the television. The mindless ease of it allows my shoulders to sink and lets me feel a little bit better.

I want to say something. I do, though I don't know what I would say, or how to say it. They've done so much for me, but here I am, acting ungrateful and just numb. This isn't the Blair they like, and I still have no idea if I can even stay here until the weekend.

"Hey. Umm." I finally prod my brain into a semblance of wakefulness so I can form the words I need. "Can I stay here? For a little while?"

"Yes." Oliver's reply is out before I've even finished asking. "You can stay here as long as you want, Blair. You know that."

"Well... I can't promise I'll be great company. And I meant. Well, can I stay until the weekend? Maybe until Sunday? I know I can't go back to campus tomorrow, and they said something about Monday, possibly, too. But I don't want to impose on you, or bother you guys, or—"

Rook sinks down on my other side, his shoulder against mine while we lean against the back of the couch. "You're allowed to be whatever kind of company you want to be," he informs me nonchalantly. "And Oliver's right. You can stay here as long as you want. We have two rooms that are set up as offices right now. If you want, you can have one of them. It's not quite as good as your own wing, but unfortunately I've hit a snag in negotiations, since we're adding that solarium you asked for as well and the two projects are difficult to accomplish at the same time. Especially with all this rain." His tone is flat while he jokes, and he flicks his fingers up toward the ceiling, as if implicating the rain in his problems.

A smile twitches at my mouth as I look down at the blanket, trying to figure out how I feel. "I won't lie... it *is* rather disconcerting how little progress you've made on my wing. But if there's going to be a solarium as well, I suppose I can curb my frustration," I say at last, a small tremble still in my voice that I can't seem to get rid of. My fingers clench the blankets, knotting the fabric in my grip without me realizing it, until Oliver's hand sneaks into one of mine and Rook leans against my opposite shoulder with a sigh.

"Stay, Blair." Oliver's sweet voice is like music in my ears as he leans closer to me, his head on my free shoulder. "Please stay, if only so I know you're safe? Stay, and I promise I'll take care of you."

I hum a reply, the last of my energy streaming out of me. Exhaustion climbs through me, faster than it ever has before, but before it's claimed me completely, I swear I hear him say one last thing, though it's probably my imagination talking, and not him.

"Stay, so I can rip him open and let you tear apart his insides while he can still feel it, wonder girl."

CHAPTER 16

My dreams are full of sharp edges and the color red. Even before I lose the full memories of them to the light of day, all I can remember is the thrill of violence in my veins, fear, and *red*.

Opening my eyes in the dim light, I see that it's still dark in the room, but the glow of the television is gone. When I turn my head to the side, I notice I'm not in their living room anymore, and fear jerks into place in my stomach as I wonder if getting out of Professor Carmine's office had been the dream, not whatever I'd just had in my head.

But a glance around the familiar room, and at the familiar body to my side, calms me before my heart can do more than race. I'm not in an office. I'm in Rook's bed. One of them must have carried me here after I'd fallen asleep, and the only reason I'm awake now is because thunder shakes the windows and lightning flickers through the room.

Lightly, I lie back down, my head on the pillow so I can stare into the calmness of Oliver's sleeping face. He looks so... sweet like this. So *kind*, like the mask he wears.

Except... it isn't quite a mask. At least not toward Rook or me. It's real for him, and I've started to learn how to tell when it's not real for other people. But that's their loss, that they don't get to see the Oliver that I do.

He's so gorgeous. Just as gorgeous as Rook, but in a completely different way. My hand inches forward until I can trace my fingers over the skin of his jaw, drawing my touch up to his hair until he sighs out a breath and a smile curls over his lips.

"I'm awake, wonder girl," he murmurs, curling closer to me until his knees bump against mine. "Do you need me to be?"

"No," I breathe, cupping his jaw in my hand. "I'm sorry. I didn't mean to wake you up."

"You didn't." His eyes flutter open, then close again. "I don't like storms."

My hand pauses, and I pull back to stare at him like he's grown a second head. "You don't?" I ask, wondering if I've heard him wrong. "Not even in the mornings, or when you don't have to get out of bed?"

He shakes his head slowly against the pillow. "Never have since I was a little kid. I had a bad experience with being caught out in one. Now I don't like them." Oliver shrugs. "It's not very deep or exciting, I'm sorry to say. But I could make it into a better story if you want."

"I don't need a better story," I tell him, but he doesn't answer. I watch as he falls back to sleep, his breathing evening out even though the storm rages on outside.

But I can't sleep. Somehow, I'm not even tired, even though it can't be past four am and I had the worst day of my life yesterday. Pain is creeping back to me, though I don't know if it's mental, physical, or both. By the time it hits, I realize I can't stay here. Not unless I want to accidentally wake Oliver again with my thrashing and inability to calm down.

Before I can change my mind, I throw the blankets off, making sure not to take them from Oliver, and crawl out of the large, king size bed. Rook's side is still a little warm when I crawl off of the mattress, so I know he was here at some point.

Silently as I can, I pad through the house, going down the hardwood floored hallway and past the photos on the walls that I assume were taken by Rook himself. He's too arrogant to let someone else's work grace his walls. Unless, maybe, it's Oliver's. That feels on track for the two of them, since in some ways, Oliver is an extension of Rook's artistic talent.

Which makes me wonder as to why Oliver isn't majoring in photography or doing more with his love of it.

A light on in the kitchen draws me to it like a moth, and I'm not surprised when I see Rook sitting with a mug of steaming coffee at his elbow as he sorts through papers spread out along the counter. It occurs to me, even when my feet are already on the tile, that he might not *want* me here. Maybe he came out here to be alone, and would rather I'd stayed away.

Before I can escape, Rook looks up at me, brows raised, and lifts a finger to gesture me towards him. "Don't run away, Love," he murmurs. "I'm not doing anything that important. Coffee?" He gestures at the coffee machine, where I can see a light on, signifying there's more in there and ready to be poured.

I hesitate at first, my mouth forming the words *no thank you*, before I realize... why *not*? It's not like I have anything to do tomorrow. Or anywhere to go. I'm just... here. Until I don't want to be here or until they've had enough of me, I suppose. "Thanks," I sigh instead, picking up a mug from beside the coffeemaker and pouring myself a cup. Normally, I'd be scrounging for sugar and ample creamer. This time, however, I don't mind the bitter burn of it. I walk to the counter to look down at the papers, unsurprised to find that they're reports from one of his photography classes, and my eyes linger on some of the photos that go with them.

They're *good*. Better than anything I've taken, and I realize instantly these are from his advanced classes, from photography majors instead of people like me who are taking the class for fun. "You know, I hear my photography professor is supposed to give our projects back soon. Or at least post grades for them," I point out with a sniff. "I think I'll drop the class if my grade sucks. That feels fair, right?" My voice doesn't sound normal to my ears. I sound...off in a way I can't quite figure out.

But if Rook notices it too, he doesn't say a word. He just offers me a seat on one of the high bar chairs that I take, still looking at the papers he's grading.

"Are these from one of your super advanced classes?" I ask, dragging over one of the photos. He glances over and examines it, then shoves a report toward me, presumably to keep them together.

"These are my thesis students. They've done proposals for their graduation projects, and I'm looking over them one last time. You'd like that one," he adds, tapping the photo I have. "She's into a lot of classical art and tries to recreate that look in photos. She likes abstract subjects, sort of like you."

"She seems talented," I admit, glancing from the report to her photo before pushing them both back to him carefully. "She's a good student?"

"One of my best," he sighs, as if it doesn't matter that much to him. "Outside of this, though, she's a bit boring. Nothing like my favorite problematic student." The grin he flashes my way is quick, though I notice how his gaze lingers on me and he reaches out his hand once more to cover mine.

"Are you all right? Can I do anything, Blair?" His voice is a low rumble, and I look up at him when he speaks, curious to see the look on his face. But I get nothing. He's always so good at being neutral, save for when I'd had a gun to Oliver's head and when he'd found me in Professor Carmine's office.

"You can wake me up from the shittiest nightmare ever," I laugh dryly, flipping my hand over to lace my fingers with his. "You can make me forget what happened, and get rid of the bruises on my face and leg." I'm happy I can't see the handprint under my sweatpants, but it burns there all the same, making sure I can't forget.

"You can make me feel like less of a failure," I don't mean to add, but it slips out before I can shut my mouth, and I close my eyes hard, trying to fight back tears.

Immediately, he yanks me forward, crushing me in a hard, one-armed hug, and pulls me off of my chair. It slides back, and I hope it doesn't topple over from the force that he's yanked me off of it.

"Oh, Love," he breathes against my hair. "You aren't a failure." There's a note of something in his voice, and I pull back again to look at his face, even though I know I won't find any emotion there.

"You're mad," I guess, not sure I'm even close to right. "At me?"

"Never at you. *Never*," he promises vehemently. "I'm angry at Professor Carmine for brushing off your concerns when you brought them up. And I'm *furious* at myself because I should've realized. I should've known. Someone should've done something when Langhorn started talking like that to people. But *I* should've been the one to do something, because you are mine." His voice makes me shiver when he says it, and I hide my face in his shirt so he can't see the effect it has on me, or the confusion I feel at all the emotion he manages to inject into that one word. "I'm not mad at you, Love. You have done nothing wrong; do you understand me?"

"I should've done something." It's like my mouth is moving

on its own, without consent from the smart part of my brain. "I should've done *something*. If I would've yelled, you could've heard me. I could've hit him, or tried harder to get away. I should've—"

"Do you know what the fawn response is, Love?" Rook gets up as he speaks, one arm slipping around my shoulders as he leads me to the living room. The light flicks off behind us when he steps onto the hardwood instead of the tile, and the smooth floor makes my toes curl from the cold.

"No?" I ask, trying to figure out if I've ever heard the term before. I let him pull me over to the sofa, unsurprised when he drags me down across him; though he gives me ample opportunity to pull away. "What does that mean?"

"People think that there's only fight-or-flight." In the darkness, the only light I have is the occasional flash of lightning to illuminate his face. I don't try to look, however. I settle against him, loving the warmth of his body against mine and the way his arms are gently wrapped around my waist. "But that's not quite true. The fawn response is just as common, and it happens when your mind is trying to minimize the trauma that's happening. The fawn response means you appease the person hurting you. It means you don't say anything, and hope that the trauma stops as soon as possible. It's the *safe* response. And it's just as valid as any other. You did what you could, Love. And it's not your fault that you froze. It's his fault for hurting you."

I stretch my arms up to his shoulders, sinking my fingers into his hair as I press my cheek against his chest, just over his heartbeat. "But you wouldn't have *fawned*," I mutter, eyes closed again. "You wouldn't have run, either. You would've killed him. So would Oliver."

"Well, you're partially right," Rook admits, combing his fingers gently through my hair and working through the tangles that had formed while I'd been at the hospital, then sleeping. "I don't mind admitting that you're right about me. I've definitely been firmly in the *fight* camp since I was a child. But Oliver?" I can feel him shake his head. "If you would've known him when he was younger, you'd know he used to be more like you than you realize."

"Oliver never *fawned*," I scoff, sure that he's lying to me to make me feel better. "He's too sure of himself. He's too quick to want a fight."

"Things change," Rook tells me. "People change. There's still a lot you don't know about us."

"Then tell me something I don't know about you." I want to change the subject, instead of talking about my *fawn* response for any longer. Though, I can't help but admit to myself that it has made me feel better, at least a little. Enough that I don't feel quite like I'm being crushed by an anvil and I can focus on the way his heartbeat sounds in my ear.

"What would you like to know? Where I went to school? Where I grew up?" His voice is full of light indulgence, and I sigh against him in thought.

"Tell me about the first person you killed." Unsure of why I say it. I don't know why I even want to know, but I find I'm suddenly eaten up by curiosity. Oliver has told me some stuff about himself. I've realized that there's definitely been some trauma in his life, and something happened that's changed him into what he is.

But that isn't the case with Rook.

"Are you sure you want to know?"

"Are you going to keep it from me?"

He hesitates for a second longer, then his grip tightens on my wrist and he says, evenly, "No. I won't keep it from you. I killed my girlfriend's mother when I was sixteen, because she slept with my mom and broke up my parents' marriage." His voice is so... flat when he says it. As if it doesn't bother him, or it's as boring of a memory as a distant relative's wedding.

"Did you mean to?"

"Yeah, I think stabbing her eight times in the stomach is a pretty clear indicator of how much I meant to." God, I don't know how he can sound so *comfortable* with it.

"And you don't regret it? You were sixteen. You didn't feel bad about it?"

"I felt bad that I left thoughts of cleanup until after," he replies, without a hesitation. "And I had to scramble to cover it up. That wasn't fun. I framed some guy in town that no one liked. It was easier than it should've been."

"Well, sure," I agree blithely, surprising myself. "That was before computers and DNA evidence, right? Before phones too, I would think. It's no surprise you were never caught."

His surprised snort is music to my ears, and he buries his face in my hair. "You're such a brat, Love," he informs me, going back to combing his fingers through my hair once more. "I thought it bothered you to hear about what we do when you aren't looking." Thunder sounds in the distance, and I hate that sleep is ready to claim me again, helped along by his fingers in my hair and his warmth against me.

"Yeah," I sigh, eyes closing hard. "Me too. Guess I don't, and I was wrong. Sorry about that." His chuckle is the last thing I hear, though I feel his arms around my waist and the blanket that he pulls off of the back of the couch being draped over me.

"You have nothing to be sorry for, Love," he promises me, and settles down on the couch while I quickly fall into blackness.

CHAPTER 17

The rain has stopped by the time my eyes open again, and I realize quickly that the sounds I'm hearing are from the television in the living room.

"Is Rook gone?" I ask when I notice he's no longer cradling me against his chest while I snore and drool on him.

Oliver nods his head, glancing at me from his spot on the sofa. He has one knee drawn up under him, his other foot on the floor, and looks utterly at ease to be here while I've been asleep. "He left an hour ago. I can't believe he just lifted you up and put you back down on the sofa without you noticing. It was pretty impressive."

"Do you not have class today?" Choosing to ignore his comments about what happened when I'd been asleep. I know I'm a heavy sleeper. He doesn't need to remind me of that, and I can only hope I didn't do anything too embarrassing while I'd been here using one of these men as a mattress and pillow.

"Nope. I made sure that I have nothing on Fridays this semester, except for Rook's class. Though obviously, I'm not going. He graciously gave me the day off from assisting." His grin is wolfish when he looks at me, but it doesn't quite reach his eyes.

That's okay, though. Because I doubt any of my smiles do either.

"He told me you wanted to know about the woman he killed when he was younger. Crazy, right? That he was always so calculating and able to cover up his own crimes?" He shakes his head. "Obviously, I wasn't capable of anything like that. Do you want to hear about my first kill? Outside of foster care, anyway. That doesn't count."

"I would love to hear about it," I assure him, rolling over onto my back so I can stare up at him. Thankfully, there's now a pillow under my head, and I'm grateful that there doesn't seem to be any puddles of drool anywhere on it. It's a real fear, as I know when I sleep on my stomach I tend to sleep with my mouth open.

It's led to some awkward instances in the past, and horrified looks from both my mother and Juniper when they'd walked in on my pillow stuck to my face from how much I'd drooled during the night.

"It was here," Oliver admits. "I was a stupid sophomore, and I'd taken Rook's class because I'd always liked photography. This boy was being an ass. I don't want to go into details, because they're not important. He didn't deserve life, anyway. And his loss was not a blow to the economy or anything, I can promise you that." He flashes a grin down at me, reaching down with one hand to press his fingers to my forehead gently, palm against my hair.

"How did you kill him?"

"I beat the shit out of him. Then I stabbed him with a piece of glass from the mirror I'd thrown him into." His eyes heat as he remembers it, and he leans against the back of the sofa as he speaks. "He really deserved it, Blair. He was the shittiest human I'd ever met at the time. So I killed him and left him in pieces on the floor. Then I killed his friend. And their other friend." The smile he gives me isn't... normal. That unhinged look slides into his eyes, and doesn't leave.

"How did you not get caught?" That's the important part to me. I know Oliver is capable of that level of violence, and it doesn't surprise me anymore.

It doesn't bother me, either.

"Rook," he laughs, in spite of himself, shoulders rising self-consciously. "He was going behind me and cleaning up my messes. I had no idea, obviously. Hell, I don't even know how he knew it was me. He just... *did.* So, in case you're ever going to try to hide something from him, remember that even I couldn't do it. So you have to do better than me." His grin widens as he remembers.

"Anyway, he cleaned up all three bodies and then grabbed me after I was walking around covered in blood. I thought I was done for, and couldn't figure out why I hadn't been caught. That didn't matter to me enough to stop, obviously. I might have been a little out of it." He flops down on the sofa beside me, his head next to mine, and mirrors my position of staring up at the ceiling. "He was crazy irritated. Said shit about how I was endangering him as well, and drawing suspicion to old crimes."

"Did you apologize?"

"Nah," Oliver shakes his head slightly. "I tried to kill him with his own knife. He slammed me into a wall, blood and all, and held me there until I calmed down. The rest is weird, sexy history. I was *obsessed* with him from the moment he did that, and I could never look away. Until last semester."

Then I can *feel* his attention on me. I feel the intensity of it, though I'm too afraid to look at him. "Last semester?" If I play dumb, maybe he'll clarify, or let the matter drop completely.

"Yeah, Blair. Last semester when I walked in and saw you? I knew you were special as hell. Then I saw you stream. I saw how much you took from my streams and you were *gorgeous*. I knew right then you were mine. And you were just so shy and sweet... I wanted to *ruin you*."

"Why didn't you?" I find myself asking, needing to know.

Oliver sits up just enough to lean over me, his eyes searching mine, and says so quietly that I almost don't hear him, "Who says I didn't?"

I open my mouth to answer, his eyes holding mine and keeping me from looking away, but nothing comes out. I don't know what to say, or how to argue with him. Because honestly... maybe he did. A normal, okay-ish person would have absolutely wanted to get away from them. But here I am, sleeping here, letting them be my support, instead of turning them into the cops.

I'm going to ask him what he means. I know that's what I want to say, but instead, other words come out, loud in the quiet of the room, previously broken only by the low noise of the television.

"Would you kill James Langhorn for me?"

Everything goes still in the room. It's like time slows down and comes to a stop, and all that moves are Oliver's eyes as he stares down at me from under the veil of his long lashes.

"Oh, wonder girl," he murmurs, sinking down on his elbows until we're barely inches apart. "I'd do anything for you. Killing Langhorn would be just as much for me and Rook as it would be for you. You wouldn't even have to ask."

"How would you do it?" I don't understand where these questions are coming from. I don't know why I'm asking, and I certainly refuse to entertain the idea that I *want* him to do it.

When he sits up, I automatically come with him, like I'm magnetized by the gravity of Oliver. When he holds a hand out to me, I take it, letting him pull me against him until I'm sitting on his lap with my face once again so close to his.

"I'd bring him home to you. Then I'd break his legs and clear out the living room. I'd want you to get to see it too. Would you want to see it?"

"Yes," I whisper. Surely something has possessed me. There's no way I'm the one saying this, or *wanting* it. "I'd want to watch."

"I'll rip him open while he's still breathing. We'll take out his insides while he watches, and I'll keep him alive while we find out what's gone bad in him. We'll look for the rotted parts of him and cut them out, and then we'll take him apart, piece by piece." His hands wander, from gripping my thighs to sliding up my ribs. I quiver under him, and though I fear the memories of Professor Langhorn's hands, instead I feel only anticipation and the warmth from Oliver's body that transfers to mine.

"What if..." I lick my lips and cut off, looking down at his mouth to avoid his gaze. "What if I want to help?"

He doesn't say anything. Not a damn word, and his hands still on my sides while both of us just breathe.

"Is that what you want, Blair?" he asks finally, his voice losing the teasing edge I'm familiar with. He sounds incredibly serious, like there's more at stake than an imaginary death in my imaginary fantasies.

But surely it's all just talk.

I don't want to murder anyone.

Right?

"Do you want me to take your hand and teach you where to carve someone up so that it hurts them? Do you want to wash your hands in his blood, and watch the look on his face when his blood is smeared across your skin?" It's impossible for him to hide his excitement. Impossible for me not to notice the tremor in his hands where he grips my sides. "Would you like me to sharpen the blade and hold him down so you can slit his throat?"

When I look up at him, the answer is on my tongue. I don't know what I'm going to say, only that I'll mean whatever it is. I take a breath, the answer bubbling up my throat, and my mouth shapes the word just as—

The front door opens, jolting both of us into looking behind the sofa as footsteps sound down the hallway. Rook stops in the entrance to the living room, framed in the archway as he looks us both over. Almost instantly his eyes narrow, gaze flicking from my face to Oliver's and back again. "What are you doing?" he asks, the question all for Oliver. "I told you to be careful with her."

"Sorry," I tell him, slipping off of Oliver's lap and back onto the sofa beside him. "We were just talking. I made him tell me about how you two met." It's not a lie, exactly, so why in the world is he still glaring at Oliver like he knows something is up?

There's no way he knows what we've been talking about for the last few minutes, or the question I was about to answer. But unfortunately, I don't know what answer I was going to give Oliver. And that's disappointing, because I *want* to know what I would've said.

I guess I'll just have to ask him again.

"Please tell me we're ordering food," Oliver groans, getting to his feet with a stretch. "I'm starving. I've been watching her sleep for like an hour. No offense, Blair, but you're not the most interesting sleeper." He gives me a lopsided grin while his eyes search mine, but I'm on board, just like him.

It's probably better that Rook doesn't know we were fantasizing about murder. Especially since I know that Oliver is easy to set off, anyway. I don't want to get him in trouble with the law. Or worse, in trouble with Rook. Hell, *I* don't want to be in trouble with our photography professor.

"What do you want?" Rook asks, finally breezing past us and into the kitchen. "Greek again?"

"Do you like Greek food?" Oliver turns to look at me, twisting to pop his back just enough to make himself wince. "Ow. That felt shitty."

"I've never had Greek food," I admit, getting to my feet as well. "I'm from Indiana, remember? There aren't a lot of good Greek places in my area."

"That's a tragedy," Oliver points out, and Rook nods his agreement. "And one we're going to fix. Get out your phone and get ready to type this in. Unless you want me to order for you? I could *definitely* order something you like."

"Not likely," Rook mutters, sliding onto one of the bar chairs at the counter. "Order your own food, Blair. He'll definitely order you something you won't love."

I snort over the sound of Oliver's outrage and sink back down on the sofa, arm wrapped around my waist as I find my phone on the end table and pull up the menu to the restaurant they suggest.

Hopefully, Rook will never know about our conversation. And I'll never have to face the consequences of what I think my answer would've been if he hadn't walked in.

CHAPTER 18

S tanding in front of my door, I realize I don't know how
to open it, or if I even want to. Instead, I rest my face
against the heavy wood, closing my eyes hard. A long
breath leaves me, and for the first time in a couple of days, I
feel the trepidation of anxiety creep up my ankles.

I have to tell Juniper what happened. Fully, not just a few
bits and pieces to keep her from breaking down Rook and Oliver's door.

I have to tell Juniper *everything*.

Well, not quite everything. I'm not about to tell her how
right she is about Oliver, or the full extent of Rob, of the *fuck rob*
fame. There are a couple of things she can't know, for her own
safety, and for the safety of the two men that I'm unwilling to
give up.

That thought sears something to life inside of me, and I
take another deep breath. I've known since Friday that my
plans to break up with them are gone. Wiped out in the same
way something else in me that I cannot name has been wiped
out of my existence.

One day, probably soon, I'll have to figure out what part of me has died and turned to dust. It feels... important. Sort of. Though it hasn't hurt me so far.

I try the doorknob that rests under my hand, unsurprised to find it locked. Even when Juniper is here, or both of us are, we usually lock the door in case the ghost that probably resides somewhere in the building decides to show up when we're sleeping. Deftly I pull my keys from my back pocket where they've been digging into me, and unlock the door so I can slip inside and breathe in the familiar smell of the scented candles Juniper likes to burn.

Today, the apartment smells like sugar cookies. It's one of my favorites of her scent collection, and I wonder if she's burning it for that reason specifically.

"Jun?" I call, my backpack slipping from my shoulders. "Are you alive, or did the ghost get you?"

"Ghost got me," she calls lazily from the living room. "This is just my disembodied voice talking to you now. Remember me fondly."

A smile twitches at my lips, and I make a quick stop by my room to drop my backpack and duffel bag there before going to the living room where my roommate is lounging on the couch.

She doesn't get up, though I can see concern and interest burning in her eyes. Her iPad sits on her lap, her knees curled under her, and a reality show of the dancing variety plays on the tv, so quiet it might as well be muted.

"You look good for a dead girl," I tell her lightly, falling into the armchair that matches the sofa in color. It's overstuffed and huge, big enough that I could probably fit Oliver here too and still be able to sleep comfortably if I wanted to.

For all his long-limbed grace, Rook is too bony. It's pretty to look at, but not as wonderful when his elbows and knees are breaking my ribs or poking me in the kidney.

"I've been working on my presentation," she agrees with a nod. "I wanted to set myself apart from the other seventeen ghosts in the building." Her gaze flicks from my face to the rest of me, then hovers somewhere just under my eyes. "Are you okay? Do you want to talk about it?"

It's hard to reply to her when the answer is more than a little complicated. I drag one knee up under me, curling my toes against the soft fabric of the chair. "I want to talk about it," I tell her slowly. "But I want to tell you about everything. Some stuff happened last semester that I kept from you. And I... want to come clean."

I can see her stiffen, and she surreptitiously mutes the television completely. "Okay... I want you to be comfortable telling me... whatever you want to tell me. I don't want you to think that you have to," my best friend tells me, earnest honesty written all over her face. "But I'm always here for you, Blair. Through whatever."

Well, I doubt that's the case, even if she says it is. She'll be with me through the things that don't involve her as much. If I told her about Oliver, about how much he hates her and that he was killing girls that looked like her last semester?

Somehow, I don't think that she'd stick with me if I told her all of that. I think she'd have me committed and have the cops at Rook's door within the hour. But I smile at her in spite of my thoughts, dragging the blanket off of the back of the armchair that we keep there for whenever we're feeling too lazy to get up and get one of our better ones.

Today is one of those days.

"I still can't go back to Wickett tomorrow, by the way," I inform her dryly. "Since, apparently, they can't fucking find Professor Langhorn." That's the easy part, and seeing her scowl of solidarity helps propel me into the next bit. "On Thursday, I had my office hour in Professor Carmine's office.

I've been doing the same thing all semester. There's this professor. No one likes him. Literally *no one*. He's weird and old and a creep who says really awkward things. But everyone has always said to just ignore him. That he's *harmless*." I sneer the word, tapping my fingers against my knee as my brain tries to make me relive what had happened on Thursday.

It hurts. The bruise on my leg burns and my face feels as raw as it had when I'd raked it against the carpet in front of Professor Carmine's desk. "Anyway, I found out the hard way he isn't so harmless." I lift the leg of my loose basketball shorts, showing her the handprint bruise on my thigh. She gasps, slapping a hand to her mouth, as if seeing physical proof of the assault has hit her harder than my words. Even the bruises on my face aren't as big of a deal as the one on my leg, and they look like they could be accidental, or quick to fade at least.

But the handprint on my thigh shows the lie in that. Or at least the reality of it. I quickly tell her a little bit of what happened, just skimming the top of everything that occurred. I don't have it in me to go into actual detail, or to tell her more than what I can quickly sweep out of my mind before it sinks into permanence.

Still, it's enough to put a look of horror on her face.

"Now about last semester," I breathe, squeezing my eyes closed as I prepare myself for it. I intend to use the same method, only telling her the easy things, so I skim over seeing Oliver's stream, and tell her how I'd started my own, and that's how I'd started making money last semester.

"If you're trying to scare me off of being your roommate, you're barking up the wrong tree, you know," Juniper informs me, a half smile on her lips. "Hell, you should've told me before. I'd be your manager, or your moderator."

I almost tell her that Rook has that covered, but stop myself at the last minute before I can tell her more than I intend to. Instead, I go into Rob and streaming with Oliver. I'd rehearsed what I'd planned to say, so when I get to the night of the assault, I make sure to keep my voice even and look Juniper in the eyes while I lie to her.

"So *fuck rob* tried to hurt me in the alley near *Starlight Coffee*. He had a gun... I was really lucky that Oliver was coming out to meet me. Oliver got the gun away, and Rob was just crazy. He acted like I owed him, like I should know him and want to be around him." I shudder, hating that I can still see Rob's face so clearly. It's hard not to note similarities between him and Langhorn. It's harder still not to wonder what Langhorn will look like when he's dead.

Not from murder, I quickly chastise myself. *I'm not talking about murder, I swear.* I don't know who I'm trying to convince with that, since lying to my own brain is difficult as hell, if not completely impossible. "He was arrested," I lie, my face even as I try to channel Rook. "I don't know. That's the last I heard. I hope to be gone and graduated by the time he's out, which I've been assured will be the case. It was just crazy. Everything lately has just been *crazy* in the worst way."

"God, seriously," Juniper mutters, shaking her head. "I'm sorry, by the way. I know I've said it before. And it's really obvious that Oliver doesn't forgive me. But I hate how I treated him last semester, when he's done so much for you."

"It's okay," I tell her, shaking my head. "Oliver is kind of complicated." He's really fucking complicated, truth be told. "And he's not mad at you. He gets you were just being a great friend and overprotective." I won't lie and say he likes her, or wants to be her friend. But I'm okay saying this much.

"Do you need anything from campus?" she asks after a few moments of silence between us. "No, wait. That isn't what I was going to ask. I mean, I'll totally pick up anything that you need. You know that. But I want to ask you something important."

I turn and look at her, blinking, and say, "Yes, I'll binge *Dance Dads* with you for the rest of the night. No problem."

She snorts and rolls her eyes at me, a frown twisting her lips momentarily downward. "That's not what I'm going to ask. I know you secretly watch it on your own. I can *see* the activity from our shared account, Blair."

"I deny any involvement in whatever you're accusing me of," I reply, shaking my head. "I would *never*—"

"Do you love him?" Her question is so out of left field, and so surprising, that I just stare at her. "Yeah, I know it might not be the best time to ask. I know you have a ton of other shit on your mind. But you have to know. Maybe, since you've only known him for six months. Do you think you *might* love him?"

I can't do anything but just stare at her. I meet her gaze with my own, mortified by the question and my inability to answer it. How could I ever be in love with someone, or two someones, that I'd only met six months ago? I'm not like them. I don't have the decision-making skills of a serial killer, since Oliver has been so sure for so long that I'm *theirs*.

But...

"I think so," I hear myself saying, my mouth once again taking over in place of my common sense. "Umm, I think..." Then trail off, looking down at the blanket that covers my hands. "I think I've never felt like this about anyone before." It's then I realize I'm not *just* talking about Oliver, though she doesn't know that. She doesn't need to. Not now, and probably not ever. There are a lot of things about Rook and Oliver that Jun would never accept, and the fact that I'm in love with two men, one of them my professor, is definitely on the list.

"Love is a big commitment. Especially when I can't sleep at night because of the nightmares." Juniper glances away, guilt on her face, but I continue to try to fix that. "It's a big commitment at any point, honestly. You know I'm not a commitment person. But..." I shrug my shoulders once more.

"God, I really think I do. It's so messed up, since I haven't known him that long." I almost say *them*, but catch myself at the last second. "Don't ask me what I'll do about it. I'm focused on, uh, learning how to sleep again first?" My smile I give her is pained, and I twist my fingers in the blanket on my lap. "Then, you know, maybe graduating. Graduating would be nice."

"The nicest," Juniper agrees sagely. "Definitely think we should work on graduating this semester." Her smile is unsure and slow to find her lips, but when I give her one of my own, it widens. "What do you want to do for dinner? I'll help you sleep, even if I have to bash you in the head with a pan to do it. I saw that on an episode of *Golden Girls*," she adds slyly. "If Mama Sophia says it's an ancient Sicilian remedy for insomnia, who am I to argue with her?"

"Oh, well, if Sophia says it, then it has to be true," I agree eagerly, unable to help the small snicker that escapes me. "Do you want to do something crazy? We could go somewhere and get sushi." I'm not normally the person to suggest actually going somewhere. Normally I'm the one that wants to stay home and order food. But I think I need to get out of here and *do something*. I need to move, and try to wear myself out before I sleep.

I've never had so much restless energy before now. Not during finals and not even when I was waiting on college acceptance letters. It's a foreign feeling, but already I'm on my feet, stretching to crack my back. "You okay with going out somewhere? If you're busy—"

"I'm all yours," Juniper interrupts, turning off the television and getting up as well. "Let me change. I probably don't look appropriate for a nice sushi restaurant." True enough, she's in old sweatpants and a tank top. And she reminds me that I, too, could do with a wardrobe change.

"Give me ten minutes to put on real pants and brush my hair," I say, and get a nod in reply as both of us move away from the living room for our respective bedrooms.

"Hey." She grabs my arm before I can enter mine, and I turn to look at her, head tilted to the side.

"What's up?"

"Thank you for telling me. And for being honest with me about... everything. I know it wasn't easy. And I'm sorry I wasn't in a place last semester that I would've listened." She cracks a crooked grin at me, and adds, "I'm going to start buying you stickers that say 'bad ass business woman,' or something like that."

"Don't get too ahead of yourself," I snort, opening my door as she lets go of my arm. "I think *maskenvy* might be taking an early retirement after this week." The words twist my chest when I say them, and I feel like I've been punched as the statement leaves me.

But I can't help it, nor can I deny it. I don't know how I'll stream again. I don't know how to work past what's happened, or if I'll ever feel comfortable enough in my own skin to let others see me without my clothes on over the internet. Even if they are faceless, nameless people that don't matter in the grand scheme of things.

CHAPTER 19

I can't lie here anymore.

Images, feelings—the sensation of a hand gripping my thigh—flick through my brain like a video-tape on fast forward.

I can't do this.

Immediately I bolt upright, unable to keep lying in my bed, alone, with the blanket feeling like it's suffocating me. I press my hand against the bruise on my thigh, my eyes closed tight as I try to force the images out of my head.

But I can't. There's no Oliver to distract me with his smiles. No Rook to tell me a story or show me what he's grading.

I can't do this, but there's no one around to help me surface before I drown in the fear and hate and *pain* that bubble up inside of me. I suck in a breath, then another, my heart pounding so hard that I feel it in my shaking palms. But I don't stop at just sitting up. Before I know it, I'm on my feet, toes curled into the carpet of my room.

I can't be here. Not right now. Not when the walls are closing in around me, threatening to press me tight, and crunch my bones to dust. I know it's not real. None of this is real.

But I still can't convince myself it isn't.

With shaking fingers and a heart that feels like it's trying to slam out of my chest, I make my way to the small closet in the room and pull out a pair of leggings and the hoodie Rook gave me last year. Somehow, through everything, it's managed to stay in one piece and not covered in blood. It's hard to pull everything on quickly, when I can barely stay still, but I manage. Soon after, I pull on a pair of sneakers and go out to the kitchen as quickly as I can, as if my room is on fire behind me.

With numb fingers and constant pauses to listen for Juniper moving around, I open the far drawer, the one closest to the entry of our apartment. It's a dumb thing to remember, but in my mind I can't forget the stupid switchblade that Juniper's boyfriend, Jesse, started carrying around last year.

"It's a utility knife," he'd laughed, showing it off to her. She'd screwed up her face in disgust and disbelief, and looked at him like an idiot before informing her boyfriend it's a switchblade, not a utility knife.

He'd left it here that day and forgotten about it thereafter. Now my fingers curl around the cool metal in the drawer, and I shove it in the pocket of my leggings, feeling the hardness of the metal sit against my hip. I shouldn't be taking it with me. It isn't mine, first of all. But it's been a nudge in my mind since I woke up, and I refuse to go outside of this apartment on my own without some way to protect myself.

I spin around before I can open the door, remembering at the last second that I should probably grab my keys and wallet phone case. I have no idea what I'm doing, or where I'm going, but I don't want to get stuck on my own without a way to call someone or money to get back. Both are on my desk, and I snag them quickly in my fingers before putting them in the pocket of my hoodie and making my way back to the door once more.

I shouldn't take the knife. I pause at the drawer, fingers on the blade. Part of me knows I should put it back where it belongs, and maybe remind Juniper to give it back to Jesse.

I really shouldn't take it. I'm not in a good enough place to have a weapon with me. No matter how small the blade. But despite how much I think I should put it back... I can't. I cannot, for love or money, reach into my pocket and drop the knife back into the drawer.

So I stop trying to convince myself. I walk out the front door and softly lock it behind me, hoping to God that I don't wake Juniper up with the noise. For a moment I stand at the door, listening for any movement, before I'm satisfied that I'm in the clear.

Juniper has no business stopping me, anyway. She doesn't understand the electricity that stings my veins, zipping through my bones like they're made of metal. I can't stay still. I can't lie down or try to go back to sleep.

I can't be alone in the dark and the quiet tonight.

My feet take me down the stairs and out of the building. It's too late to be wandering down the streets of St. Augustine. It's after midnight, I know, and probably closer to the 1 am mark if I'm being logical. Sure, it might be Monday and not exactly a day where the city is full of people looking for a good time, but it's still the *city*. It's still dangerous.

Except, that thought makes me want to laugh in an unpleasant way. If it's the city that's dangerous, why did I get hurt in one of the safest places possible?

If the city is so dangerous, why does it feel safer than my university or even my bedroom tonight? Sure, Rob found me at night in an alley near my apartment. But even Rob wasn't *from* St. Augustine. All the stranger danger warnings I'd been told.

All the rules I'd grown up with to keep myself safe seem... pointless.

Why should I have to learn and follow the rules, or learn how to protect myself, if I'm going to lose in the end and get hurt anyway, in spite of them?

Unconsciously, my hand slips into my pocket and I find myself gripping the switchblade, one end of it digging into my palm. My eyes flit from sign to sign, and I'm not quite sure where I am by now. My phone says it's one twenty-two in the morning, so I know I've been walking for at least a half hour. But somehow, the trepidation or anxiety that should come along with that is missing from inside of me.

I don't feel anything at all, except for the dregs of fear from the nightmares that I'd had in my own bed. I'm afraid of going back to sleep. *Terrified* of the dreams that find me when I close my eyes.

Without thinking, I swerve into the building with the brightest sign, barely realizing what I'm walking into until I glance up and see a long bar at the other end of the room.

Whoops.

I hesitate at the door, not sure if I should stay or go. I certainly didn't mean to come into a bar, of all places. Even with Juniper, I barely come to bars. Alone feels...*strange*. But then again, I feel strange tonight. Maybe it's meant to be.

Without a word, I try to shrug some confidence into myself as I stride to the bar. I look okay with what I'm wearing, and as it's near closing on a Monday night, no one else here is dressed to the nines either. It's mostly middle-aged men sitting at tables or at the bar itself. Dressed in jeans and long-sleeved shirts, they talk quietly as the sound from some game that was obviously pre-recorded plays on the television above the well-stocked bar.

Even the bartender is a man. He glances up at me as I stride up to the bar, giving me a once over as his eyes narrow in concern and question. "Can I see your ID?" he asks, before I can get a word out.

But then again, I wouldn't have known what to say. Silently, I fish out my ID from my phone case, handing it over. He scans it, checks my birthday, and compares me to my picture before sliding it back to me across the bar. "You're a student?" he assumes, though I have no idea how he'd know. St. Augustine isn't exactly a college town. The only way I can see him thinking that is that my license is from Indiana.

I nod anyway, after a moment of hesitation. The man closest to me swivels on his bar seat, his eyes dark as he looks me over and then pats the bar next time. "You're out late," he tells me kindly, gesturing for me to sit. "Do you normally go to sports bars on a Monday?"

"Yeah," I laugh lightly, feeling less confident than I'm pretending to be. Then sink onto the bar seat, hooking my legs around the bar under me that's meant to be just a footrest. "I, uh, have chronic insomnia. I have to find new things to do. The haunted cemeteries are getting boring. Ghosts only have so much to say." I'm rambling, I suppose, but both the bartender and the man next to me grin. The bartender even snorts, and comes to stand in front of me, resting his hands on the bar.

"What can I get you? We are closing in about forty-five minutes, just to let you know."

"Umm..." I don't drink much. Mostly just for the holidays, or at the parties Juniper and I have gone to over the years. And even then, it's either wine with my parents or cheap beer at frat parties. "Can I just get a beer?" The bartender cites what they have on tap, and I pick one at random that sounds like a small town IPA.

Sure enough, when the amber liquid is poured in the glass and I take a sip of it, I nearly vomit. It's an IPA all right, and one of the strongest I've ever tasted. I'm not a fan of the bitterness, or the strong aftertaste that lingers in my mouth.

But that's not very important to me right now. It's more important to just have something to do. Something to focus on that isn't my nightmares.

Closing my eyes hard, I suck in a breath before letting it out in a harsh sigh. The knife weighs heavily in my pocket, and after a bit of awkward conversation, the man beside me leaves me alone and goes back to watching the game.

For lack of anything else to do, I copy him. My eyes flick between two screens over the bar. One plays a basketball game, while the other shows a race track. Neither sport particularly interests me. And obviously there's no betting going on for these. For all I know, these games happened weeks ago, or maybe today.

But it doesn't really matter. Even though I'm watching them, my attention going between both as I sip my beer, I just don't care. I can't get myself to really focus on either of them, and I'm just so exhausted from the past few days that it's hard for me to think about anything other than my own issues.

God, I'm a mess right now. I'll have to go home soon. I know that, especially as the adrenaline leaves me and takes some of the stinging electricity with it. Part of me aches for sleep. I know I'm tired. There's no way I'm *not* tired. But I still don't know how I'll close my eyes.

Absently, I look at my phone, half considering calling Oliver or Rook and asking if I can come over. But the thought makes me recoil as soon as it crosses my brain. They can't be the only thing getting me through the day. They can't be my everything, because if they leave or I leave, then I won't be able to keep going.

I can't let that happen to me. I can't—

"A little late for you to be out, isn't it?" The voice comes from a man on my left who levers himself onto the barstool there. His arm brushes mine, and I eye him shrewdly, eyes narrowing.

Already he's touched me twice, and by the way he's leaning into me, I know he's trying to 'accidentally' touch me again. His grin is slimy, his eyes cold and not quite meeting mine. He's older than anyone I'd ever date. Probably in his mid-forties. Nothing about him reminds me of Professor Langhorn and yet...

And yet the knife in my pocket weighs heavily against my hip, and it's so hard not to reach down and flick it open, to press it under this man's chin and—

"Is it?" I ask evenly, coolly. I'm numb, not afraid like I should be. For some reason, I don't fear this man, or the way his hands inch towards me on the bar. I should. I *should*, because he's the same kind of person as Langhorn is.

But something in me itches for him to touch me. Because if he does, then he'll give me a reason. A motive to do something reckless. Then I really can pull the knife out, and—

I stand up quickly from my seat, backing away from him and watching his face fall open in confusion. Belatedly, I realize that I've already paid for my beer, and even the bartender is looking at me with bemusement on his face.

I can't stay here, though. I can't stay here with this man.

Because the knife in my pocket is begging to be used, and I know that I'll do something that I might regret if I stay. Already I have a plan in my head. How I'll get him out of the building, and where I'll cut him. Will his blood be hot when it hits my skin? Should I cut off his finger, to make sure he knows never to touch a girl again?

I have to get out of here.

I don't bother with an explanation. He doesn't deserve one, and with my teeth gritted together, all I can think of is how to get out of here. Thankfully, I'm not frozen. I *run* out of the bar, unable to stop and care about what anyone thinks or what they might say about me when I'm gone.

I can't care about that right now. I can't care about anything except getting out of here. Somehow, I find my way back home without really seeing where I'm going. My apartment building looms in the distance within twenty minutes, and in another five I'm back in front of the door, my breath coming in heavy pants as I double over and clutch my sides. I don't normally *run* unless I'm being chased, and my stomach is on fire right now. But the pain helps clear my head. It helps me forget the knife in my leggings, and slowly I drag myself up the stairs to my apartment, softly unlocking the door and trudging to my room.

Without bothering to change, I fall onto my bed with a groan, all of my energy sapped from my body. I can't move. I can barely think. And when I finally fall asleep, I've completely forgotten the knife in my pocket that my fingers are still wrapped around, as if some part of me is afraid it's going to move on its own like a living thing, instead of the inanimate object that it is.

CHAPTER 20

I don't *mean* to be on *funxcams*. It isn't really my intention to watch anything. I certainly haven't been interested in porn lately, and if I was in some kind of mood, I'd just go stare at Oliver.

But... I'm not.

Here I am, chewing on my thumbnail, and flicking my eyes over different sections of the site. I'm putting off looking at the little live notification in the corner that tells me one of the streamers I follow is currently streaming.

I'm not dumb. I only subscribe to *one* person. It feels wrong, somehow, to even consider watching him. It feels like I shouldn't want to watch him be sexy. That I should close myself off and maybe become a nun.

But fuck, I don't want to be a nun. I don't want to be celibate for the rest of my life, or guilt myself into not watching Oliver's stream. In an act of self defiance, I click the notification and let it take me to his stream, where he's just started.

Well, he's been going long enough that his shirt is off and his jeans are unbuttoned. His words falter when he sees my name pop up in his chat, and for a moment he's quiet. As if he wants to say something but doesn't because it isn't just us.

"Hello there, *finalistgirl*," he greets at last with a low purr. "It's been a while since you were here. Not that I'm at all disappointed." He tilts his head first one way, then the other, and I swear there's an urgency, an excitement to his movements that isn't usually there.

He pays attention to his other viewers, talking to them and taking their suggestions when they tip. But he talks to me as well, and whenever he gazes at the camera with that little tilt of his head that I love, I wonder if it's because he's wondering what I'm thinking.

My lip curls in a small grin and I hit the tip button, sending him ten dollars. It's not the biggest he's gotten, but I know his rules.

"Thanks so much, *finalistgirl*," he tells me, full of enthusiasm. "Seriously, it means a lot. Do you have a request for me, darling?" I'm pretty sure he's never called anyone else darling.

Which is how it should be.

That thought feels too possessive. Too committed to him being mine, but with no one else here, I don't have to explain myself away, except to my own brain. My fingers move across the keys as I grin, and when I hit enter, I get to watch him read my message in real time.

I'd love to see you in ears and a tail.

While it was originally his and Rook's thing to say to me, I remember very distinctly how Oliver had mentioned that he'd been the one wearing a tail before me.

I want to see it in real time.

"Huh," he murmurs, sitting back in his chair. "I think I'll have to ask you to take a raincheck on that, *finalistgirl*. Unfortunately, I'm not sure where mine are. But you don't mind waiting for me, right? You don't *really* mind?" He reaches into his pants as he says it, drawing out his length and stroking it slowly.

Everyone else in his chat rushes to tell him that *they* don't mind, and beg him to show them more. With my eyes glued to the screen, I watch as he touches himself, answering questions as he does. He's always been so good at this, and even just watching him causes heat to pool between my thighs. It's a relief, I think, that I won't have to be celibate for the rest of my life if I don't want to. And that I can watch Oliver like this without getting lost in other, worse thoughts.

In fact, those worse thoughts are becoming darker, more twisted than they have any right to be. And instead of all focusing on what happened to me, so many of them are beginning to circle around the idea of what *I* want to do to *Langhorn*.

Sucking in a breath through my teeth, I realize Oliver has said my name. Or at least, my screen name. He repeats himself when I send a question mark in the chat, and when he does, I snort.

"Is this okay for you, *finalistgirl?*" His voice is tight, and I can tell that he's close. Part of me is sure the reason he can get off so quickly and without a lot of effort is because of how much he loves being watched. Part of me thinks he's just always ready to go and turned on by way more than he should be.

Like violence. And blood.

And death.

"I could finish with your name on my lips, to make up for not having the ears and tail for you." He's teasing me, like he does everyone else. But there's an extra undercurrent in his voice that I don't think anyone else can recognize.

Still grinning, I type in my reply and send it without stopping to reconsider.

I suppose. Just this once.

He laughs outright at that, head hitting his headrest as he leans his shoulders back against it. "So kind. So benevolent, wonder girl." He doesn't seem to notice the slip, and I wonder if it even *is* a slip. "Watch me carefully, now. This is totally for you." He puts more effort into his movements, his hips rocking up into his hand. I'm captivated, even though I've seen this show so many times before.

It never gets old. My lips part and I breathe through my open mouth, nearly panting in time with Oliver as he gets himself off. True to his word, he comes with my screen name on his lips, and settles back against his chair, chest rising and falling as he breathes.

"You are all my *favorite* people." He laughs as I put the laptop on my bed and lean back against the headboard. I know this won't be the first time he gets himself off for the camera during his stream. He's more relaxed now. With a kind of boneless grace that I could never match. "You especially today, *finalistgirl*."

I thank him for that, and keep my computer open as I get up and do the chores in my room that have needed to get done for days, all while listening to how he talks to everyone else and works through the hour of his stream with professional ease.

I pause in folding laundry when my phone vibrates against my leg. With Juniper in the other room and Oliver just done with his stream a few minutes ago, I'm not exactly expecting anyone to try to get a hold of me. After all, it isn't like I have a plethora of friends.

When I fish my phone out from the abyss of blankets, however, I see that it's Oliver. And more than that, it's an image sent from him. My brows lift, and I open the message, only to choke on the air I was breathing.

It's Oliver. Naked. On his bed, with a pair of cat ears on his head. His hair hides the base of them, and the auburn fur is only a few shades lighter than the curls they rest in. With his head tilted to the side and a sly look on his face, he's certainly the sexiest cat I've ever seen.

I save the picture for future, uh, research, and then focus on figuring out what in the world to text back to him. Clearly my laundry isn't going to get done. Not now, anyway. Not when I definitely have more important things on my mind.

Well hi, I text back finally, barely able to tear my eyes from the photo. *This is unexpected.*

Is it? He texts back within a minute. *I wanted to show you. And you know you don't have to tip me, wonder girl. Do you like my ears?*

I fucking love his ears. And while I know I don't have to tip him on his streams, it would've looked weird if I'd just made a request like the random assholes who show up in his stream and demand something for nothing. He usually ignores or mutes them without saying a word to their whining. Hell, sometimes I wonder if he's installed Rook as a moderator on his streams so his bigger, meaner counterpart can boot them instead.

It feels like something Rook would enjoy doing, after all.

Depends. Do you have a tail to go along with them? Belatedly, I wonder if he's going to show me his ass next, complete with a tail butt plug. But instead, when a picture comes through, it's of him licking his palm, doing his best impression of a cat ready to groom himself. I snort, rolling my eyes and giving a quick shake of my head. What a lovable idiot.

Somewhere. I haven't used it in a while. I'm sorry, he apologizes. *But if you're that into it, I'll dig it out for you. As long as you wear the ears and tail I got you last semester. You don't mind, right? Tell me you liked it, at least a little.*

I liked it, I assure him quickly. I definitely don't want him thinking I don't. *And I love your ears. You're the cutest cat to ever walk the planet. Though I think golden retriever ears would suit you more. And a dog's tail that you can wag like the real thing.* It isn't my fault that he consistently brings to mind thoughts of a golden retriever with his happy-go-lucky, ride-or-die attitude. I like him all the more for it, really. I'm certainly not complaining, and never would.

Oliver is perfect, after all. Maybe not to other people. Especially people he murders. But to me? He and Rook are the perfect, most complimentary pair of people I've ever witnessed.

When he sends me another picture, it pulls me out of my thoughts and I bark out a surprised laugh before I can stop myself. In the picture, he's licking Rook's cheek, both of them looking at the camera with opposite kinds of reactions. Oliver is clearly thrilled. Rook is clearly... Well, he's definitely not thrilled. I wonder if he'll throttle Oliver. Lovingly, of course, but still.

You cannot tell me he let you do that of his own free will, I text him back, kicking the rest of my unfolded laundry back into the basket and laying the folded pieces on top. I have no desire to finish it right now. Not when Oliver has all of my attention.

Well... maybe not, Oliver agrees. *But he's fine. A little fun won't kill him.*

Yeah, but are you sure he won't kill you? The edges of a smile twitch at my lips. I feel better than I have in a week when I'm joking with him here, but I ache for this to be in person, instead of so far apart. *By the way, hurry up and build me my wing,* I add, my words are beyond reckless. *I want to move in before the next century.*

He doesn't text back.

My stomach plummets, heart sinking, and I worry for one

solid moment that I've really fucked up. I've taken things too far, to a level he's not comfortable with, and now he's looking for ways to deescalate the situation. *Shit.* I hadn't meant to do this. I hadn't meant to ruin—

My eyes flutter over the words of his text the moment it comes through, and I relax even before my brain has fully processed the words.

I am getting Rook on that right now, wonder girl. You know you could like. Steal an office, yeah? Or one of our bedrooms? Seriously, I'll kick Rook out of his room temporarily if it gets you in the door. The problem now, of course, is that I can't tell if he's joking. I can't tell if this is him being serious, for the most part, or if he's just going along with me because he thinks I'm making a joke.

Two options come to mind, though neither of them is completely what I need right now. Unfortunately for me, magical crystal balls that can tell me his thoughts were out of stock at Walmart, so that leaves me with only my lackluster mortal senses and decision-making skills. So, unfortunately, no mind reading today.

I could joke with him. Or rather, make it clear that I was joking.

Or, on a more serious note, I could be clear that I'm *not.* I could take this to a more earnest place, even if it's just to see how genuine he is before I decide what to do with that information.

But joking is the easier, less risky option.

What the hell, I think to myself, biting down on my bottom lip until it stings and my eyes threaten to water from the discomfort. I'm feeling stupidly reckless this week, and knowing is important to me. I'm tired of playing guesswork with him, or not knowing where we stand.

I wouldn't make you kick him out. That feels suicidal, I tease, sending the first message and furiously typing the next. *What if I really did want to move in with you? Just hypothetically. Are you joking when you talk about it? You know I'm joking about the wing. And the solarium, I suppose.*

Again, he doesn't reply right away. I can't help but wonder why, and what he's doing with his time. I've seen him text, so I know he's a faster texter. But I can't help but think that either he's going over his replies as carefully as I'd gone over mine, or he's asking Rook for guidance on what to do.

Either option is... interesting. Though it's possible that neither of them is true. When he does reply again, I take a deep breath before I read it, just in case I've read this entire situation wrong and he isn't going to give me the answer that I'm hoping for.

Wonder girl. You don't know how much I want you to live with me. Rook says kidnapping you and bringing your stuff here is wrong, but I am going to put it on the table. We have a four bedroom house, and you could literally make any part of it yours. You want my room? Done. Rook's room? Maybe not. But anywhere else is yours.

You're just saying that so I wear the dog ears and tail for you when I'm over there next, I say, hating myself for resorting to a comfortable joke.

But Oliver doesn't let me fall back into my humor. *Maybe a little. But not really. All I need is for you to say the words. Stand outside your apartment building and I'll move you in no matter what time of day or night it is. I'd do anything for you to live with us. And Rook is nodding, so he is definitely agreeing and not just choking on a pomegranate.*

Our photography professor eats pomegranates? That's definitely the most shocking part of that statement.

Don't question it. You know by now how weird he is. But seriously. You're welcome here whenever you want. Short term, long term, medium term, or something way more permanent. We would love you to live with us, Blair. Under any circumstances that make you comfortable.

Ah, so, I can request Rook to sign the deed over to me?

He says no. But I'm willing to fight him for you, if that's what it would take. I'd lose, just so we're clear. You'd lose too. But we can say we tried?

His response actually brings a laugh to my lips. Everything he says lightens my heart a little, and before long, I'm actually grinning. God, why did I ever leave their house? Staying with them had helped me so much, and now being stuck here instead, in an empty bed and darkness that feels like it suffocates me when the lights are off is absolute torture.

And, apparently, sends me into spirals of considering things that I definitely have no business considering.

We would try so hard. And fail. So hard, I agree, knowing that would be the most likely outcome. *But right now I'm going to go figure out dinner, okay?* I'm starving, but somehow this is the first time all day I've felt like eating. *I'll talk to you later?*

Anytime, Blair, he replies. *Have something good for dinner. Get pancakes. I'll reimburse you for the fancy pancakes. And seriously, you know you can text or call us anytime, right? We're here for you whenever. However. Whatever that means to you.*

If you keep saying shit like that, I'll think you're serious, I threaten, again trying to lighten the mood of the conversation. In reality, he has me so shook up that I sometimes can't see straight. I want him—both of them—so badly that it *hurts*. But with the bruise still so plain on my thigh, even considering it makes me feel wrong.

Like I haven't earned it, or don't deserve to want them in all the ways I do.

I do mean them. Get food, Blair. You're not you when you're hungry. I grin at that as well, and send one more quick message to wish him a good night before throwing my feet off the side of my bed and coming to a halt when I'm up and leaning my weight on them.

I don't want to be here. The thought hits me hard, and the smile falls from my lips. I don't want to be in this apartment, even though Juniper is here more than she isn't. I love her to death, and she's my best friend in the world.

But she isn't what I need right now, and I don't know how to change that.

CHAPTER 21

I t's strange to be walking back onto campus. Stranger still, to stroll into the art department like it's nothing. I feel... jumpy. Weird, I think. Like I shouldn't be here. Obviously I won't have office hours in Professor Carmine's office anymore this year, and I haven't decided if I'm willing to continue being her teaching assistant, truth be told.

But everything just seems to be going by me so *fast*. It's only mid-February, but in reality there are only three months left of the semester. Instead of only a few days off, thanks to Professor Langhorn going MIA, it's been a week since I've been here.

A *week* since I've set foot in Rook's classroom, and five days since I've even seen Rook *or* Oliver. I'd told them that I had to work on my thesis, which isn't a lie. Without completing it, I won't graduate with honors.

I can't lose that. I *won't*. So I've pushed away the longing that I feel every time I think about them or talk to either of them on the phone. I've pushed away the need to feel their hands on my skin, and every time I glance at the bruise on my leg I will it to fade faster.

It feels wrong to let them touch me with it still there. As though another man's mark is burned into my skin, and until the burn is healed, I can't let anyone else lay their palm there or anywhere else.

It fucking sucks, but I haven't been able to change my mind, no matter what I do. I also can't help wondering if there's something wrong with me. Shouldn't I be repulsed by the idea of either of them touching me after what happened a week ago? Thinking of Langhorn makes my skin almost visibly crawl off of my skeleton, but when I think of Rook and Oliver?

It's the exact opposite.

For a while, I don't realize I'm standing in the middle of the arts department with my eyes on Professor Carmine's office. When I *do* realize what I'm doing, I shake my head and pick up my feet, like I'm trying to find my balance in mud or quicksand. I pull my bottom lip into my mouth and look around, almost wishing I hadn't gotten here twenty minutes before Rook's class starts.

To be honest... I'm nervous. Not just about seeing them for the first time in days. But also because I don't know how good this project really is. I don't know if it's worth me turning it in, or if I should fake being sick while I run home. I'd like to think he'd give me extra time, but that seems somewhat unlikely, given that he knows I'm doing better than I was.

"Oh, Blair. I didn't know you were coming back in today." The voice sounds more surprised than anything, and I turn to see Professor Carmine standing in the area near the lounge. She's too slow to wipe the concern off of her face, and her confusion about why I'm just standing here. She must be shaken up, because normally she barely gives way to any emotion, let alone surprise.

I give her a wan half smile and shrug my shoulders. "Well, I couldn't keep hiding in my apartment. I was starting to count the ceiling tiles," I joke, as if I can just brush this off so easily. I can't, obviously, but I don't want her to be weird around me.

I don't want anyone to be weird when they're around me, or feel sorry for me.

"Blair, I'm..." She glances down, her brows drawn, as if she hasn't heard me. "I owe you an apology," she tells me at last, finally meeting my eyes once more. I glance around as she speaks, making sure there's no one else on this side of the hallway. Thankfully, there isn't, but I know that could change relatively quickly. "I'm sorry," she goes on.

"Why?" My attention snaps back to her, and I can feel my eyes widening. "Why are you sorry, Professor? You didn't do anything. You weren't even there, and you helped me when you found... me." There has to be a more delicate way to put that, and I shift my grip on the strap of my backpack uncomfortably when I realize how it sounds.

"No. I should've listened to you," she disagrees. "He'd gotten worse this year. Professor Langhorn had started acting more erratically than he had been. It had been brought up at meetings, of course. But he has—*had* a lot of fans among the faculty. Everyone thought he'd leave on his own, or we'd help ease him into retirement. He was harmless. Or so we thought." Guilt oozes off of her like sweat, and I open my mouth to say something to absolve her of it.

Except I can't find anything to say. She *knew* the things he was saying to me, other students, and other professors. She *knew* he was off.

And yet she, and others, did nothing about it. If they had, maybe I wouldn't have ended up with my clothes torn on the floor of her office, unsure if I'd ever be able to pick up the pieces.

If she had done something, if anyone had done something, would my dreams be full of knives and blood?

For some reason, the knife from home is in my pocket again. It weighs heavily against my hip, though I'm sure it's not noticeable to anyone other than me, thanks to the tee I wear over it that hangs past my hips. Tucked in the high pocket of my leggings means that it's unnoticeable.

It's only there for *me*. Not anyone else.

"It's okay." The words don't sound like my voice. They sound brittle, hollow, and unconvincing. But I know that even if I repeat them a hundred times, it won't get any better. Because it *isn't* okay. It'll never be okay until one day I take the knife out of my pocket and—

"Blair." Oliver's warm voice curls around me just as his arm does. He pulls me against him, arm wrapped around my shoulders, and I stare up at him with a smile.

Only to see that he's... not smiling. Our sides are pressed together, and between us I can feel the press of the switchblade against my hip. Can he feel it too? Surely not. Or if he does, I doubt he knows what it is.

"Hello, professor," he greets, beaming at professor Carmine in that way of his that tells people he's either dumb or just way too friendly. "I'm not sure if you remember me? I'm—"

"Oliver Greer." She regains her composure instantly when confronted with his overbearing friendliness. Her lips purse together and she looks at him with dislike. "I remember you from my Intro to Art History class. What was it? Five years ago now?"

"A little closer to seven, actually. I graduate this year, though!" he tells her excitedly. When I move to pull away, his grip tightens on my shoulders, but thankfully Professor Carmine doesn't notice.

Is he mad at me?

He exchanges a few more words with my professor, though I can tell she'd rather him not be around, before finally she excuses herself with one last look at me and heads for her office.

The same one I'll never be able to look at again.

Once more I move to step away from him, and once more he holds me tight against his side, his arm like a band of iron. It should scare me, I realize, though only confusion and a small thrill of surprise flit through my body. I turn my face up to see that he's staring at me, and a jolt makes my stomach flip.

"What's wrong?" I ask, my voice soft. "Are you mad? Did I do something, or—"

"What's in your pocket, Blair?" he asks, going suddenly serious.

Immediately I freeze. My entire body goes still, and except for my heartbeat, I could probably be a statue. My breathing comes shallow as I stare at him, and part of me wants to look around him, in fear that Rook is here already as well.

"My phone," I lie, unsure of why I do it. "It's just my phone."

"That's not your phone, wonder girl." He doesn't sound angry, exactly. But there's a guarded, cautious look on his face. "We're going to walk to Rook's office, okay? Just like this. And you're not going to reach for your pocket. Understand?"

"Are you high?" Is my plaintive response. It earns me a snort, but nothing else, and just as forcefully Oliver wheels me around and walks me to Professor Solomon's office, forcing me to keep step with his longer strides.

When we're there, he all but shoves me inside, and Rook glances up as he closes the door firmly behind him to lean against it. Effectively trapping me between the desk and himself.

"What are you doing?" I snap, just as Professor Solomon lays down his phone, attention fully on us.

"What *are* you doing?" he repeats, his attention going to Oliver when he realizes I've just been shoved in here. "We have class in twenty minutes. If she feels up to it—"

"What's in your pocket, wonder girl?" Oliver demands, his eyes not leaving mine. His mask has fallen in the last couple of seconds, but it isn't anger or insanity that I see in his face. It's cold, calculating concern. Like he's trying to figure out what the problem is that he's about to deal with.

I reach for the knife, my fingers fluttering around my pocket, before I realize what I'm doing, and drop my hand with a huff of disbelief. "Why do you care what's in my pocket?" God, I know I shouldn't be trying to keep this from him. But for some reason I'm too afraid of them knowing about it, to be honest. "It's not a big deal," I added, looking away from him when I can't stand his gaze any longer. "Seriously, it's not."

"She has a knife in her pocket, Rook," Oliver says slowly, his voice quiet in the dim private office. "When I saw her she was standing in front of Professor Carmine's office, just staring around. And there's a knife in her fucking pocket." Is that a hint of worry I can hear in his voice? The anger I expect doesn't show. Just that strange, worried sound that has him talking low and fast.

Rook gets to his feet slowly, coming around the desk until he can sit on the corner nearest me. "*Is* there a knife in your pocket, Blair?" he asks me steadily, one of his hands coming up to circle my wrist in his long fingers.

I can't lie to him, just like I can't lie to Oliver for a third time. Dropping my gaze to the floor, I nod, though I scramble to look for an explanation in my mind that will make this seem not as bad as it really is. "I wasn't going to do anything," I whisper finally, letting my professor lift my hoodie and reach into my pocket. "Seriously. I've just been... taking it with me. Sometimes. Some places."

"Some places like where?" His voice is still just as steady, but there's a demanding note in it that warns me not to lie or try to get out of this.

God, he's going to kill me.

"You'll think I'm insane," I admit, sinking down into the chair that sits across from his desk and putting my head in my hands. "*I* think I'm insane, and I'm the one living in my head. I just..." I let out a breath, then take another one. "A few nights ago I woke up freaking out. I didn't realize how hard it would be to sleep alone and I just... I just had to get out. I don't know why, but I grabbed the knife. It's not even mine, by the way. It's Jun's boyfriend's that he left at our place last semester. So I just took it with me to the bar, and then this guy talked to me—I didn't do anything!" I add, when I see Oliver's face fall in shock. "I literally did *nothing*. It's not a big deal. I know how to control myself, and I know my own mind. I wouldn't have done anything. It's like a security blanket I've just been carrying around. I'd never use it."

Wouldn't you? a treacherous voice in my brain asks in a soft whisper. This voice doesn't sound like Juniper's, or my mother's. It sounds like my own, though a different version of me than what exists here and now.

Would I?

"Blair, if someone catches you with that, you'll get expelled," Oliver murmurs, sinking down beside my chair. "Seriously. I don't think it's okay for you to be carrying it around. At least not right now."

"Definitely not right now," Rook agrees, though he eyes me carefully, as if there's more he wants to say. "I'm keeping it. I'm keeping it here, and I'm taking it home with me. You can't have it back. It's not even yours, after all. Don't argue with me,

Blair." He eases to his feet, ignoring the irritation on my face and the verbal arguments he's cut me off from.

"You're certainly one to warn me off of a murder," I snap, tossing my photography project onto his desk half-heartedly. "Seriously, *you two?*"

"I'm not warning you off of murder, Love," Rook replies firmly, leaning over the chair to trap me in it before I can move. "I think we both know I wouldn't do that under the right circumstances. But I *am* going to keep you from getting yourself hurt or expelled. Or arrested." His hands tighten on the armrests of the chair, eyes fixed on mine and not letting me look away. "Do you understand, Love? No matter what I have to do, I am not going to let you go around stabbing people you don't like with a stupid, dull switchblade. So drop it. You aren't getting this back, and you're going to class with Oliver."

"You're not my father," I point out, my heart slamming in my chest. "You can't—"

"No, I'm not. Because your dad would probably frown on murder," he replies in what could almost be called a sneer. "I'm helping you. And I know you're just nervous right now. Too nervous to see that, I think. So please, *please* take what I'm saying to heart. Do you hear me, Love?" His face comes closer, and I feel his breath on my lips when he opens his mouth and says, "No more knives at school. No more going to bars after midnight. Can you promise me that?"

I shouldn't.

I can't.

Something in me itches and aches and *burns* to do it again. To have that comforting weight on my hip and know that with just a flick of my hand, I could end someone's fragile little life if they ever try to hurt me again.

But I can't say that. I can't admit to them that I've considered it. That I've fully thought about what it would feel like to kill someone and have their blood on my hands.

So I close my eyes and count to five before reopening them, though I can't meet his eyes. I play it off as embarrassment, not dishonesty, when I nod and repeat what he'd wanted from me.

"I promise, okay? I won't carry a knife around, and I won't go to a bar after midnight. Can I go now?" My breath catches in my throat when he doesn't pull away immediately, and I wonder if he's going to call me on the lie that I've just told.

Instead. he just... doesn't. Rook kisses my forehead and helps me to my feet before turning and clapping Oliver on the shoulder. "Can you both just go to class, please? I'll be in there soon. And I'd be grateful knowing you're both in the same place."

I don't argue. Not when Oliver agrees, and not when he tugs me out the door and toward the classroom that we don't need to be in for another ten minutes.

Because he doesn't understand. Maybe neither of them do.

And I can't be sure I'll keep the promise that I'd so freely given to get out of Rook's scrutiny.

CHAPTER 22

I'm trying so hard to keep my promise that I think it's going to kill me.

Lying in bed and staring at the dark ceiling does nothing for my tumultuous thoughts. In fact, whenever I close my eyes, things are worse. All I can see is the office of the woman in charge of our school's Title IX accreditation, and therefore works as the school's coordinator in all aspects of sexual harassment or assault on campus.

With scrubbed white walls and carefully placed trinkets on her desk, it had been strange when the owner of that office had walked in and turned out to be a woman who, from her outfit, had yet to leave the sixties behind. Ms. Beck had sat down in front of me on her side of the desk, offered me a piece of candy like I was five and she was a bank receptionist with a bowl of old, dusty suckers in front of her while Rook sat beside me and stared at her, unimpressed.

I know that the rest of the school is confused about why I've chosen him as my professor-chaperone-counselor for this.

Everyone had expected me to choose a woman. As if I'd be more comfortable around a female professor than a man. To be fair, none of them know that I have a relationship going with him, but the looks I'd gotten today when Ms. Beck had looked between us hadn't made me feel better.

Then she'd dropped the ball on me, when it was obvious I hadn't wanted any fucking candy.

Professor Langhorn, unfortunately, still has friends here at Wickett. Apparently, a few reports were... misplaced. It had seemed to burn her to say it, and I curl on my side in bed as I remember the way her face had pinched painfully at the words. *But we're taking care of it. You don't need to worry about it.*

I didn't need to hear that part from her. My brain had buzzed and burned over the idea that people *liked* him enough to lose the report of what he'd done to me. The fact that the school could lose their Title IX accreditation hadn't even occurred to me until Rook had brought it up in a low voice to her, and Ms. Beck was quick to push aside our concerns with another pinched smile in my direction.

I don't think we need to escalate this any further, Professor Solomon. She'd sounded so fucking condescending when she'd said it, and had looked at me with a widening grin. *We've got it taken care of.*

I wondered then, as I do now, how long—and often—the school has known his 'friends' in the office had pushed away the consequences of what he'd done. How *could* they, when I'm here, a living witness, and sane enough to know I didn't imagine it?

How could *anyone* like him enough to forgive what he'd done?

Before I can stop myself, I fly out of bed to walk around the room. The hardwood is cold under my bare feet, but I barely notice. I can't notice now, not at this moment when my brain is too busy buzzing like a cloud of flies has moved in to settle somewhere behind my eyes.

For over a week, I'd managed to keep my promise to Rook and Oliver. I haven't gone out again. Not before midnight or after. For *a week* I've tried to be what I'm supposed to be, even though something in me is different and stirring and *hungry*.

So the news about Langhorn, and how he's on the cusp of getting off with no more than a slap on the wrist, has me fucking ravenous. It's a strange, gnawing feeling in my stomach that I can't explain. As if I haven't eaten in weeks and the pain of emptiness is about to end me.

I can't sit still tonight, like I've forced myself to do every other night. I can't do this right now.

Without waiting to feel bad, or to make sure Juniper isn't up, I throw on real clothes, my shoes, and head out the door again. This time without the comforting weight of a knife at my side or any idea of what I'm going to do with myself.

I'll figure it out. And it's only this once. Just this once, because my day was shit and I can't be blamed for needing to get up and get out of my apartment.

Just this once, and I'll never do this again. Even if I have to tie myself to the bed.

When it happens again, I tell myself that it, too, is the last time. That I only need once more to get it out of my system. I walk the streets and find a bar, sitting there and waiting for someone to do something. To say something.

To be the kind of person that I can't stand. But nothing happens. Nothing can, really, when I don't even know what I'm angling for. There's no weapon in the pocket of my leggings, and nothing I could do if I found what I was looking for. So the second time I just go home, go back to bed, and try to sleep until the sun comes up.

The same things happen with the third, fourth, and fifth

time until, by accident, I have a schedule going. Once a week, then twice a week, I prowl around St. Augustine' streets at night. Looking for something. Waiting for someone, though I'm not even sure what that is, if I'm being honest with myself. All the while I try to be normal, I try to act like the broken, festering piece inside me is fine, and try *so hard* to focus on how much I care about Rook and Oliver, all the while knowing I'm lying to their faces.

It isn't until the end of March, a week before spring break, that I stop by a small pawn shop on my way home from school and pick up the blade that I've been eyeing in the glass counter display. It's so cheap that I barely blink at the price. Instead, I fork over the twenty dollars and shove the switchblade into my pocket with a small word of thanks, and a promise to have a good day. The old lady running the shop doesn't give me a second look, and I don't give her a reason to.

I even swear that I'm not going to take it anywhere, like that means anything right now.

Guilt swirls in my chest at how I'd promised both of them I wouldn't do stupid shit like this anymore. I'd sworn to myself as well, but here I am in my room again, with my leggings and t-shirt on and the knife in my pocket, ready to go along my pre-established route once more.

Maybe I should've taken up the school's offer to see our campus therapist.

Maybe if I had, then I wouldn't be here now, heading to a bar with a knife in my pocket and a feeling that I can't describe in my chest.

As usual, Juniper is asleep. I hear the low sounds of the television in her room, but I know by now that it's just the noise she goes to sleep listening to. Not an indication that she's actually awake. I barely stop to listen this time. I barely bother to be careful and as quiet as possible.

It's not like anyone's caught me so far. Nothing will change just because I'm half-willing her to come out of her room and stop me.

There's nothing to stop me from, I remind myself firmly, locking the door behind me. Like usual, I take the stairs, the nervous energy in my legs taking me down them quickly. Normally I'm not a stairs person. I put going up and down stairs in the same category as *running.* Unless the elevator is broken and the serial killer on my trail is catching up, I hate them.

But at night, when I feel full to the brim of electricity that gives me more energy than I can stand, the thought of taking the elevator down makes me shrink away in dislike.

I'm out of the building quicker than I would've been if I'd waited for the elevator, and I easily fall into the tracks I've taken once or twice a week for the past three weeks. The air is much warmer than it was when I started this routine, making the need for a hoodie non-existent at this time of year. Even my leggings feel too-warm, though I need them to hide my knife and give me a pocket for my phone and keys.

It's crazy that I barely have to think about where I'm going. Over the past month, I've established a bit of a route. The three bars that I've found form a circle around my apartment building, so I'm not ranging too far in any direction, and if one is empty, I'll just go to the next, or the one after. I haven't had a night when I wasn't able to find a place that had what I was looking for, and I'm sure tonight will be no different.

The first bar, the Wet Seal, is my least favorite of the three. I don't like the bar itself, or the stickiness of the floor or tables. I try to stay here as little as possible, though it's definitely been the best for highlighting the worst kind of people I've come across so far. Bartenders who only know how to be rude seem to make up the entire roster of employees, and men with no manners or sense seem to be the vast majority of the customer base.

But tonight it's empty. Well, not empty, but the games playing above the bar tug on the attention of the three men sitting at the long, wooden counter. One of the bartenders, a blond man who I have a particular dislike for, glances up at me with glittering eyes, like he's less than happy to see me.

Lucky for him, this isn't where I want to be tonight.

Back outside, I pause in the breeze, taking a deep breath before I take another step. Which promptly makes me realize my shoe is untied, and with a roll of my eyes I kneel on one knee, fingers deftly moving to re-tie the knot as I look around the street to see if anyone else is out roaming as late as I am.

Out of the corner of my eye I do see some movement, but when I turn to face behind me where I swear something had flickered out of sight, there's nothing. No person, no movement, and no shadows that look like they shouldn't be there.

For a moment I consider backtracking, to see if there is someone there or I'm being followed. But the absurdity of that sets in and I snort, shaking my head. Who in the world would be following *me*? No one knows why I'm out here, after all. And I'm not exactly the most enticing target for someone, unless they're drunk. In a t-shirt and leggings, I could pass for just about anything. Nothing about me sticks out or makes people notice me.

That's what I'm going for, anyway.

Blinking, I realize that I'm still standing there, head cocked to the side as I stare back down the street. I must look like an idiot, and I give a quick shake of my head before I pivot on my heel and keep going down my pre-ordained route that I know will take me to Raven's Nest.

Out of all three, it might be my favorite. Maybe. If I can

have a favorite sleazy sports bar that serves mostly old beer and shitty fried food. Though I'd never tried food from any of the three places I frequent, I've seen other people order wings, fries, and other appetizers that are drenched in cooling, congealing grease when served.

No thanks, I've thought, every time I see it. *I like my internal organs working and right where they are, actually.*

While it's only a five or so minute walk to my second bar, I take my time tonight. I don't normally, though I busy myself with pulling my hair back into a long and thick ponytail, the volume courtesy of how much I'd been tossing and turning in my bed before I'd come out here tonight. I should be tired, with how poorly I've been sleeping lately.

Well, except when I sleep with Rook and Oliver. While it's only happened a few times, and I've been maybe a little distant since I started breaking my promise to them, being in their house, in their bed, is still the best sleep I could ever ask for. The nightmares never come. The strange, gnawing hunger isn't a thing, and I don't have this kind of electric, painful energy that pushes me to do stupid shit at night in the city.

I look for opportunities to glance back over my shoulder, a spot between my shoulder blades itching like someone's gaze is boring a hole into my back. It's probably just me, just my fear of being caught by someone I care for, because every time I look, there's absolutely no one there. Hell, there's not even a trace of anyone behind me. No shadow, no movement, and nothing else to suggest I'm being followed. The streets are empty enough that I'd be able to tell. I'd know if there was someone, I think.

Right?

Thankfully, when I open the door to Raven's Nest, I can let out a breath and stop worrying about that. It would be incredibly difficult to follow me into the bar without me noticing. Especially one with a mirror above the main counter, reflecting the faces of the customers back at them should they look up. Here, at least, I'll know if anyone is looming up behind me or skulking around like they don't belong.

But who would even bother? One of the bartenders from Wet Seal? That seems like a stretch, and it's not like anyone here can read my mind to know what I think about when a man with alcohol on his breath leans in and huffs it all over me, his hands reaching for a touch he thinks I won't notice.

As my steps take me to the bar, I'd be an idiot not to recognize that there's something different about tonight. My restless energy is magnified, evolved, and has become something that sings through me. My hands shake when I put them on the bar, but I busy myself by trying to look normal instead of stopping to focus on it.

For five weeks, I've been so good at controlling myself and not letting this go too far. It's been a game for me. An awful, danger-filled game that's almost gone too far more than once. But tonight feels like the stakes are higher. As if I'm playing competitively, instead of still learning the ropes.

What if I took this further tonight?

What's *stopping* me? is the real question. If I don't hurt anyone, then no one will know what I'm doing. Even with my mind full of ideas, it's so damn easy to fall into conversation with a man at the bar, my drink in hand. There's no way for him to know that it's just coke without the rum I swear is in there. I never drink when I'm out like this, unless it's a beer I can sip away at for the hour I tend to hang out.

I'd decided early on the only way this would work was if I was smarter than my opponents, and that means not drinking like they do. I can use that to my advantage, and their detriment.

Sure enough, the man whose breath stinks like a mix of old, cheap beer and the whiskey he's been shooting has no idea that I'm not drinking. I see his eyes dart to the coke I'm sipping, and know that he's assuming there's a fair bit of rum in this, judging by the way I grin up at him shyly, with a tinge of merriment to my cheeks.

It's scary how easy this has become, if I stop to think about it. How I've learned exactly what to say to make them let their guards down. How I can pretend to be just a little bit tipsy, and how much men want to believe that I'm drunker than I would realistically be, even if this glass was full of alcohol.

It sucks for most men that they're so stupid.

"I'm Jan," I introduce, when the man tells me his name. I've worked my way through the *Brady Bunch* girls' names twice now, and this is my third time using Jan. Next time, or at the next bar, I'll be Cindy instead. The man mumbles something about me having a nice name, but his eyes aren't on my face.

They never are.

He stares at my chest like he's going to spontaneously gain the power of x-ray vision. I let him, glancing off to the side to see that the bartender has walked away to the edge of the counter. The man in front of me, Henry, says a few other things, but by now they wash over me like water.

I don't care about his stupid, hopeless flirting. That's not what I'm here for.

But that's all Henry wants to give me. His hands stay on his glass or limp in his lap, and it's only his gaze that wonders. Disappointment sinks into me every time he leans away, and I can tell he's getting drunker by the minute.

At last I excuse myself, glancing around the room until I can find someone else. Normally, this is when I'd leave. I don't want the bartender thinking that I'm a prostitute, or something worse. The only other women here are engrossed in the game, and in each other. Obviously, I'm something different, I just don't want to be different enough for attention.

I'm almost out the door when I see him. The man sits by the side door, at a small table that barely fits him, let alone the other chair that sits cock-eyed on the other side of it. He looks like he hasn't showered in days, and his eyes glitter at me with both lust and resentment.

And that makes him exactly what I'm looking for.

I turn like I was going his way anyway, and sit down across from him with a wry, apologetic smile on my lips. "Can I sit here for a moment?" I ask, leaning in so I don't have to talk too loudly. "I'm sorry. It's just... I don't normally do this, or come out this late. But I couldn't sleep," I admit, trying my tried-and-true methods of explanation.

"Couldn't sleep?" The man tilts his glass back until he can down the rest of it. "Why come here? It's not exactly a great place. The liquor sucks too," he adds, wrinkling his nose at the now-empty glass. "The bartenders can't make shit, and this tastes old."

"I don't know. It was just open, and I was..." I shrug my shoulders again, looking to the side. "Sorry. I can leave, if you want? I'm not trying to bother anyone." The sadder I look, the easier this normally is. Once or twice, things have taken a weird turn, with someone wanting to actually help me or be there for me.

But not often.

And not with this guy. He leans closer to me over the table, the puff of his stale breath sneaking into my nose like curdled milk. He definitely needs a shower, and to do laundry considering the stains on his shirt. And unlike the man at the bar, he doesn't keep his parts to himself.

His knee bumps against mine under the table, and when I

don't move or protest, he does it again, leg actually pressing against mine for a few seconds before he grins at me.

"What's your name, pretty girl?" he purrs in a voice that's the opposite of seductive. If this is his attempt at flirting or being sexy, he's pretty awful at it.

"Jan," I reply, resting my hands on the table in front of me. I offer him another wan smile, and ask, "What's yours?"

"Jeremy. You don't have to leave, Jan. But you do look tired." I've never had someone move this fast before. Normally they want to talk a little, or have some kind of conversation where they ask me friendly questions, only to not actually hear a thing I've said.

But not wonderful, perfect *Jeremy*. He breathes in my face with lightly wheezing breaths while I try not to look disgusted, and I use that moment to think about what I'm going to say to seal this devil's deal.

"You're right, I need to go home. I should've gone home an hour ago, but..." I offer him a nervous grin. "It's really late, and I'm kind of afraid to go home alone. I don't have the money to hire an Uber, so I guess I'm waiting here until dawn." Sitting back in my chair, I give a nervous laugh. "Guess it's a good thing this place doesn't close on Fridays, right?"

"Right," he agrees, his gaze sharpening. "But you don't want to be waiting around here all night. Look, this is all I've had." He brandishes the glass at me again. "I'm not even tipsy. Do you want a ride home?"

Does this actually work on anyone? It's desperate, at best. Predatory, at worst. Even if I were actually drunk, there would be no way I'd fall for this.

I make a show of being unsure. Of shaking my head with a pained look on my face. "I can't ask you to do that. I wouldn't be able to pay you back for gas."

"Seriously," he assures me. "I was going to leave soon, anyway. I don't mind."

Again, I hesitate. I can't seem too eager, though I doubt he'd even know that something was up if I did. I look away from him and at the table, mentally counting down from ten as he fidgets in front of me, waiting for the answer he's praying for.

"If you're sure," I agree at last, rising to my feet. "I would really like to sleep in my bed." He replies with some nonsense, some reassurance, that I barely hear. The blood rushes in my ears, and I follow him out of the side door with my gaze on his and my heart pounding, sending icy electricity through my veins.

This is it.

I've never gotten this far before. I've always quit or chickened out before I could be alone with one of these men.

This is it.

I know that when I'm out in the parking lot alone with him, I'll have to be fast once I know we're alone. He could still overpower me if I'm not. Switchblade or no.

But he's slow, and drunker than he thinks. His steps wobble on his way through parked cars, and I'm elated when I realize that he's parked at the very back of the small, poorly lit lot. Far enough away from the lights of the door that no one looking out will be able to see us in just a few more steps.

My hands clench at my sides, feeling too empty, and I surreptitiously pull the switchblade from my pocket to grip against my palm.

A few more steps. Just a few more steps and this really *will be—*

Hands on my shoulders jerk me around roughly, so hard that I have no choice but to pivot on the sidewalk. A surprised sound, more breath than anything, leaves me, and I tilt my head back, looking up into the shadowed face, the dark curls, at a mouth that twists up at the edges to say—

"Oh no, my pretty little killer." Rook's voice is an absolute purr in the darkness, and his grip tightens once I'm crushed against him.

"This is not how we do this kind of thing."

CHAPTER 23

My heart nearly stops. I don't know how to reply, or even what to do. It has never, in all the times I've done this, crossed my mind that Rook *knows*. Or that either of them might suspect. The pieces of tonight slam into place, and I narrow my eyes at him, not trying to get away.

"You've been following me," I accuse softly. "I saw you outside of the Wet Seal."

He leans forward to nose my cheek, his lips close to my ear when he says, "I've been following you for a month. I hate to tell you this, my darling, lovely girl, but you're not as subtle as you think you are. But you aren't just here to play tonight, are you?"

Distantly, I hear the sound of Jeremy's indignation and surprise. I look up and over my shoulder, face nearly brushing Rook's as both of us stare at him with miles of disdain.

"Who are you?" he demands, glancing between us. "Do you know her? I was just about to take her home—"

"She's my girlfriend. And she doesn't need a ride from

you," Rook assures him, while I just stare flatly, no longer interested in poor, stupid Jeremy.

"Lucky for you," I mutter, though Rook's grip twinges, as if telling me to be quiet. Guilt flashes through me and I look down, not trusting myself to even look at the man whose throat I may or may not have been about to slit.

"Seriously, it's time for you to go," Rook adds, still not breaking his hold on me. "But thanks so much for looking out for her. She really appreciates it."

Thankfully, Jeremy gets the hint. Though I hear him mutter a few choice words about me, and about Rook, before he gets into his old pickup truck and slams the door hard enough to make it shake. I eye it dully, wondering if the thing is going to fall off. Quickly, his engine starts up and he leaves the parking lot with tires squealing, just in case we didn't know how put out he was by Rook's appearance.

"You can let go now," I point out once he's gone, my ears picking up only the sounds of the parking lot. "Seriously, anytime." He's mad. I know he's mad at me, and I can't look at him when he pulls back enough to study my face.

"Knife," he demands, one hand outstretched, palm up. It occurs to me that he isn't afraid of me in the least, even though I'm the one holding the blade and possibly, maybe, a little unhinged tonight. Without argument, I drop it on his fingers, and watch when he brings it up to the light with a scowl. "Love, we have got to get you past this fascination with switchblades. Did you even sharpen this?" He flicks it open and studies the short blade, before closing it once more and pocketing it. "They're impossible to clean, by the way. It's one and done at best. A jail sentence at worst."

"You're mad at me." It should come out as a question, but it's not. I know he's mad at me, because he *has* to be.

Except the look on his face when he meets my eyes is just

bemusement instead of anger. "Mad at you?" he repeats, reaching up to brush my hair back from my face. "I'm concerned, because this is unsafe, but I'm not mad at you."

"Why?" I don't mean to make it sound like a demand, but when the word comes out, it's too abrupt. Too sudden, like I'm accusing him of something. "*Why* aren't you freaking out right now? Rook, I wanted to *kill him*. You know that, right? I have a knife and I've been walking around bars for a month, even after I promised you I wouldn't." The words pour out of me, and when I look up at him once more, it's through a hazy veil in my eyes.

I don't realize until I blink that it's tears obscuring my vision. But when I blink again, they fall from my lids, coursing down my face and leaving sticky, hot trails in their wake. "I *promised you* I wouldn't do this. I literally promised you, in your office, that I'd stop. Then I broke that promise pretty fast."

"Within what, a week and a half?" he agrees airily, watching me.

"You knew?"

"Might I repeat, politely, that you aren't as subtle as you seem to think? And I don't know how many times I have to tell you that you're too much like Oliver for your own good." His smile is crooked, but he really doesn't seem mad.

My brain scrambles for an explanation, throwing out every single one it can find as my heart flutters in my throat. My fingers flex around nothing, palms clammy as I stagger a step away from him and glare down at the ground. "You don't want me around," I assume, throwing it at him.

"Never said that."

"You think I'm crazy."

"Definitely never said that. But I do think you're reckless, in case that's your next question." He gives me some space as I walk away, though he follows before I've gotten far. "Could we not finish the night at O'Leary's?" he requests, naming the last stop on my nightly bar tours. "I don't know how you stand the bartenders there. They grate on me, quite frankly."

I freeze, unable to take another step. He really *has* been following me.

"Does Oliver know?" I ask, without turning to look at him.

"Yep. He came with me to follow you a couple of times, but he was tired tonight."

"Is he mad?"

"No, Love." I can feel him behind me, barely inches from me as he adds, "Neither of us is mad at you. How could we be?"

"What does that even mean?" I whirl around again, nearly hitting him with my elbow. "You should absolutely be furious with me! Look what I'm doing!" I throw my arm out toward the bar, as if he's somehow forgotten. "And you *know* what I've been inching towards! I've been lying to you every time I come over, or have dinner with you. Every time I sit in your class, I'm *lying* to you. You should be furious with me!" More hot tears slip from my eyes, but he doesn't get angry or upset. Not even when I'm basically in his face and shrieking like a banshee.

"Actually..." Rook reaches up to gently circle my wrists with his long fingers. I hadn't realized my hands had found their way to his shirt, but when he grabs me, I release the fabric from my white-knuckled grip. "I don't think you're crazy at all. Or unreasonable. I understand why you want a knife. Even if I'm planning a lecture, PowerPoint included, on why you will not be carrying a switchblade." His voice is dry, even, and more patient than I have a right for him to be. "You come here looking for men who are willing to do what both Rob and Langhorn did to you. You want the excuse to hurt them, because without that, you'd never let yourself kill someone. That's honestly a lot more noble than you think it is. Certainly more noble than what Oliver's got going on. But you're doing this all wrong."

"Because I shouldn't be doing it at all?" I mutter dryly.

"Because you're doing it in a way that's going to get you killed or caught. And I can't have that."

My surprise must be evident on his face, because he chuckles softly when I look up at him, wide-eyed and speechless. "Who am *I* to preach morals to you, Love?" he asks me flatly. "Like Oliver, I'm less noble than you when I look for my outlet. I don't follow you to stop you from hurting someone." Again he pulls me to him, so he can hold me against his warmth. "I follow you to stop you from hurting yourself."

It's like a reflex, I can't help it. I don't mean to, but in the next moment my arms are around his shoulders and I bury my face in his shoulder, shoulders trembling as I cry out every bit of frustration, every flinch of fear, every feeling of absolute anger that I've kept hidden for months. I cry out my feelings about people *liking* Langhorn enough to hide what he'd done, and Wickett University not finding that to be a big deal.

I cry until I have nothing left but dry, itchy eyes and exhaustion, and Rook lets me without a complaint.

"I think there's something wrong with me," I murmur against his now-soaked shirt. "That there's something *broken* inside of me. I haven't been the same since what happened. I think..." I take a deep breath. "I think it started to break last semester, with Rob. Maybe it would've healed, but now it can't. It's *gone*."

"It's not gone, Blair. You haven't lost yourself." Gently he disentangles me from his shirt, ending my imitation of an octopus suction-cupped to him. "I'm afraid it's a bit of a walk back to my car," he admits. "But I'd rather you come home with me, instead of going back to your apartment. In fact, I'll insist you do."

"Because you don't trust me not to off the first weirdo I meet?" I ask, letting him guide me back down the sidewalk, taking me on a shortcut back to my apartment.

"Something like that," he agrees. "But you already knew the answer before you asked the question, so you can't hold it against me."

I can't, and he's right about that. But I appreciate it when he doesn't push me to talk. Instead he just walks, his steps steady and even, and keeps an arm around my shoulders as both a warning and a comfort.

"If I agree to go home with you, can we stop for milk-shakes?" I ask dully, leaning my head against his chest briefly as we walk. "And not fast food milkshakes. I mean that twenty-four-hour place a few blocks from here."

His snort is barely audible. He leans over and presses a kiss to the top of my head, and I can feel the chuckle that reverber-ates through him. "Yes, Blair. I will get you whatever you want on the way back. As long as you're coming with me."

"I said I would," I mutter, and fall into a natural silence that lasts back to my apartment.

Thankfully, he lets me run upstairs with the promise of being back in a few minutes and not shimmying out the fire escape. Not that we have one. I jot a note on the table Post-It stack, then run to my bedroom and throw a few pieces of clothing into my backpack. With my laptop and iPad in there as well, I'm back into the kitchen, quick as a flash, but this time, I stop.

Juniper leans against the table, reading my note before her eyes flick up to mine. "You're going to Oliver's? This late?" she questions, eyeing me with concern. "Are you okay?"

"I'll... be okay," I tell her, not wanting to lie anymore tonight. "Trust me?"

"Implicitly." There's no real suspicion in her tone or in her face, and she takes a step back. "I just wish you wouldn't keep so many secrets from me."

The words stop me in my tracks and I turn to look at her over my shoulder, stomach twisting with guilt at how much I've lied to her over the past year. But if she knew...

It isn't just our friendship at stake. If it was, I'd come clean with her in a heartbeat. But when it's also her *safety* I worry for, and Oliver's safety, I find that my hands are tied and there's no other real recourse.

"I'm sorry," I tell her, but she only shrugs again.

"You'll tell me when you're ready. Or you won't. But I *do* call being maid of honor at your wedding, just so you know."

My smile grows to match hers, and some of the weight that drags at me lifts. "Maybe I'll be a bridezilla. Then you'll really regret saying that," I snicker, adjusting my backpack more comfortably on my shoulder.

She snorts her disagreement and heads back to bed, bidding me to have a nice night and giving me an eyebrow waggling look before she disappears into her room. I wait, listening for a few seconds, then I swallow my resentment for the lies I've told her and open the door, making sure to lock it behind me before I walk to the elevator.

CHAPTER 24

I don't find the heart for conversation until Rook has made good on his promise and my fingers are curled around an extra large, double chocolate brownie milkshake with caramel swirls. It's thick enough that I have to use a spoon to eat it, and I swirl the spoon in the chocolate as I swallow the mouthful I already have.

Rook sucks on a chocolate malt, relaxed in the driver's seat of his SUV. There's another cup in the console, a chocolate-cherry-almond milkshake that he swears is Oliver's guilty pleasure. I, for one, don't understand the inclusion of almonds, but who am I to judge?

My legs feel restless, and I resettle them multiple times before giving up with a sigh and sitting up straighter. "I was going to break up with you and Oliver that day," I say, unsure why the words leave my mouth. I can't take my eyes off of my drink, off of the swirls that I can barely see in the darkness of the St. Augustine night.

For a few moments, Rook doesn't answer. His silence draws my attention, but I don't have the energy left to worry about what he's going to say. His hand flexes on the wheel in front of him, and I swear he works through three or four different thoughts before he says, "I know."

A thrill shoots through me, though it's dampened by exhaustion. "You did not. You're just saying that. There's no way you knew."

His sigh is long-suffering, if a little bit fond. "I hate to be the continuous bearer of bad news, Love. But you're really not as subtle as you think you are. You're also rather easy to read. Well, for anyone who knows what they're looking for. You'd been looking for a reason and figuring out how to put distance between us since the semester started."

"Yeah," I finally agree, my voice soft. "But I notice you're saying that in the past tense. Like you don't think I am anymore."

"I think we both know the answer to that, but I'm more than willing to be the one to say it if you need to hear it."

I fiddle with the cup in my hands, fingers running over the soft styrofoam as he pulls into his subdivision. "Pretend I'm an idiot," I whisper. "Tell me what the answer is." My eyes dart to the side, to the shine of the switchblade that sits beside Oliver's cup in the console.

"You stopped putting distance between us that day. Especially when you saw Oliver in the hospital room." The last part of that is a shock to me, and I turn to him, mouth open, to ask for clarification.

But then my brain supplies the answer, and I know exactly what he means.

I hadn't been able to take my eyes off of Oliver when his humanity, his kindness, had slipped away like water through an open drain. He'd become a different person. Someone who was willing to kill the man who'd hurt me.

It should've terrified me. But instead, I'd wanted him

closer. I had wanted him to stay, and I'd tried to catch another glimpse of that for hours.

But it isn't *just* that. Not anymore. They've been more supportive than anyone else. Even now, with Rook tracking me around the city to make sure I don't do anything stupid.

"I'm sorry," I sigh, tilting my head back against my seat. "I know I'm being a real problem for you."

"Stop," Rook orders mildly. "Haven't I told you before how often I've had to keep Oliver from doing the same thing you are right now? I have practice, and you're not a problem, Love." The SUV slows as he pulls into his driveway, and when I open my eyes, I see lights on in the house. "At least, not one I'm bothered by. You should know by now how I feel about you."

I *don't* know how he feels about me. Not in simple words, anyway. I know he wants me around. That he wants to ruin me. He wants everything I want to give him.

But does he want me to stay forever? Does Oliver?

"Please let him know I didn't manhandle you much." Rook's plaintive request brings a grin to my face, and I watch almost ruefully as he plucks my switchblade out of the console and pockets it as he gets out of the driver's seat. He sees me staring and snorts, then gives a small shake of his head. "Don't even think about it. And I'm telling you right now that if you try to take this or any other weapon out of my house, you're not going to get to leave. I won't have you roaming the streets if I can't trust you, Love. I won't have you getting hurt."

My eyes go down and away, but I unbuckle my seatbelt and slide out of the SUV, my feet thumping on the ground a moment before I drag my backpack off of the floor of the vehicle. Slinging it over my shoulder, I follow him up the driveway, only a touch surprised when the door opens to show Oliver standing there, in a pair of sweatpants and a faded gray tee.

He kisses Rook on the cheek, going up on his tiptoes to do

so, but the latter just shimmies on by, leaving Oliver to pin me with his eyes that are full of judgment and concern.

"I hear you were having another field trip. A much more involved one," he remarks, holding a hand out to me. I take it, head tilted to the side as I observe his face, wondering how he really feels about that.

"Yeah, who knew Officer Rook would come after me for touching the exhibits at the museum?" I joke, letting him pull me inside. He yanks me harder than I expect, and as he lets the door close behind me, I stumble into him, his arms wrapping around my waist as he buries his face in my hair.

"Shit, wonder girl," he purrs against my temple. "What were you thinking? What if something had happened?"

"You mean... What if I'd killed that guy?" I ask carefully, stomach flipping around like it's on a trapeze. "Is that what you were worried about?"

"What? No? Fuck some other guy." He shakes his head, eyes closed, when he presses his forehead to mine. "But you're rushing. You're going to hurt yourself, or get caught. I worry..." He looks at me, his green eyes dark in the dimness of the hall-way. "I worry you don't understand what happens when you kill someone. You'll never be able to forget it, Blair. You'll *never* be able to go back. Do you understand?"

"No," I whisper, aware Rook is near when he slides an arm across my shoulders and takes my backpack from me. Loud enough for him to hear, I say, "But you don't understand how much I need this. I need..." What in the world *do* I need, exactly? "It's like I need to fix what's going on in my brain. I can't sleep, I can't—"

It's a good thing Rook takes the milkshake in my hand as well. Oliver crushes me to his chest, holding me tightly enough that I can barely breathe, let alone speak.

"Come on." Rook's voice is soft. "You can do this somewhere other than the doorway." I expect him to drag us into the kitchen with strict orders to not eat on the furniture. Instead, when all is said and done, I'm situated between them, sitting with my legs tucked under me in the middle of Rook's king size bed.

"You're going to find me looking for ways to break in so I can sleep here," I joke quietly. "I actually get to *sleep* while I'm here." I go to take another spoonful of my milkshake, but Oliver's hand on my wrist stops me and shows me his surprisingly serious expression.

"Blair, you don't have to break in." His voice is soft but firm. "You never have to break in. Why don't you just *stay*? You could sleep here every night—"

"But I have to learn to sleep alone!" While I don't mean to snap at him, or to bristle at his words, I stare at him, willing him to understand. "I have to learn to *be alone*. I can't rely on the two of you to get me through everything, or to chase away the memories and the bad dreams." Then I lift my hand and drop it, not knowing what my plan with the movement even was. "I can't make you guys do that for me. Even if you want to. I have to figure some of this out on my own. You understand, right?" I look between them, fingers crossed, and see that Oliver, somehow, doesn't.

"I do." Rook reaches out to touch my face, leaning against the headboard beside me and already half done with his milkshake. "I understand that you need to learn for yourself. But It's only been three weeks, Blair. Barely that. You can't expect to go back to normal just like that, when you're still working through this. What's wrong with leaning on us for a little while, hmm? Or do you not trust me to help you when I think you're ready to find your way back to your comfort zone?"

The words are surprisingly heart-wrenching. I look at him,

his silhouette blurring in my gaze. God, I don't want to cry again.

"I wouldn't be able to see it like he does," Oliver admits, slinging an arm around my shoulders and pulling me back against him. "But I'd take his word for it. We don't want you dependent on us or miserable, Blair. But we do want to help you. Give us some credit for that, won't you?" When he leans forward, I turn without thinking and quickly press my lips to his.

Surprised as he is, it takes Oliver a few moments to respond. Before I can worry that he doesn't want my mouth on his, he kisses back voraciously. Fiercely enough that I can *feel* every beat of his enthusiasm and adoration for me.

Moments go by before I move, but I don't break away from him fully. Meeting Rook's gaze again, I let Oliver pull me back against him, though it means relinquishing the ability to perch on my folded legs and instead moving them to the side, still folded.

"So explain to me why I can't have my cool switchblade back. Or, better yet, tell me why I can't kill someone with it," I challenge, with my eyes on Rook. "Did he tell you he was practically *offended* by my weapon of choice?"

"God, I would hope so." Oliver shudders. "A switchblade? In *this* century? Why don't you just, I don't know, hand yourself over to the cops and save them the extra steps if you want to be that easy to find?"

Blinking, I stare at him in confusion. "Are we an anti-switchblade family? I need to know these things."

Rook's hand on my thigh makes me stop. He takes my milkshake and puts it on the nightstand with his own, and the next thing I know, he's on his knees in front of me, prowling closer.

"We don't like them because they're too hard to clean. And

they're a little obvious," Rook purrs, reaching up to catch my chin between his fingers. "We prefer not getting caught. And we'd like you not to get caught either. That's why you're not going to use a switchblade. I get that it feels cool to have in your pocket. And it's an easy, convenient option. But that's not how we do things."

As I watch, he lifts the hem of his shirt, showing the waistband of the sweatpants he'd changed into when we got back to their house. From the curve of his lower back, he pulls something free and brandishes the black-covered object to me. "You'll use a real knife. Not a switchblade, and we try not to use guns. I'll tell you what I've told him. If you're not close enough that you feel their last breath leave them, then you don't deserve the kill in the first place."

"Oh," I reply, unsure of what else I *can* say. He unsheathes the long, slender blade and holds it out to me, hilt first.

I take it, surprised when I hear Oliver's sudden intake of breath behind me. Before I can look at him, Rook snickers.

"Ignore him, Love. If you want. He likes my knives quite a bit." His fingers skim along my thighs, though when he gets close to the not-quite-faded handprint, I push his hand away. Sure, maybe it's barely visible, but to *me* it's still there.

To me, it's just as obvious as it always was.

"You really like these?" I murmur, turning to glance at Oliver over my shoulder. "Like, in more than just a murder way?"

"In so much more than a murder way," he promises, reaching out for it. I don't give it to him. I curl my hand around the hilt and catch his hand, unwilling to let him go.

"I need to tell you something." With the promise of sex or without, I can't keep this from him any longer. Especially with Rook already aware.

"Anything," he purrs, nuzzling my neck. "Anything, anytime. What do you need to tell me, wonder girl?"

"I was... looking for a reason to break up with you." I expect him to tense, but the only sign of hearing me is his hand on my shoulder that's stroking nonsensical designs over my skin. It stops for a brief few seconds before his movement picks up again. "But let me guess. You already knew too, didn't you?"

"You are rather easy to read." He smiles apologetically, his other arm wrapping around my waist as he pulls me back against him as tightly as he can. "Sorry, Blair."

"You weren't going to do anything?" I look between them again, eyebrows raised. "Either of you?"

"You needed to figure things out for yourself." It surprises me that Oliver is the one that says it. But he's so serious when he does, and kisses my shoulder sweetly. "Either you had to decide that you didn't want us in your life. Or you did. But I had faith you wouldn't leave us. I had faith because I'm so fucking cute."

"You are incredibly cute," I agree, nodding sagely. "But would you like to know what really changed my mind?" Rook might know, but by the bemusement on Oliver's face, he doesn't.

"You."

"Me?" He blinks, looking between us, and I don't miss the sweet, affectionate smile that crosses Rook's lips. "I know I'm great, and I don't doubt it. But how?"

"It's weird," I admit, my words only partially a warning that what comes next isn't quite normal. "Incredibly weird. It was that day, when you were at the hospital with me." His smile falls, though he looks at me with such concern that my heart hurts. "You like, let your mask slip. Your nice-face. Just for a few moments. I watched you become something else and I just..." I shrug, not sure how to explain it. "I loved how cold you were. How you weren't going to let anyone argue with you. Maybe I'm crazy and just attracted to dangerous men."

"Super dangerous man. That's me," Oliver agrees with a snort. Rook scoffs in disagreement, rolling his eyes even as he curls closer around me.

"Do you think I'll ever be normal again?" It's definitely not what I mean to ask either of them. "Do you think I'll stop dreaming of murder?"

"What kind of murder are you dreaming of?" I hear Oliver set his own cup on the opposite nightstand from mine, and before I can register what he's doing, the hand around my waist tugs me onto my side on the bed, my face parallel with Rook's.

"That seems like an awful question when you say it out loud." I laugh anxiously, my heart thrumming in my throat.

"Is it?" Oliver noses at the back of my neck, and as I watch, Rook brings the knife up that he holds once more, skimming along Oliver's arm that rests over mine. I feel him shudder, and when he presses his hips into mine, I realize he really does like this a lot more than a normal person would.

"I dream about slitting men's throats," I admit in a soft whisper as I watch them. Oliver's grip tightens on my shoulders as Rook continues to draw the blade along his skin, but I sense both of their eyes on me when I say, "I dream of how easy it would be to end a man's life."

"Easy and complicated," Rook murmurs. "The after might not be what you think. I think you'll have a hard time once the adrenaline wears off." I stir in disagreement, but his eyes pin me in place. "Don't argue with me. I have a little bit of experience with this."

"Yeah, just with Oliver. That's not exactly a ton of—"

"*Oliver* is the third prodigy I've trained. It just so happens he's the one I kept, and the one I thought would be my last." I don't miss the flash in his gaze when he adds, "But I don't mind being wrong."

"I'm not a serial killer." The words are out of my mouth before I can stop them, and my eyes flick back to the knife again.

"No one is when they start." Oliver laughs darkly. "Maybe they'll give you a cool nickname on the news. Maybe you'll sound terrifying when people start hearing about all the disgusting, slimy men you've killed."

"I'm not a serial killer," I say again, just as unsure as the first time. Rook brandishes the blade in front of me, and even though a shiver trails down my spine like fingers, I'm not afraid of him.

"Would you like to feel it on your skin?" he purrs deep in his chest. "I don't think you'll like it as much as Oliver does. But that's only because he's obsessed with knives on his skin." A low laugh meets my ears from behind me, but I ignore Oliver. "Still, it doesn't hurt."

"I figured, since he doesn't mind it."

"That's not a good thing to go off of. Our dear Oliver is an absolute sadomasochist."

While that takes a moment to process, it isn't exactly a shock to my brain. Still, I find myself nodding, and my eyes never leave the long blade as it drags down Oliver's shoulder again, then slips against my skin.

I can't help the soft breath that leaves my lips. It doesn't hurt, not in the least. The blade feels almost like a feather, if that feather was made from steel instead of soft keratin. My fingers tangle in the blankets under me, and I barely notice Oliver's hands on my hips, pushing my shirt up with slow and cautious movements, until Rook murmurs for him to stop.

My eyes snap open, and I wonder when I'd closed them. Some part of me is remembering how long it's been since I've slept. And exactly what time it has to be. "No," I say sharply, reaching back just as Oliver moves his hand. "No, I..." My heart beats rapidly in my throat, and I look carefully at both of them before I say, "I *want* you to."

Even Oliver hesitates. His hand comes back to my hip, but he doesn't move it. Rook's movements don't cease. He continues to flick the knife up over my shoulder, dragging it up my jaw until he can skim it lightly across my nose.

It doesn't scare me. Sure, it makes me super aware of the blade and the fact that if he pushes it down at all, he'll cut me. And I don't want him to cut my face, but I'm still not about to tell him to stop.

Finally, he drags the blade down under my chin, and with the flat of it, he pushes my chin upward and forces me to meet his eyes. "Are you *sure?*" Rook asks, the concern on his face readily apparent. "You don't have to. We're not going to push you to—"

It's a stupid thing to do, given the knife. But I trust his reflexes enough to assume he won't stab me in the throat when I move toward him, my hands going to his collar and pulling my upper body closer to him. I crush my mouth to his and feel the flat of the blade between us, pressed against my chest harmlessly.

He hesitates for half a second more, then he's kissing me back, carefully slipping the blade away from me as he devours my lips and presses his tongue between them. Oliver takes that as his cue as well. His hands come back more confidently on my hips, pressing my shirt up as he touches as much of my skin as he can.

Within seconds it feels like he's magicked my leggings off of my body, leaving me half naked between them and much more able to feel his eagerness through the fabric of his sweat-pants. His hips move against me, hands sliding down, but I catch one of them when it gets too close to the faded handprint on my thigh.

"Does it hurt?" he murmurs, not trying to pull out of my grip.

I shake my head when I pull away from Rook, glancing between them with a frown on my face. "No, it's not that.... It doesn't hurt anymore. It feels bad. Like, *wrong*," I amend. "Like I shouldn't let you touch it, because it's from *him.*"

"Oh, wonder girl." Oliver buries his face against my throat and shakes free of my hand. A moment later, his fingers come down on my opposite leg, but this time it's *Oliver* gripping hard. It's Oliver digging his nails into my skin while he nips at my throat.

And nothing about it feels wrong in the least. My mouth falls open in a gasp, only for Rook to catch my lips again. He moves closer, pinning me between his body and Oliver's and giving me nowhere to go.

But I don't want to go anywhere. This is perfect. Beyond perfect, since my head is swimming and I'm sure I'm dreaming. There's no way their hands can feel this good. The prick of the knife blade makes me flinch, but that feeling curls into delight in my stomach, causing more heat to pool in my thighs. The blade moves up my arm and over my shoulder again. Between them, they move me onto my back, with Oliver dragging my shirt up and over my head to leave me only in my bra.

I'm not sure I've ever felt more vulnerable, or safer.

"Tell me if you need us to stop. We'll stop," Oliver intones, repeating most of Rook's sentiment. Carefully, sweetly, he draws my hands up above my head, pinning my wrists with a light grip while Rook lifts himself up on one arm to hover over me.

I can't see anything but them. Every breath that I draw into my lungs is air I'm sharing with them, and they block out the rest of the world when they hold themselves over me, caging me with their presence.

I don't fight Oliver. My fingers curl as Rook drags the knife down my throat, over my clavicle, and teases my skin while Oliver watches. On my left, Oliver moves, rocking his hips against my thigh while he watches with rapt attention and almost without blinking. I watch too, my breathing shallow and quick. It doesn't hurt. None of it hurts. But God, it's exhilarating to see the shining, dark grey metal skim along my skin in different, random designs. Once in a while, I feel the sharpness of the edge as a slight amount of pain, but it certainly isn't a bad thing.

It makes me look forward to that, and dread it in equal measure. Every time the tickle turns into a scrape, I can't help the small, full body flinch that shoots through me.

But neither can Rook help the soft smile and quiet purr of approval that comes from him every time I do it. "You're so gorgeous, Love," he murmurs, hooking the blade in the front of my bra. "I'll buy you a new one," he declares, seconds before he *rips* the blade outward, pulling a yelp from my throat when the blade cuts through the thick fabric that holds the cups together.

Oliver is quick to help, jerking the separated pieces off of my shoulders and throwing it somewhere else in the room.

"Maybe I didn't pack another bra," I tell them, my thighs pressed together as the heat pooling between them turns into something much more demanding.

"Maybe you didn't," Rook agrees, curving the blade over my breasts, giving each one of them a plethora of attention before he circles inward, getting closer to my nipples. "Maybe I don't really mind."

"He definitely doesn't mind," Oliver agrees, his low voice a growl against my ear. He watches the path of the blade, his hand moving along my leg and slowly shifting inward. With a touch, he urges my thighs apart, hooking my knee to the side so he can trail his fingers along the sensitive skin of my inner thighs.

"I bet you could fuck her with the hilt of that," Oliver murmurs, his eyes gleaming in the light from the bedside lamp. "I bet she'd love it."

"I bet she would too," Rook remarks. "But not tonight. Unless you're volunteering to get fucked with it so she can *watch*." I can tell Oliver is considering it, and when Rook also realizes it, he rolls his eyes and chucks the knife sheath at his boyfriend. "Not tonight," he says again, more firmly.

"Fine, fine." Oliver's fingers slide into me, curling once they're inside and bringing a groan to my lips. It's been *weeks* since I'd done this with them. Or anything even half this good.

I missed this.

The thought burns through me, prompting me to pull free from Oliver's grip so I can turn to him, one hand in his hair, and drag his mouth down to mine. At the same time, his fingers plunge deeper, and on my other hip I feel the tease of Rook's fingers instead of the blade of his knife.

When I'm done with Oliver, I turn away from him, doing the same with Rook and dragging my fingers through his hair until I can grip him tightly. He welcomes it, curling into me, and brings one hand up to cup my cheek as he kisses me as fiercely as I kiss him.

"Will you fuck me? Please?" I ask both of them, eyes flitting from one to the other. "If you don't want to—"

"It's too late to think we don't want to," Rook purrs, and Oliver murmurs his agreement.

"And we always want you. *Always*," Oliver growls against my throat, his free hand curling around my shoulders until he can grip my throat. "Who do you want first?"

"That's an unfair question," I laugh. "Since 'both of you' isn't an answer."

Rook's eyes slide to Oliver's, narrowing, before he looks back at me. "It could be," he murmurs, nuzzling my jaw. "But it'll hurt at first. Do you want to take both of us, gorgeous girl? At the same time?"

Right before I ask what he means, it slams into place. The fact that it took me so long makes me feel like an idiot, and I open my mouth to tell him maybe next time, when fear clenches a fist around my heart.

But... *why not?* If it hurts badly, I can tell them to stop. I *want them.* Both of them.

"Have you ever both fucked someone before?" I ask, glancing between them. Oliver is the first to shake his head, a rueful smile on his lips.

"You're the first girl either of us has fucked in a few years," he admits, kissing my shoulder. "But I'll be so good for you, wonder girl." The undercurrent of excitement in his voice isn't lost on me. "If you'll let us, we'll be so careful."

"I've done it once or twice," Rook assures me. "And it's not like it's complicated. But you're going to have to stretch her better than that, Oliver," he tells the younger killer, who grins.

"Challenge accepted." Oliver snickers, another finger entering me. Before I can react, Rook captures my mouth. All I can do is focus on the way he's trying to suck my soul out between my teeth while Oliver scissors his fingers inside me and curls them against that spot that makes me wiggle.

"Make her come," Rook growls in the scant moment that he pulls away for air. I feel his hand wander down my body as well, stroking over my skin until he can press it just above my slit. "She'll be more relaxed, and it'll work better in the long run." His quick, dark grin is full of savage excitement, and when he captures my mouth again, I can feel the urgency of his lips.

He swallows the sound of surprise I make when his fingers slide against my clit, and desperation pulses through me as they work together to bring me over the edge as efficiently as they can.

It's embarrassingly quick, and obviously not difficult for them in the least. I shriek into Rook's mouth as I come, one hand behind me so I can clutch any part of Oliver I can find.

"Good girl, good *fucking* girl," Rook purrs. He lets go of me to pull off his shirt, and a few seconds later, his sweatpants are gone as well. It's rare I get to see him completely naked, and every time I've spent as much time looking at him as I can, trying to memorize every curve and plane of his body.

But he doesn't let me this time. As soon as he's dropped his clothes onto the floor, Rook grips my waist and yanks me against him as he rolls onto his back, settling me over him so that my knees slide to either side of his thighs.

"You're going to get to be on top. Isn't that exciting?" he teases, grinning wickedly up at me. "It's so rare for you."

"Next time, I get to top Oliver," I huff in reply, a smile growing on my lips. Nervousness still dances in my veins, and my fingers curl in the blankets. I don't know what to do, and I'm nervous, though I trust Rook implicitly. "Tell me what to do."

"I just need you to relax. For you to *trust me*," Rook murmurs. "I'm going to fuck you, and Oliver's going to fuck you as well." I can feel Oliver moving, and I shiver when his hands find my hips, fingers digging lightly into my skin.

"Let me help you," Oliver breathes. "I'll do all the work for you, Blair. You just have to relax." For someone who's never done this before, it occurs to me that he's already really good at this. He guides my hips downward until I feel Rook's tip brushing against my slit. I hesitate, but Oliver doesn't. He drags my hips further down, startling a gasp from me when Rook's length enters me.

But it's not one of pain, and it doesn't take much for me to be fully on board. I let my knees slide just enough that I can stretch out against Rook, my body flush with his warmth. I can feel his strength, and he urges my arms up until I'm clutching the sheets above his head.

"Just like that," he promises, starting to move slowly inside me. I'm used to taking him, but it's been *weeks*, and I'd forgotten how much I love this. How much I love *them*. "Go *slow*," he warns Oliver, who's kneeling behind me with his hands still on my hips as I move with Rook. "Be gentle."

"I'm always gentle with my wonder girl," Oliver teases, and Rook stills, wrapping an arm around me. Then I feel Oliver's cock slide against my folds, just over where Rook's still inside me.

"Tell me it won't hurt," I murmur, dragging one hand down to curl it in Rook's hair. "Tell me it'll be fine."

"It's going to hurt some. But it's going to be *more* than fine," Rook growls, reaching up with one hand to grip my hair as well. "Come here, Love. Let me distract you." He doesn't give me a chance to think about it. He jerks me down into a kiss, just as Oliver starts to work his length into my pussy as well.

Rook's right about the first part. It does hurt, especially as he forces himself inside, and I can *feel* how tight it is with both of them there. My body burns to accommodate both of them, and I can't help the whimper that leaves me.

"Shh, it's okay, wonder girl." Oliver's voice is strained, and he trails his fingers down my spine. "I'm almost there, I promise. God, you're so tight. Rook, she's so fucking tight, I can't—" He makes a guttural sound that goes straight to my core, pushing a shudder through my body before he finally, *finally* bottoms out with his hips against my thighs.

"Holy shit," he says, sounding strangled. "*Shit,* Blair. This is —" He swallows the words with a shiver. "Tell me you're okay."

Rook lets me up for air so I can reassure them both I am. Though I swear I'm seeing stars in my vision from how intense of a feeling this is. Still, the words pour out of me, breathless, as Oliver moves slightly, sliding against Rook inside of me and causing the latter to growl.

"Fuck," Rook grates out under me. "*Fuck,* Love. I didn't think you could be any more perfect, but here you are. You really were made for us."

"You're telling me," Oliver laughs, just as hoarse. "I'm going to move, okay? More than this. Are you okay with that?"

I nod once, then again, jerky movements as I let my weight fall back onto Rook and find his lips with mine once more. His arms come up under mine, encircling my body, pressing me to him just as Oliver makes good on his word and starts moving in earnest.

He has the most freedom of movement between us, and he uses it to his advantage. His hips slam into mine, causing me to rock into Rook and aiding both of their movements as they fuck me.

The pain fades quickly, though the intensity does not. I'm *too full*, too out of my mind to register more than how good this feels and how impossibly full I am.

"She's so good. She's just—" He breaks off to suck in a breath, his fingers gripping me so tightly I know I'll bruise. But tonight, I welcome the marks. I *welcome* the opportunity to wear their marks instead of Langhorn's, and mentally will him to hold me tighter. "I'm going to come." It's only been maybe a minute, but I can feel how much he trembles. "She's just so tight, and she's so fucking hot. Tell me you're going to come too. You want us to fill you up together?" he asks, jerking on my hips again.

"You want us to, don't you?" Rook edges, his grip tightening to the level of Oliver's. While he isn't moving as much, being trapped under me, I can feel that Oliver isn't the only one about to come apart. Tension sings in every single one of Rook's muscles, causing him to tremble under me.

"Tell me what *you* want," I challenge, by way of answering. "Because you both know how much I want everything you'll give me."

"What I want is to fuck you until you're dripping with our cum." Rook's voice is harsh in my ear, and he nips the tip of it sharply. "I don't want to let you out of this bed for days. I want us both to fuck your cunt until you need it. Until you *beg us* to stretch you like this." My whimper seems to cheer him on, and he snarls once more, giving another light nip.

"I want you to realize you're made for us too, Blair."

Even if I have an answer, I don't get to say anything. Oliver curses and slams into me once more, then again, until he loses control and shudders, coming inside my body with unhinged enthusiasm. But Rook isn't far behind. His movements pick up, and he slides against Oliver, causing the other to whimper. Then he sinks into me one last time and comes as well, as deeply as Oliver and just as overwhelming.

"Don't think you aren't going to come too, Blair." Oliver laughs, a dark edge in his voice as his hands slip over my hips, one of them going between us until he can rub his fingers against my clit. I don't expect it, and any strings of control I'd been holding onto *snap* just like that.

I come, and immediately it's different from any other orgasm I've ever had in my life. It tears through me, my body unable to do more than clamp around both of them. The intensity of it has me falling against Rook's chest, no longer holding myself up with my arms. But he doesn't seem to mind. If anything—judging by the way he holds me tighter while Oliver fingers me through my orgasm—he likes it. He *wants* me here, between them, unable to do more than nearly faint from pleasure.

It's a jolt when Oliver slides free, leaving me feeling empty once my orgasm has finally finished ripping through me. He leans over me and helps me up and off of Rook, holding me as we sit on the bed.

"Oh, okay, ow," I hiss, leaning back. "That kind of smarts."

I don't expect Rook's chuckle, or for him to yank me back against him so I'm laying down again. This time it's Oliver who goes to the bathroom and gets a towel, one that he uses to help me clean up when he comes back.

"How are you feeling?" Rook asks, settling me under the blankets and against his body once Oliver finishes.

"Like I've never come so hard in my life," I reply, watching Oliver slide into the bed, under the blankets as well. He latches onto me like an octopus, his arms around my waist and snuggling up to me.

"Same," he agrees with a nod. "So much same."

Rook murmurs a reply, but I'm fading too fast to really know what he says. It's too easy to just... let go. Even though sleep is what I have an issue with back at my apartment. I never sleep like this on my own, and I'm never able to fall asleep so quickly, or without tossing and turning.

Yet here I am, between my two favorite men, ready to sleep away all the exhaustion that's been building in me for the weeks that I've been stalking men at bars and putting myself into dangerous situations.

CHAPTER 25

Movement behind me, along with soft, needy noises, pulls me out of what I hope has been a sixteen hour sleep. I open my eyes and find I'm staring at the bedside table, one of the milkshake cups still there and teetering too close to the edge for my comfort.

God, I have to work on my senior project. With spring break looming around the corner, and the threat of April pressure that will weigh on me until graduation, I'd wanted to be much further into it than I am.

More noises remind me I'm not alone, but I reach out to adjust the styrofoam cup before I sit up, still naked, the covers pooling at my waist.

Gazing behind me makes me thrilled to be alive.

Oliver is on his back on the far edge of the bed, Rook over him and whispering in his ear as he fucks into him. I can *feel* their adoration for each other. It rolls off of them in waves, and I draw my knees up under me, unable to look away.

It's clear pretty quickly Oliver doesn't know I'm awake. His eyes are screwed shut, hips arched, with Rook's hand around his throat holding him in place. Scratch marks on Rook's chest show me Oliver's in a feral mood, and while I can't hear what Rook is saying to him, I have a pretty good idea of what it might be.

My professor turns to look at me slyly, a small grin on his face. "Look what you did, my love," he purrs, eyes glittering. "You woke up our precious girl."

Oliver's eyes snap open and an apologetic grimace morphs his features, stopping somewhere between apology and pleasure. "Shit, Blair, I didn't mean—"

"Don't apologize," I breathe, crawling across the bed toward them. I glance up at Rook, looking for approval, and get a quick nod before I lean down to nip at his lip, drawing away before he can kiss me. "This is better than my alarm clock by a mile."

Rook's snort is soft, but when he starts moving once more, it's with a renewed vigor that has Oliver howling. "He feels so good," he chokes out. "You want him after me?"

"No, *God* no. My pussy is closed for business today, *thanks*. You abused her last night." He can't help his huff of a laugh, and a second later he's coming with Rook's hand gripping his throat so hard I'm worried he's going to pass out.

But Oliver loves every second of it. Even when he's nearly choking with breathlessness around Rook's hand and scrabbling at my wrist. Even when Rook curls a hand around his spent cock and continues to tug and tease at him past the point of pleasure, moans falling from his lips like rain.

During all of it, I can tell Oliver adores it. He trusts Rook implicitly, and Rook's attention never once leaves his partner. All of that adoration, all of that affection, pours out of him shamelessly.

They *love* each other.

It's almost strange to sit here with Oliver gripping my wrist as I watch the two of them. I'm secure enough to admit to myself that I *am* envious of this relationship they have.

What would it feel like for them to love me like they love each other?

I'm so lost in my own thoughts that I don't notice when Rook rolls off of Oliver. I *do* notice when he's suddenly in my space, his hand coming up to grip my jaw as he leans in close, as if he's going to kiss me.

Instead, even though my lips are parted in anticipation, he shoves his fingers between my lips and presses them to my tongue. "He tastes sweeter when you're watching, don't you agree?" he asks sweetly, watching as I clean his fingers with my tongue. He kisses me when I'm done, swiping his tongue around my mouth as if he's trying to taste every bit of Oliver I've found on his skin, before whipping around and slamming his mouth against Oliver's, giving him a taste as well.

"Are you sure you don't want to come, Blair?" Oliver asks, finally sitting up just so he can drape himself against my lap, his mouth tantalizingly close to the space between my thighs. It's on purpose, I know. And so is the kiss that leads to him mouthing my sensitive skin, just beside the handprint bruise from—

I blink.

There is no bruise. Nothing at all mars the pale, smooth skin of my thigh, though I could swear it was there ever so faintly last night.

Wasn't it?

My fingers inch along the spot, but the only marks there are the ones Oliver has left. He follows the movement with his eyes, frowning, and when he opens his mouth it's to say, "Did I hurt you last night? I'm sorry—"

"Don't be sorry." Easily, I drag him up so I can nuzzle his face, a smile working its way across my lips. "Seriously, don't ever be sorry. You didn't hurt me." I don't want to say that I'm wondering if the last of the fading bruises was in my mind and he helped my brain see that it's gone.

I don't want him to think I'm *that* nuts.

"I can't," I add, disappointment on my face. "I'm exhausted from last night and I haven't slept well in forever. Plus, I *have* to work on my senior project today."

Rook stirs at that, his professor senses tingling. "I can help you," he offers. "I did offer to mentor you, and you haven't really asked for my help. Should I be offended? Does this mean you aren't incorporating photography into your senior project?"

"It may mean I'm not quite as far in my project as I want to be," I mutter, sliding out of bed and looking for my clothes. I find them in a pile, though I don't intend to put them back on since I brought perfectly good lounge clothes. Still, I hold up my bra, eyebrows raised, and look at Rook with it draped over my finger.

He doesn't even *try* to look apologetic. Rook shrugs one shoulder, looking as innocent as can be, and says, "You know it was hot when I cut it off of you. And I said I'd buy you a new one. My credit card is in my wallet. I'll just flat out give it to you, Love."

"That seems dangerous. What if I go on a shopping spree?" I ask, going to my backpack that sits by the bathroom door and yanking out a t-shirt. I hesitate, seeing that I'd also brought leggings, but decide last minute I'd rather steal clothes from Oliver.

Rook, though I would love looking like a prim and proper professor, is slightly too lean for me to wear anything of his. Oliver, on the other hand, is just a smidge more muscular, enough that his clothes fit me perfectly.

"Oliver, can I steal a pair of sweatpants?" I ask, glancing up at him hopefully.

"You can steal my entire soul. *And* his credit card," Oliver informs me, climbing out of Rook's massive bed. He strides beside me and grabs his own clothes, putting them on quickly and pressing a kiss to my cheek. He pads out of the room and immediately my eyes are drawn back to Rook as he flops down on the bed, once more on his back.

"You can steal my credit card for a shopping trip," he bargains. "I doubt you'd make a dent in my bank account, *wonder girl*," he uses Oliver's nickname teasingly, and I lift a brow at his cheeky tone.

"Oh, yeah?" I demand, hearing Oliver's steps fade as he walks to the other side of the house, where his room is. "And what's the catch?"

"That you pay me back for every single purchase. Every hundred dollars means I get a whole night to try out one of my many, *many* kinks with you. Once we hit a thousand, I get to make good on my threat and you're my pet for the day, sick little puppy." The pet name from last year sends shivers up my spine, though I try to look like I'm barely affected by it.

"If you're going to say yes, I'll go shopping with you," Oliver bargains, coming back in and handing over a pair of sweatpants. They're my favorite pair, which I'm sure he knows, and the softest black fleece I've ever worn. "Just so I can run up the bill and have you here forever."

"Have you ever considered just, I don't know, asking me to move in with you? Instead of trying to trap me with great sex?" I demand without thinking, yanking on his pants. I hate knowing that I'll be stuck working all day, but if not today, then when? I haven't felt this awake, or this *normal* in a long time.

"All the time. Pretty sure I've brought it up," he replies.

"Yeah, you've brought it up as a joke."

"No, Blair." He reaches out to catch my arm, his eyes on mine. Rook gets up and brushes past us, going into his closet and re-emerging wearing a pair of faded, well-fitting jeans.

I stare at him, wondering why he can't be lazy like us and wear a pair of damn sweatpants more often.

"He's right. We're never joking. Not for a long time," Rook informs me when he sees my gaze on him. "Do you want help with your project before breakfast?"

I'm happy about the change in subject. Happier still when Oliver drops my arm and tells me he'll get his notes in case I want to use them.

It isn't that I don't want to move in with them; it's not that at all.

It's that I don't know how to handle the offer, knowing it's real now and not just a joke or something they've said in the moment.

Do I want to live with them?

How could I *not?*

"Yeah, but only if you want to? I don't want to give you more work on a Saturday." I smile apologetically at him, lifting my backpack and hooking it over my shoulder, since I doubt we're going to work here in his bedroom.

I'm right. Rook beckons me with the crook of one finger across the hall to a good size office that's clearly meant to be a bedroom. He gestures to the seats at the desk, and I take the one that isn't sitting in front of the computer with its dual monitors.

How very tech savvy of him.

"Show me what you're looking to do. Show me a proposal, or just your ideas," he begins with a sigh of contentment. I can't help the small smile, nor do I protest when Oliver steps in and hands me his notes. He sits down on the floor near my leg, promising me he won't be bored, and leans back against me so that I can play with his hair while Rook glares and continues his first round of thoughts on my ideas.

All the while, as I work through ideas and problems and finally come to a solid plan for what I'm going to do, I wonder how in the world I could ever have expected to get along without this.

And pray that I never have to.

When my phone rings, I initially don't notice. I'm too wrapped up in both my senior project and the other work I've been putting off for the last couple of weeks. I'd initially planned to keep putting it off, but when Rook saw the folders in my backpack and asked about them, he'd drawn himself up and become morally offended with me.

I blink up at the ceiling when my phone rings again, resting my Apple pencil on Rook's desk. He's graciously let me use his desk for the weekend, and with both of the guys doing other things, I've had peace and quiet for over an hour now.

Well, until this.

I know my mother's ringtone without having to look at my phone, but when my eyes finally slide to it, I feel myself tensing. I haven't been ignoring my parents, per se. But I'd be surprised if they haven't noticed the distance I've put between us.

I consider telling them. Briefly, I even think that it would be a good idea. But reality crashes down the moment I pick up my phone; I sigh before tapping the screen and pulling it to my ear. "Hey mom," I greet, false cheer in my voice. She's never been able to see through it, though she promises everyone that will listen that she can read me better than anyone.

It's too bad that's not true.

"*Happy Saturday, Blair,*" my mother answers, clearly

thrilled I've answered the phone. *"I won't keep you. I'm sure you and Juniper have plans."* A stab of guilt goes through me at that. *Plans* is my normal excuse not to talk for long. But worse, I haven't had real plans with Juniper for a long time.

Instead, all my plans revolve around two amazing, sweet, psychopathic men.

"Yeah," I laugh, sounding apologetic. "We're going to be out most of the weekend. I'm doing a photography thing and we're looking at some local historical places for it. It's... kind of boring." While my project really is about the historical sites of St. Augustine, and comparing architecture of it versus other centuries and places, Juniper has no idea what I'm doing and isn't doing it with me. "What's up?"

"I just wanted to talk to you about spring break."

My heart sinks in my chest at her words. I gnaw on my lower lip as I think, kicking myself for forgetting that I usually go back home to spend the week with them.

But I don't *want* to go home this year.

"Mom, would it be a problem if I didn't come home?" Thankfully, there's no long-term plan in place. No vacation or show for us to go see. "Just this one time. You'll see me in, like, two months anyway. I just have so much work, and I'd really like to stay and do my senior project."

"Of course that's fine, honey." My mother is nothing if not supportive. *"We understand. I just wanted to check and see what your plans are. At least try to do something fun for me, okay?"*

"Okay Mom," I say, unable not to smile. I ask her how her day is going, falling into the pattern of easy conversation with her until she tells me she has to go find Dad.

"Love you." My voice is soft when I say it, the longing in me to tell her is stronger than it ever has been. But I know what will happen, and the shit storm that will unleash.

I'll tell her after graduation. When I'm done and free and she can't yank me out of college.

She hangs up, and I set the phone down, resting my head in my hands as all of that nervous, electric energy floods me all over again. In the way it hasn't since just before Rook's arms wrapped around me in the parking lot last night, stopping me from making a big mistake.

CHAPTER 26

I t doesn't fade. The nervous energy stays with me all day, no matter what I do. It sticks in my bones and against my insides, plastering to every bit of me and making me fidgety while I work to get to where I'm supposed to be for my work.

I suck in a breath and tangle my fingers in my hair, elbows thumping onto the desk in front of me. I'm done, mostly because I feel like I'm going cross-eyed from staring at my work for so long. "God," I mutter, getting to my feet. I'm definitely done for now, no questions asked. From the office I go out to the kitchen, where I've prowled multiple times today to find food and something to drink.

To my detriment, both of them are in the kitchen, talking in normal tones as Oliver roots through the fridge, pawing for something unseen.

"Hello, sweetheart," Rook purrs, snagging an arm around my waist and dragging me to him. He moves to kiss me, but stops, suspicion narrowing his gaze as he looks at me. "I see," he murmurs, grip not loosening. "You're not okay. What happened?"

"Nothing?" I blink at him, my eyes wide, and try to look innocent. "I am a-okay. Absolutely fine."

"Yeah, like anyone believes that." Oliver snorts, slamming down a Gatorade on the counter. "Do you want one? We have red and purple. The superior flavors," he informs me, a goofy smile on his lips. Whatever has me glowering clearly isn't a problem for him, and he sidles closer to me.

"My mom called," I sigh, sitting down when Rook loosens his grip and press my face into my hands. "I'm just tired. It's fine. It's *fine*." I repeat the words, though I know the only person I'm trying to convince is myself.

Both Rook and Oliver clearly aren't going to believe the words, but that's fine, too. They don't have a reason to, and they're not the ones with electricity shocking them from the inside out, telling them to *do something* before they're devoured by the gloom inside them.

God, when did I become so fucking dramatic?

"Hypothetically," I say, circling the cap of one of the Gatorade bottles with my finger. "If I were to... leave. In the middle of the night. For a nice, brisk walk in the cool night air—"

"No." Rook lays a hand over mine. "*No*," he says again, carefully. "You can't do this again. There's a reason I brought you home last night. Did something happen with your mother?"

"She just wanted to know what I was doing for spring break. I'm not going home. I can't go home. It's not just the amount of work I have, since that was basically a lie." I still have some work, but I'm also fast once I know what I'm doing. That's not what I'm worried about. "I just can't go home and see them now. They don't know what happened. They'd blow up my entire life if they did. So I just... told her I was busy." I shrug my shoulders. "Nothing happened. But that feeling is back again. I'm starting to feel like I can't sit still or stay in one place. I'm craving my bar loop." I snort. "Don't suppose you'd give me my switchblade back?"

Rook shakes his head even before I'm done speaking. "You know the answer to that without me giving you a real one. You aren't going out, and you're not getting a knife. Especially not that switchblade."

"Okay, *okay*," I sigh heavily, getting to my feet. "Could I *at least* go take a shower, Master Rook?"

"As long as you don't shimmy out the window, darling girl. Then you can do whatever you want." I wave at both of them, pivoting and heading back towards Rook's bedroom. Even so, I can feel their eyes on me the entire way. But I refuse to turn and give them the satisfaction of knowing I feel guilty about all the thoughts flitting through my head.

Standing in the hallway makes it easy to hear the grandfather clock that Rook probably rescued from last century. Even in the dark, when I can't see it, I hear the heavy ticking as the pendulum swings side to side. When he'd seen me staring at it earlier, he'd told me it was a family heirloom. I hadn't thought to ask if it was from *his* family, or he'd carried it out of a victim's house post-murder.

As unrealistic as that seems, I wouldn't actually put it past him.

Neither do I think for a second that either of them are sleeping. I'm not an idiot, nor am I blind. I know they think I'm going to do exactly what I'm doing. Just as I know there's no way in hell I'm going to waltz out of here, with or without a knife.

But I have to move. I can't stand at the end of the hallway

forever, just like I can't waver on this for the rest of the night. I've known for hours what I would be doing once midnight came. Though, whether I'm actually successful is another matter.

My soft steps take me into the kitchen, where the night-light on the wall gently illuminates my loose, long-sleeve tee and the leggings I'd worn last night as well. I glance around, using the light to show me what I need to see, and immediately I can tell which shadows don't belong.

I don't go for the door. With my luck, it's booby trapped or Oliver is going to launch toward it at the last second to take me down. With my luck, they've figured out how to lock the door from the outside with force of will alone, and they're just waiting for me to figure it out.

"Nice night we're having, isn't it?" I remark, standing in the middle of the mostly dark living room. "I was actually thinking about going for a stroll."

Immediately, the shadow on the sofa stirs and Oliver is up before I can do more than glance his way. "What are you doing, wonder girl?" he murmurs, resting his face against mine. "Did you really think we wouldn't know?"

"I figured you'd be here," I tell him. "And I knew I wouldn't get far. I won't lie; I'm interested to know what your plan is if I'm irrational and can't be talked into submission. Will you throw me over your shoulder and drag me back down the hallway?"

"Yep," he tells me, still nosing at my jaw. "Then I'll tie you to the bed, get you a milkshake, and read you as many bedtime stories as it takes for you to go to sleep."

It's not the answer I'd expected, but it's better. It's *sweet* of him, in all the ways that Oliver really is the sweetest guy I've ever met. "Brownie caramel swirl?" I ask, eyebrows lifting even though he can't see it in the dark.

"Absolutely."

It's Rook's turn to get up. He strides past me, making me wonder if he's mad at me, before I hear the jingle of his keys on the table being picked up and pocketed. "I'd like to go to a closer bar, if it's all the same to you," he tells me, running a hand through my hair lightly. "If I find us a decently sleazy one for you to prowl around, would that still suffice, Love?"

I can't help but stiffen. I wish that I could see him, or that I could turn on the lights. Is he serious? Is he fucking with me, or what? "You want to... take me to a bar?" I ask them, and I see Oliver's nod in the dimness. "At night... For me to look for men who really deserve a knife in the throat?"

"Yep. I don't know why you think we'd push you away from this," Oliver says, an arm hooked around my waist like he can't stop touching me. "But there are some rules."

"No switchblades," supplies Rook, leading the way to the door. I'm still so bewildered that I let them push me along, and by the time we get to the door, I'm just as confused as I had been previously. "No blades at all, actually. You don't get to kill anyone tonight. You get to do what you've been doing, and you get to tell us what it is you *want*."

"I think what I want is pretty obvious. Which sounds pretty bad every time I have to say it out loud, huh?" Thankfully, neither of them answer. I crawl into Rook's backseat, flopping onto my stomach as I close the door behind me. If I have to ride in the back, then I'm going to enjoy it. "Why do you want me to talk to you about it? I don't understand what this accomplishes."

"First of all, it gets you to calm down. I wouldn't be able to keep you here tonight short of tying you up, like Oliver said. I know that and so do you. And I'm not mad about it, but neither of us can let you put yourself in danger anymore. Second of all, I'm trying to figure out what you *want*. Yes, I get the basics of it. But I need to figure out why, so I can help you." Rook's voice is even and calm when he speaks, and he never once sounds even impatient with me.

"Maybe I just hate all men and want to rid the world of most of them. You know, I'll use that song as my theme song to hum when I'm on the hunt. You know?" I know I sound dumb, but it helps me not be so nervous to speak lightly like this. Humming the melody a couple of times for practice, I then add on the words. "Reuben, Reuben, I've been thinking, what a great world this would be. If the boys were all transported, far beyond the Northern sea."

Oliver laughs when I do it, but Rook takes a second before saying, "There's more verses to that, isn't there? Some about girls being taken beyond the sea, and the last one saying how *sad* it would be if all the boys were gone? You'd miss us, you know. So don't be so quick to ship us off to Antarctica."

"I'd let you stay," I murmur, flopping over onto my back so I can stare at the shafts of light that pass against the roof of the car as we drive. "I'd miss you both too much if I sent you away."

When he parks, it's behind a low brick building with light pouring from the windows behind dingy shades. I can see the dirt from the outside of the building when I wander close, and I'm pretty sure no one has ever bothered to clean these windows, judging by how they're smeared and smudged to hell and back.

Rook's hand appears on my shoulder, gripping me comfortingly. "I won't let you get hurt. Even if that means kidnapping you and never letting you out without a leash."

"That's hot."

"It wasn't supposed to be."

I snort at his ensuing sigh, and when he leads both me and Oliver to the entrance to the bar, it's... surreal.

Are we really doing this?

Are they really supporting me by taking me to a dive bar like the ones I've been prowling around for the past few weeks? It's certainly not the reaction I ever could've expected. Hell, if I realized they would go with me, maybe I would've actually invited them.

"I don't know how this is going to work," I say, stopping in my tracks. "I can't go in with you. That's not how I do this."

"Then don't," Oliver suggests, flashing me a wolfish grin from a face that's less of his normal mask than usual, though not quite as bad as what I've seen. "Don't come in with us, but maybe don't forget that we're not going to let you slit any throats." He steps past me, but quickly turns and kisses me hard, eyes glittering, before walking into the bar with Rook and leaving me outside, the closed door in my face.

It takes a few moments to get myself under control. I'm nervous, first of all. But past that, I really don't know how in the world I'm going to do this with them here. Will I feel awkward? Will I be too nervous, knowing that they're here and watching me?

Before I can keep going with my what ifs, I suck in a deep breath, close my eyes, and count to twenty. By the time I'm done, I feel a little better, and I've managed to sink into the familiar headspace that I've become pretty acquainted with over the past few weeks.

The itch is back, causing my fingers to twitch with antici-pation. I know what I'm doing. I've done this before.

Rook and Oliver are just an added bonus. At least now I know I won't lose myself, or do something stupid. More than that, at least I know I'm not going to get my own throat slit in a parking lot if something goes wrong.

With more confidence and less indecision, I push open the door to the bar, looking around with insecurity etched into every line of my body. I take in my surroundings as I walk, eyes wide as I gaze at the sports memorabilia around the room like I actually give a shit that it exists. Like so many of the crappy bars I've seen lately, this one is dedicated to sports and has two TVs above the bar itself, where two separate games are playing.

I'm surprised to see Rook sitting at the bar in front of one of them, his head tilted back to stare at the screen as if he's interested. For as long as I've known him, which admittedly isn't that long, I've never thought that he was someone who's actually into sports. It takes longer to spot Oliver. He's on the other side of the bar, a drink in his hand, as he looks at his phone and gives off an air of being absolutely exhausted.

It's crazy how good they are at seeming so... normal. They don't even glance at me as I approach the bar as well, my fingers curling over the old, sticky wood that makes my nose scrunch. But my attention is pulled from them almost immediately, and any worry I'd had about their eyes on me fades as I look between the other men at the bar.

My nervous helplessness intensifies. I hunch my shoulders as I ask for just a coke, this time not hiding the fact that I'm not drinking. It's worked a couple of times before, and sure enough, a middle-aged man to my left leans in a little closer, telling the bartender that he'll cover it for me.

Almost immediately, even before he asks if I'm okay, I realize that he's not what I'm looking for. He actually cares, instead of seeing me as a victim. I excuse myself from him and wander the bar unobtrusively, keeping my attention on the way the men in here look at me.

I can usually tell, after a few times of doing this, which of the men in the bar are what I need. Sure enough, I lock eyes with a man who doesn't look like he cares. His gaze is narrowed, and I know I've just caught him looking me over, judging my figure and my body under my skin-tight leggings and the shirt that's pushed up my arms to the elbows.

For a few moments I waver, like I don't know what to do. My feet inch toward his table, and I finally make myself look like I've resigned myself to this before closing the distance between his table and mine. "Can I sit here? Sorry, I get it if not. I don't want to bother anyone, I'm just..." I trail off, an apologetic smile on my lips. "Feeling a little lost tonight."

Predictably, the man offers me a seat at his table. The only other seat, and the chair is close enough that he can brush his knees against mine. He does it once, then again, leaving his leg there for a moment longer than before as I worry my lip with my teeth.

"My boyfriend broke up with me," I say, my words soft and unsure. "I left. I know that's dumb, I just... left." My shoulders lift, then fall. He touches my leg with the hand that's under the table, watching my face to see if I notice, let alone care.

I do, but not in the way that he thinks. It takes a lot of focus to not move away from him, then I close my eyes hard as if I'm really struggling with something. "I need to go home, but I couldn't get an Uber yet. I'm just trying to wait it out for a few minutes, you know? It usually just takes a bit. I'm just *tired*." I make sure to put that into my voice as well, wanting him to buy the entire act.

He does. But it's not because he likes me, or has any sympathy. I can feel the brush of his hand every once in a while, reaching as far as it can. Drunk men are never patient, and this one in particular is more rash than most.

It's only a few minutes later that I feel myself nearing the end of this. I can just *tell* sometimes, with the men who are drunk, and this one is trying oh-so-hard to look empathetic.

"Look, why don't you stop waiting for an Uber?" he

murmurs, lifting his hand to rest it on the back of mine. "I can just take you home, sound good?"

"No, I can't ask you to do that," I shake my head. "I live like twenty minutes from here. I don't want to make you go out of your way." He's also drunk, and I would never let a drunk man drive me anywhere. But that probably hasn't even occurred to him, truth be told. The wood-bordered walls, their surfaces painted a dark green, draw my attention as he tells me that it's fine. He *promises* he was about to leave too, and that he doesn't mind taking me home.

"Can I pay you back?" I ask, getting to my feet as he heads for the door. "I can pay you. Do you have Venmo, or PayPal?" When I follow him out the door, I forget about Rook and Oliver. It doesn't even occur to me, as my blood rushes through me so tumultuously that I can hear it in my ears. His steps lengthen in his excitement, and I follow after him while I try to hold myself back.

God, it hurts not to have a knife in my pocket, weighing comfortingly against my skin. It hurts not to be able to do more than tease myself with this little taste.

The man turns, a grin sliding over his lips as he stops beside an old, beat up sedan that's parked close to Rook's SUV. "We can figure something out. Just get in, and you can show me where I'm going."

It doesn't even occur to me to *stop*. I don't stop to think that I can't go any further than this as my fingers touch the door handle, ready to open it and oh-so-innocently slide inside the car.

But I don't get to. An arm wraps around my waist, yanking me back against someone's warm body. I stiffen, shocked for a few seconds and unsure of what's going on, before Oliver's scent washes over me and I relax in his grip.

"Rook was right," he murmurs in my ear. "You really do get

carried away." He glares up at the man, a wolfish grin on his features and his eyes cold. "This one's mine, friend," he chuckles. "You can't have her."

The man's face falls in shock. He glances at me and I shrug, my own smile apologetic. "Sorry, kind of," I chuckle, and the man doesn't answer, past what looks like him grasping for the right thing to say.

At last, when his door is open and he's half in, the man snarls a quick *"fuck you,"* just as Oliver yanks me back into his arms to make sure I'm not going to have my feet run over.

I'm still snickering when he whirls me around and shoves me up against Rook's SUV, which unlocks behind me as Rook saunters out from the bar, keys in hand.

"You're adorable," Oliver purrs, grasping behind me for the door handle. "Ever been fucked in the back of a car? I so want to fuck you back here after that. Do you know how hot you are when you're setting up to kill someone? *Fuck,* Blair." He finally gets it open and lifts me up by my waist, setting me on the seat and crawling in after me.

I don't think he can or will make good on his idea of fucking me, though he does shove me against the far window, caging me with his body as his mouth slants against mine. "Blair." He laughs. "Oh, fucking *wonder girl.* You're too perfect to exist."

"Sure she is," Rook agrees, turning the key in the SUV's ignition to get the engine purring to life. "We just need to get you past this, and thinking straight again." He doesn't leave the parking lot. He turns and looks at us, resting his shoulders against his seat. "Tell me what you were thinking," he orders curiously, eyes searching mine.

"I just think about what I need to do to seal the deal," I admit, hooking my fingers in Oliver's shirt and yanking it over his head. "I think about how *easy* it is. How these men are so predictable and disgusting. Sometimes I think about how fucking easy it would be to kill someone. To just drag a blade across their throat." Reaching up, I drag my thumb against Oliver's throat to simulate my point. "It just seems too easy. Like there should be more resistance between them and death, you know?"

Oliver is warm as he pushes forward to kiss at my throat, pushing my knees open so he can settle between them.

"I do know," Rook agrees, as he shifts into drive. "I know, because you're right. And you need to understand that it *is* that easy. But you'll never forget it once you do it. So think hard before you push this to another level, Blair." His eyes are dark in the mirror, and I take notice, pushing Oliver away from me for a moment so I know what he's saying and can focus on it.

"Because if you keep going with this, you're going to have to accept that you're never going to be the same again." He goes quiet as we drive, and Oliver calms down as well, no longer kissing me like I'm about to die or like he's trying to devour me.

But he pulls me into his lap, my head on his thighs as he runs his fingers through my hair. I stare up at the shafts of light again, thinking. But I'm not able to fully work through my thoughts before they halt and go back on repeat.

"Is there something wrong with me?" I ask the ceiling, too afraid to look at either Rook or Oliver. "I think sometimes that I'm broken inside after... that. It's like I'm missing something that used to be there. Something that kept me from doing things like this."

"There's nothing wrong with you," Oliver assures me. "Unless you think there's also something wrong with us."

"Darling, there is a *lot* wrong with you," Rook cuts in smoothly. "Love, I think you should ask yourself if it matters, and what it means to you if the answer ends up being yes.

Maybe something did break. Maybe that thing inside you that kept you from doing this *is* gone." Rook sighs, then takes another breath just as my heart twists in my chest. "But that doesn't make you any less perfect for us, or any less able to accomplish anything in the world you want to do."

His words are... sweet. My eyes close hard, and I turn to face Oliver's stomach, brushing my nose against his bare skin. I don't know what to say. I don't *have* anything to say, and this is the easy, safe option.

At least until I figure out what to do or where to go from here.

CHAPTER 27

"I'm dying for spring break." Juniper's voice is coated in exhaustion, and when I peer at her over our shared library table, brows raised, I see that she *looks* as tired as she sounds.

"You've got, like, less than twenty-four hours left before you leave," I point out. "What time are you and Jesse flying to Cancun tomorrow?"

A grin curves her thin lips upward, and the gleam in her eyes shows me just how excited she is. Though I'm not sure how much of her excitement is for Cancun, and how much of it is instead for spending uninterrupted time with Jesse.

Frankly, I think it's more of that one than the actual destination. I'm also starting to think that he's going to propose to her on this trip.

God, I hope he does. I know, or at least I think, that she'll say yes. Even with their problems early this semester, they're still glued together so tightly it would be impossible to pry them apart. Good for them, is what I normally think when I see how in love they are. I *hope* they're married this year.

"Eleven. I got lucky and my last class was canceled after our Friday exam. So I'm done at nine-thirty, instead of two. You'll be okay?" She looks up at me with sudden worry, like a new idea has just struck her. "If you need me—"

"You are not going to cancel," I inform her sharply, pointing my pen in her direction. "Repeat after me. You are *not* going to cancel. Not for me or for anyone else. Don't stop at the side of the road to pet a strange dog on the way to the airport. Don't even *think* of canceling your trip to stay home and coddle me all spring break. If I have an issue, I already have a solution."

She thinks about it, trying to figure out what I'm going to say. "It's something to do with Oliver, isn't it?" She sighs at last, head in her hand. "You must really love him, to spend as much time with him as you do."

Juniper is obviously right. My problems end with me going to spend time with them. And any of my current issues can be solved by launching myself into their bed whenever I'm starting to freak out. It's not a perfect solution, but at least it's working for me until I can get my feet back under me after what happened. "I will absolutely go crawl into Oliver's bed if I have an issue," I assure her, a sly grin crossing my lips. She snorts, and then the rest of her words make it through my brain.

"*Love him*?" I choke out, nearly strangling myself on the words.

Juniper tilts her head, looking surprised at my indignation. "Yeah. Love him. You do, don't you? There's no way I'm wrong. I've never seen you like this for anyone, Blair. I didn't even know you could *get* like this over a man."

"I don't..." My words die in my throat when I think of Oliver. I love things *about* him. Like his charm, his friendliness, and his enthusiasm.

And the way his mask slips off, taking all of that kind, friendly nature with it.

I love things about Rook, too. His sternness, but mostly the way he cares so much about me. He's so careful with me, and so considerate.

Until it's not me but someone else, and his eyes become so cold they could freeze the person looking at him.

Okay, I admittedly love everything about them. But I'm not sure I'm ready to admit that. I'm *definitely* not going to admit it to Juniper, when I haven't even told her I have two boyfriends instead of just Oliver. "I don't know," I say finally, knowing she's still watching me. "But hey, be careful in Cancun, okay? Don't get like, enchanted by some really hot guy on the beach, then get flown back to some country in Europe to become a billionaire's victim at a rundown hostel."

Her eyes narrow as she processes the warning. "That's so... specific of you. Were you watching *Hostel* in the living room this morning? Was that the screaming I heard?"

"Uh, yeah. *Hostel 2*, because it's the only one that really matters out of them," I clarify, even though I know she really doesn't care and wouldn't have watched it with me, anyway. Even though she enjoys horror, and likes the paranormal side of it more than I do, I'm a gore lover.

Which, when I think about it a little too closely, says something about me that maybe I'm not ready to accept.

"I'm done studying." Juniper closes her laptop and gets to her feet, shoving it into her pocket. "What about you? Are you going to stay here?"

"Yeah, just for a few minutes," I tell her, glancing at the work I still have to do for my classes before spring break starts. "My photography professor is an ass, and I have to get a few more things done for him." It's not exactly a lie, but I wonder if Rook's ears burn when I talk about him.

I hope so.

"Sounds like an absolute jerk," Juniper comments, slinging her tote bag over her shoulder, and looks at me once more before she heads around the table, going toward the stairs. "By the way..." she trails off, glancing at me as if to gauge my mood. "I heard something about Langhorn."

With suddenly trembling hands, I lay my pencil down before looking up at her. "That he was let out of the psych ward?" I ask, figuring that's the rumor that's been going around.

She searches my gaze, opens her mouth, then closes it again. I know she wants to say something about it, but clearly there's something about me that warns her off. "I shouldn't have said anything. Are you mad?" She waits for my expression to even out, and for me to shake my head, before she adds in a hurry, "See you later. Try not to die doing work before spring break."

I just wave, wondering what she'll want to do for dinner.

It's easy to submerge myself in my work, barely listening to anything around me, until my phone vibrates in the pocket of my sweatpants, startling me out of what I'm doing and making me drop my pen.

Glancing at the time, I'm surprised to see that it's been thirty minutes since Juniper walked out. To me, it seems like it's only been two or three at most. Blinking, I let my eyes flick down to the actual text, and a breath leaves me, stress clenching my stomach tight.

Are you sure you don't want to come home?

It's from my dad, and he's always been harder to say no to than my mom. I *love* spending time with my dad, and I've probably been closer to him for most of my life. The only reason we don't talk as much now is because he's just... quiet. He's not a talker, especially when it comes to the phone, and what I normally get from him is a weekly text reminding me how proud of me he is and how much he loves me. We talk once a week as well, and it hits me that we haven't done that now in three weeks, twisting my heart into a painful figure eight.

My fingers hover over the keyboard, my lungs constricting to force me into shallow, guilty breathing.

Sorry Dad, I reply, sending the message off quickly. *I have some stay at home plans for spring break. And I just want to power through these last projects that need to be done before the end of the semester. I'm dying to see you at graduation, though.*

To me, my words sound fake. I mentally cross my fingers as I watch him type his reply, wondering if he'll call me out for what he has to see is a lie. Surely he can't think I'd rather stay here than go home, even if just for a few days.

Okay, Blair. No problem. I'll miss you and go boating in your honor. The text makes me crack a smile. It's so very my dad.

Have a nice time. Or at least try to take a few breaks. Love you, kiddo.

I'm not a kid, and I've been trying to remind him of that for years now. But this time I don't protest. I only tell him I love him, and to take lots of pictures of whatever boating trip he's on.

Instead of my phone going back into the pocket it had come out of, I place it on the table near me, checking once more to make sure it's still on vibrate. It definitely wouldn't be great for it to beep out a random Disney tune anytime my mom or dad texts me.

Back to work I go, diving into the homework I have left, and finishing up the touches on my project that I wanted to have done a week ago. Really, I wanted to avoid any last-minute stuff, but now that it's crunch time, I find that I'm more motivated than I normally am when I'm *not procrastinating* until the last possible moment.

By the time I feel like I'm close to being done, the sun is setting, from what I can see out the window to my back left, and I feel like I've been here forever. With a groan, I flop forward, stretching my arms out across the table.

At least now I can go home and take a break. I can chill, watch a movie, and have whatever breakfast food for dinner sounds best. If I know Juniper, she won't be home tonight. At least not for long. She'll want to spend as much time as possible with Jesse, planning their trip and talking about what she needs to bring. Of all the over-planners I've known, my mother included, Juniper is by far the friendliest I've been around.

My phone vibrates once, making me think I have a text. It's probably my mother, or my dad again, wanting me to—

It vibrates again, taking itself towards the edge of the table as if in threat. I grope back for it, picking it up before it can fall, and bring it to my ear without looking at the screen, though I know enough that I can answer it without looking.

"Hello?" I ask lightly, quietly, still expecting my mom. "This is the international bank of Blair; how may I help you?"

I'm not expecting the *laugh*. Oliver giggles in my ear, the sound fading into a snicker that echoes between my ears. Immediately I know that this isn't people-friendly Oliver.

This is the insanity that he hides underneath.

"Blair, Blair." He can't be drunk, I know. But he sounds like he's happy enough to pass for it. "We have a surprise for you." He's panting, and I swear I hear something muffled in the background, but I could be hearing things.

"Are you... okay?" I ask, shoveling my textbooks, notebook, and iPad into my backpack so I can sling it over my shoulders. "You sound off. Like, really off. You good?"

"I'm so good," he promises sweetly. "Oh, do I have a surprise—" He's cut off by the phone leaving his mouth, though I hear his protests as the phone is taken away.

"Sorry, Love." Rook's sigh is weary, and I can *feel* the glare he's giving Oliver, even across the phone. "I told him to calm down first before he called you. Did he catch you at a bad time?"

"Uh, no," I reply, taking the stairs down from the third floor, where the tables and work areas are, to the first, so I can leave. "I'm just doing all of this extra credit for my jerk of a photography professor."

"Careful. Oliver and I went to the trouble of getting you a gift we think you'll enjoy. Where are you?"

"The library?" He's being so confusing. His voice sounds off, too. Like he's been doing something that I might not approve of. But unless he's smuggled me one of the queen's diamonds, I don't see why. "I'm about to go home. I don't have any classes tomorrow, so I'm just going to sleep in—"

"Spend spring break with us." The invitation comes out in a rush, and it's so unlike Rook to be so impatient that I'm shocked to silence until he says my name, looking for an answer.

"Yeah, umm. Maybe? Like, just come over to your house, and—"

"No. I have a cabin a few hours from St. Augustine. You trust us, right?"

"Sure. Maybe not when you're weird like this, but sure."

"Spend spring break with us. I promise you'll enjoy it."

It's such a weirdly timed request, but it's not like I have anything better to do. Unless they're planning to murder me, which of course would qualify as something I *don't* want to do with my spring break.

"Okay," I find myself saying, as I take off at a jog toward the bus that will take me back to a stop near my apartment. If I get there in the next few seconds, I'll definitely be able to hop on.

I do, jumping onto it just as Rook says, "Pack a bag. Old clothes and whatever else you want to bring on vacation. I'm going to come pick you up tonight."

"Tonight?" I repeat. "What time?"

"Late. Just be ready for me, Blair? Please?" He sounds so endearing, so hopeful, and so... strange that I just don't know how to refuse.

"Okay," I find myself saying, in spite of myself. "I'll be ready to go in a couple hours."

CHAPTER 28

S liding into the passenger seat of Rook's SUV feels...
surreal, at best. There's something different about him
tonight, and when I give him a sidelong glance from the
corner of my eye, it takes a few moments for me to realize
exactly what it is.

He's *excited*. His hands grip the steering wheel tightly, and
he can't quite sit still, though his movements are small and
quickly aborted so that I won't notice.

But I *do* notice. It's hard to really explain how the gleam in
his eye is different, or how he just seems like a slightly different
person than the Rook I know. It reminds me of Oliver, and
when he loses his mask.

But I've never seen Rook lose *his* control like this.

Does that mean murder is afoot?

I open my mouth to ask, but something about him puts me
off of it. He still hasn't said anything, even though my seatbelt
is on and we're driving away from my apartment building. My
duffel bag and backpack are in the back, both packed haphaz-

ardly, because I have no idea what we're doing or how long we'll be gone.

"I, umm, burn easily," I tell him, lights playing over the inside of the SUV.

He glances at me, confusion on his face, and I realize he's been lost in his thoughts. Did he even remember I was here before I spoke up?

When I meet his eyes, he must realize the same thing. He sighs, his body relaxing like the strings holding him tight are loosened just enough for him to have a little bit of slack in his muscles. He frowns apologetically and reaches out a hand to brush my hair back from my face. "I'm so sorry, Love," he purrs, sounding like he means it. "What did you say?"

"I *burn* easily," I repeat slowly, though I know he's paying enough attention now that he doesn't need me to take things slow for him. "Because I'm *pale.*"

"Deathly pale," he agrees sagely, when my words get through to his brain. "Did you bring sunscreen?"

"Will I get to go swimming?"

"Do you *want* to go swimming?" he arches a brow and readjusts his too-tight grip on the steering wheel once more. "You can swim if you want. But not tonight."

"What, we aren't a fan of night swims in this car?" I drawl, tapping my fingers on the door handle. My heart flutters in my chest, though I'm not quite sure why. I don't understand what we're doing here, or why he's so wired.

But it must have something to do with me.

"We have a two-hour drive," he tells me, glancing at the clock that shows it's closing in on midnight. "And I want you to get some sleep, because it's probably going to be a long night."

"Because we're doing something... cooler than night swim-ming?" For some reason, it hits me now that Oliver isn't in the car, though I turn to look behind me just to make sure he's not hiding on the floorboards. I should've realized it when I got into the car, of course. But with Rook's strangeness and the weirdness of the night, it had just slipped my mind. "Where's Oliver?"

"Because we're doing something that's going to take a while. *If* you want to. He's already at the cabin keeping an eye on things, so please don't worry about him. I'd like to talk to you about it when we're closer, and I'm sorry I dragged you away from your bed at the last minute. Do you think you could get some sleep?"

"Don't apologize for dragging me away for a sex holiday. I *assume* this is a sex holiday, and not you sacrificing me to the Eldritch god that gave you your photography ability." That makes him snicker, and his grip relaxes by degrees, until he looks almost normal.

"Take a nap, Blair." His words are firm, but he can't just make me go to sleep with a single command and nothing else. Still, I wouldn't mind the quiet time. My eyes hurt after all the work I'd done earlier, and if we really are doing something—though whatever it is has to be the biggest surprise of all time for him to act like this—I could use at least some quiet time for myself.

As he turns back to the road, I lean my seat back, press earbuds into my ears, and watch the play of light across his face as he drives, imagining all the things that he could have planned. Doesn't he know that the only surprise I could ever really want from them is more of a commitment than whatever we have going on? Though, if I'm being honest with myself, I'm a big part of the reason things aren't more serious.

God, I suck with relationships.

Rook's hand gently shakes me awake, being careful not to jostle me more than he needs to. My music, still loud in my ears, startles me into wakefulness before it suddenly stops, and I sit up, looking around blearily as I suck in a long breath.

"Where are we?" I murmur, blinking a few times in the darkness. We're nowhere near the city, that's for sure. In fact, I don't see any lights at all, except for a few rogue streetlights that have the nerve to show themselves along the wooded road.

"This is Jekyll Island," Rook informs me, his hands now resting on the steering wheel instead of gripping it. "We're almost to my cabin."

"Is that North or South Florida?" I wouldn't know, especially since I'd fallen asleep before we got on the interstate.

"It's Georgia." His answer has me staring at him in surprise, and I wonder why in the world he has a cabin in *Georgia*, for fuck's sake.

"Why?" I blurt out, not knowing what else to ask.

"Because it's nice, it's secluded, and no one bothers me here. I've had it for a few years." He sucks in a breath and turns on his brights, though I'm not sure why they were even off. This road isn't taken care of too well, and potholes jar me semi-regularly as we drive.

"Let's talk before we get there." I've never heard him sound this serious, except for the day in Professor Carmine's office that I *refuse* to allow back into my brain.

"Talk about...?"

"About what's going to happen when we're there."

There's a thrill that makes my heart flutter. Even though I don't know what he means, my fingers clench in my lap, one hand pressing against the front of my phone. Removing the earbuds from my ears and carefully wrapping the cord around my phone in order to busy my hands. "I'm not in danger, right?" I force myself to ask quietly, though if I am, I'm not sure I even want to know.

Or that he'll tell me.

But Rook's startled glance tells me that he's not expecting the question. He nearly veers off the road, and one of his hands reaches over so he can lace his fingers with mine. "*Never,*" he informs me fiercely. "Never in your life when you're with us, I swear. But this is going to be a lot, and if you can't handle it, that's okay. It's more than okay. We'll take care of it, if you can't."

God, this is sounding more and more cryptic by the moment. Biting my lip, I stare at him in the darkness, only able to see his profile and wait for him to continue.

"You always have the right to say no, or stop. Or just to walk away. If there's something you don't want to do, or can't, then you just say the word and it ends."

"This is sounding like a really questionable sex getaway," I admit, unsure if that really is what's going on. I assume I'm here for other reasons, too. Like the *surprise* that Oliver had mentioned. But for the life of me, I can't figure out what that is.

"It's not a sex getaway," Rook corrects automatically. He pulls into a long, gravel driveway that winds into the woods and makes me question my safety and my sanity. I'm *really* riding in a dark car, at almost two in the morning, to some part of Georgia that I couldn't even find on a map.

Yeah, I definitely need therapy.

"Okay. Not going to lie." I press my feet against the floor of the SUV, toes curling in my sneakers. "I'm kind of freaking out."

"Don't freak out." He turns slightly until a medium-sized cottage comes into view. It looks freshly painted, the white boards gleaming in Rook's headlights. Seconds later he's parked, and he turns to look at me, one hand coming up to cup my jaw. "I would never let anything happen to you, Blair," he promises me, eyes locked on mine in the darkness. I can feel it more than see it, and I lean into his hand even as my heart speeds up again until it's trying to choke me. "And Oliver would skin me if you got hurt. We both know it."

I have to smile at that, and the soft taunt gives me the strength to slide out of the car, leaving my stuff for later as Rook tells me to. I can tell he's nervous as well, by the almost-jerky nature of his strides and the way he keeps glancing at me. Like he isn't sure I can do this.

Whatever *this* is.

At the door, he stops me again and kisses me hard. His mouth is desperate against mine, only confusing me more in the moment, then knocks twice on the door.

Steps from inside draw my attention, and when the door opens to expose Oliver, I reach for him, but stop.

There's blood on his face, streaked across his skin. There's a feral savagery to him, one that tells me what he's been doing or looking to do, and there's no warmth in his eyes until he looks at me and grins. The problem, of course, is that it's not the grin of my happy-go-lucky boyfriend.

It's the rictus, soon-to-be-bloody smile of a psycho. "Did you tell her?" he breathes, reaching up to touch my face lightly with hands that shake. "You didn't, right?"

"I didn't tell her," Rook tells him, iron in his voice. "And you better not have started without us." When Oliver glances at him in confusion, Rook swipes at the blood on his face.

"What? No. No, I was cleaning up from earlier. I didn't touch anything," Oliver promises, his gaze coming back to mine like he's magnetized to me. "He told you that you don't have to, right? That you can back out, or we can do it for you? That it's okay—"

"I told her everything we discussed, my love. You have to move, or she'll never get to see her surprise." His tone makes me glance at him, but coldness climbs my body from my extremities.

"Wait." I reach out and grab Oliver's hand, unsure of what I'm trying to even ask him. I swallow once, then twice, nerves and fear winding up my body. "Wait, please. I'm kind of freaking out. Tell me again you're not going to hurt me. That you're not—"

Oliver surges forward, a hand on my face, and crushes his lips to mine as hungrily, as urgently, as I've ever felt him. More so, in a lot of ways, and that doesn't help me calm down.

"I *promise*," he growls in his throat, tone husky. "I swear to you, Blair. That this is *for* you, and you will never, ever be in any danger with us. We would never hurt you." His words, along with Rook's, serve to calm me down enough for me to at least step in the door with him, willing to face whatever surprise called for me to leave in the middle of the night and have all of these cryptic instructions bestowed upon me by them both.

When I suck in a breath, the air smells... strange. Cold, and almost stale, but I attribute that to this place being unlived in for most of the year. Oliver tugs me forward by my hand, giving me time to look around the sparsely decorated but still cute cabin. It's more modern than I'd expected, and I spy a small kitchen and breakfast nook before I'm pulled past it, down the little hallway, and into the main, open space that would normally serve as a living room, I think.

The first thing that catches my eye is all the plastic. There's a tarp on the floor made of thick clear plastic, and sheets of it overlap, going to the walls where they're held tight with blue painter's tape. Volumes and volumes of plastic, enough to wrap a truck in, cover the furniture and climb a few feet up the walls on all sides.

All stemming from one piece of furniture in the middle of the room that isn't covered.

The blocky legs of the chair are chipped and old, and the duct tape wrapping someone's legs to them is bright silver and tight enough that I wonder if they're cutting off his circulation. My eyes climb his messed and torn clothing, and I know before my gaze reaches his face exactly who I'm looking at.

James Langhorn, tied to an old chair and gagged with duct tape, sits in the living room of Rook's cabin. Judging by the setup, the coldly rational part of my brain tells me they've probably done this before.

"Oh," I whisper, and take a step back, straight into Rook's embrace. He wraps me up in his arms when my eyes find Langhorn's, nuzzling the side of my face comfortingly.

"He was let out yesterday." Oliver's voice is manic with pleasure, and he's like the cat that ate the canary as he prowls into the room, barefoot, to circle his captive. "He was let out, and told he could just go *home*. Go *home*," he sneers, sticking his face close to Langhorn's. "After what he did to you and two other girls?" My sound of surprise makes Rook hold me tighter, as if he's afraid I can't support myself.

"Other girls?" I repeat, feeling numb. Every part of me is cold, frozen to the spot. I can't move or do anything except stare.

"Yeah," Oliver says grimly. "All in the span of a week. Poor, old Professor Langhorn. The hospital says he had a psychotic break. That maybe he couldn't help himself." He sneers the words close to the old man's face, teeth bared. "That's what he told us earlier, anyway. That he couldn't help himself. But that makes him no better than an animal. A *rabid* one." A knife appears in his hand, coming from somewhere on his person. "So I think that means we treat him like we would a dangerous old hog."

I watch the knife descend as if it's in slow motion. I watch him press the blade against Langhorn's cheek, and I even think I can see the blade indenting his skin between his whiskers, though logically I'm probably too far away for that.

"Wait," I hear myself saying. "*Wait.*" I don't want Oliver to cut him. I don't want to see him bleed to Oliver's knife while I'm watching.

Carefully, like *I* might break or fall on the plastic, I creep toward them, one foot set carefully in front of the other. My heart beats against my ribs, like a bird trying to escape the cage that's kept it prisoner for far too long. I've never felt it beat this hard, and I wonder offhandedly if my heart could burst.

Slowly, I reach one trembling hand up, gripping the edge of the duct tape on his face as I truly meet his gaze for the first time.

Langhorn is terrified. There's a scrape across one cheek, and dried blood on his temple, but apart from that, he's pretty unharmed.

He makes a noise of protest, but I don't listen. I slowly peel the tape back, not all the way, but just enough so that I can see his mouth and he can speak.

"Help me," he gasps, panting through his lips. "Don't let them hurt me, Blair. Don't let them—"

"Shut up," I whisper. "Or I'll let him cut out your teeth."

Oliver shifts beside me, the grin on his face growing wider when I say it.

"I didn't mean to—"

"*Shut up,*" I say again, more forcefully this time. But he opens his mouth again, and frustration fuels me, fuels my hand that grips the edge of the duct tape that's still on his cheek.

I rip it off as hard as I can and as fast, yanking a strip of facial hair and skin along with it.

He screams. The sound ripples through me, but I don't feel the horror and revulsion I'd expected. Instead, it makes me shudder, and a tingle goes down my spine that makes me think of how it feels whenever Oliver shoves me down onto his bed, his hands all over me, and I realize I'm about to have some of the best sex of my life.

"Why did you hurt me?" I ask, when he's finally forced to take a breath for more air.

"I didn't—"

"*Why did you hurt me?*" I demand, my voice sharp. I can see Rook prowling around behind him, and from the corner of my eye, I see him surreptitiously flip the plastic off of a stool that's been dragged close behind Langhorn.

Knives sit on top of it. Small knives, like a scalpel, a medium hunting knife, and something bigger, longer, with a serrated edge that I would use to chop up a side of beef, instead of an old man.

But I'm always open to learning new things, so I would never assume that any of these aren't capable of doing a number on a human's insides.

"The hospital said I had a psychotic break," he pants, dark eyes locked on mine. He still reminds me of the buzzing of flies, and I'm not close enough to smell his rotted-meat breath. Memories surge behind my eyes, and I shake my head as tears threaten to well at my eyelids.

"No, that's not good enough. *Why did you hurt me?*" I all but scream, getting in his face this time. Now I can smell his fetid breath, and I can hear the wheezing whenever he drags air into lungs that don't deserve it.

"Okay, I'll tell you. I'll tell you whatever you want, Blair, *please.*"

"Don't say my name," I remark offhandedly, shaking my head. "Don't you *ever* say my name."

"Just tell them not to hurt me, make them let me go, and I'll give you whatever you want."

His words ring in the empty air. They're absurd. They're fucking *ridiculous* enough that a startled yelp of laughter tears from my throat.

"Let... let you go?" I repeat, feeling my eyes widen. Blood rushes in my ears as I lift my arms to gesture at the walls around us. "You think for a second they'll let you *go*? Even if I told them to, even if I said I couldn't do this or couldn't let them, what do you think would happen? If we let you go, then you'll tell. And you are *not* getting them locked up. You will *not* take them from me like you took *parts of me*."

I sound hysterical. There's no way I don't sound hysterical when I'm nearly screaming at him.

"Now tell me why the fuck you hurt me, and maybe, just maybe, I'll tell them to kill you quick. I'll let them give you the fastest death, even though you don't deserve it."

His eyes dart around the room. He looks at Oliver, and tries to look at Rook, before his eyes fall on mine again. There's a cunning in them I don't expect, and even now I see he's looking for a way out of this, when there is none.

"I'll tell you," he says finally, softly. "I'll tell you whatever you want to know—"

"I've literally told you so many times what I want to know. So fucking say it. Say it, or lose—"

"Because you were there. Is that what you want to hear?" Now he's the one interrupting me, and his panting becomes frantic, as do the glances around the room. "Because you were *easy*, all right?" I'm not sure whether he's surrendered to the fact that he's going to die, or he still thinks he's going to get out of it. "Is that what you want to hear, *Blair*?" He sneers my name when he says it, but it only makes me flinch this time. "You were so scared, so easy and so quiet. I knew you wouldn't scream. If you had, he would've been there." He jerks his head back at Rook. "I should've known you were fucking him. I should've known that a whore was fucking any professor she found. What was wrong with me, huh? What's so different, other than me being older than him? The truth is, you were the easiest target I've ever seen, and I was *right*." He spits the words at me and I stumble back, falling onto my ass on the plastic that crunches and bends beneath me.

Oliver slides into my place, his hand gripping Langhorn's jaw and forcing him to shut up. "She told you not to say her name," he purrs, reaching back for whatever blade Rook is handing to him. "I heard her, and I know you did, too. And I know you speak English, *Professor*." When he brings his hand back, I see that he's holding the scalpel in it. He forces the professor's mouth open, and shoves the scalpel between his lips, not caring what he cuts along the way.

Then Langhorn screams. I can see Oliver's hand twisting, his movements precise, but Langhorn just screams and jerks back, unable to do anything else when Rook grips his hair and holds him still.

"What are you—" I swallow the question when Oliver jerks back, his hand covered in blood, and Rook lets Langhorn's head fall. He chokes, spitting blood from between his lips, and Oliver chucks two small white shapes onto the plastic that rattle and roll, finally coming to a stop so I can see...

He'd cut out two of Langhorn's fucking *teeth*.

When he moves to do it again, I lunge to my feet, one hand on Oliver's arm. "Wait," I say, eyes wide. "Wait, Oliver, please."

He turns to look at me, his gaze softening. He searches my face and frowns, some of the light dying from his eyes. "It's okay, Blair," he murmurs, leaning in to press his forehead to mine. "It's okay. Let us do it for you, okay? It's fine that—"

"Let me try."

He stands there, frozen. As if he doesn't know if he's heard me right. Rook is still as well, eyes on my face, and it's not until I reach up, my hand outstretched for the scalpel, that Oliver moves to hand it to me.

I turn slowly, the coldness in my body overwhelming when I look at Langhorn. This is supposed to be the hardest part, isn't it? The part where I look at a man I want to kill, remember he's a person, and chicken out. But that's not what I see when I look at him. I see nothing more than swine. Nothing more than a dying piece of trash that's outlived its usefulness.

His gasps of pain and soft cries don't bother me, the same way the rain doesn't bother me. If anything, it heats my blood, sending it rushing through my ears, and Oliver holds his mouth as I lean into Langhorn, the scalpel in my left hand.

"I was easy?" I repeat quietly, unsure if he can even hear me. "I was *easy*? Like this?" I'm not as precise as Oliver. The scalpel cuts Langhorn's mouth, scoring the roof of it and then his tongue. I'm not being particularly careful not to, but the blood in his mouth streams outward, the rest of it choking him. I can see the holes carved out of his gums by Oliver, and I move the blade beside them. But I don't intend to carve like he did. Instead, I *push*; the scalpel jabs into his gum under the tooth behind the two that are missing. Like I'm sawing something in half, I jab the blade back and forth, wondering if I can cut the nerves that hold it in place.

"God, I bet this hurts," I tell him, glancing up at his eyes again. He's screaming wordlessly, unable to make more than sounds of agony as I cut him. I yank the blade out of his mouth, cutting him up as I do, and reach in with my free hand to grip the tooth I've almost sawed out of his gum. Slowly, so slowly that it's cruel, I yank it out, feeling the rip of whatever holding it in place, protest, then give way under my fingers.

The sound he makes when I drop the tooth and the rest of

what's attached to the floor is barely human, but it sure is interesting.

"Can I do whatever I want?" I ask in a voice that doesn't sound like my own. "Does it matter?"

"You can do whatever you want," Rook tells me, drawing my attention to his face. He's *pleased*, I realize instantly. He's so pleased that he can barely contain it, and while that should bother me, instead it causes a swirl of pride to curl in my stomach.

Wordlessly, Rook hands me the medium-sized knife off of the table, just as Oliver flips the big one in his grip.

"Let me show you," my professor purrs when I glance at Langhorn, unsure of what to do. "Let me help you, darling girl." He strides around to me, running his fingers up my arm. "My perfect, perfect girl," he goes on, kissing my temple. "You're such a sick little darling, aren't you?"

"I want to hurt him," I murmur, eyes still on Langhorn. "I want to hurt him more." There's a fire in my bones now, lighting me up in ways I've never felt before. Oliver grins when he looks at me, and I wonder how I look right now. How I must seem.

Do I look like them? God, I hope I do.

Rook makes good on his word. He helps me, showing where to cut to provide the most pain with minimal damage. And Langhorn *screams.* He can't talk with his mouth full of blood, but his screams echo and ring through the room, bouncing back at him from the walls as I cut him. It lasts for hours, some part of my brain thinks, but the other part of me disagrees. The other part of me thinks I've only been here for a couple of minutes, even though I'm trembling and sweating, blood coating my skin up to my elbows.

Langhorn is a mess. If he didn't look human to me before, he certainly doesn't now. Covered in blood and barely still conscious, the cruel old man is nothing like his former self.

And now, when I'm no longer getting any kind of reaction, it isn't fun anymore.

I lean back in Rook's grip, sighing in disappointment. "I'm done," I tell him, reaching an arm up to hook it around him. "He's gone, anyway. I don't care anymore." Those are my words, coming from my mouth, but I'm not sure I've ever said anything so cold.

"Then can I end it with you?" Oliver looks almost like he's shivering with excitement, and he holds the large serrated blade out to me. "I won't take this from you," he promises. "I just want to hold you when you do it."

Rook releases me with a kiss to my temple, letting Oliver grab me up and press the blade into my hand. I take it, curling my slippery, sticky fingers around it, and while he guides my hand, I reach forward, pressing the blade to Langhorn's throat as he leans back in the chair.

"You have to do it hard, with *intent*. Don't stop once you start, wonder girl," he purrs in my ears, hands going to my waist. "Don't get scared or have a light touch—"

His words slam to a stop when I press the blade tighter to Langhorn's throat until I see a dribble of blood... and I *rip* it to the side, tearing a gaping wound into the man's throat that sprays bright red blood at both me and Oliver, coating my face and shirt, making me turn away but only succeeding in getting it in my hair as well.

For a brief moment, everything is quiet except for my heart and the pleasure that slams through my veins.

Then the silence breaks. Oliver whirls me around, a snarl of delight on his lips, and crushes his lips to mine. He yanks me away from Langhorn's cooling body, and I don't have time to wonder why.

Rook is suddenly behind me, his hands on my hips as he nips at the shell of my ear. "You perfect, terrible thing," he murmurs in my ear. "You're so gorgeous covered in blood."

"You're sexy with murder in your eyes," adds Oliver, pulling away enough so that he can rip off my blood-soaked shirt and bra. Rook takes the hint and goes for my leggings, and in record time I'm naked, though I make sure they're not far behind.

The blades clatter to the ground, and thankfully Rook has the brain to shove them away before he comes back to me, his fingers on my hips.

"Fuck me," I breathe against Oliver's lips, though I turn to kiss Rook, repeating the same epithet against his. "Fuck me, please. I know he's dead and doesn't know but—"

Rook doesn't need the rest of my answer. He kisses me harder, holding me against him with one hand while the other delves between my thighs. His fingers, no longer bloody thanks to how meticulously he's wiped them off, slide into me without resistance, and before long he's thrusting them into me and stretching me open with no problem, while I writhe in his grip.

Oliver runs his hands up my body, streaking blood along my fair skin and nipping at me whenever he seems to feel like it. His sharp teeth scrape my shoulder, my throat, and finally my face as his long fingers wrap around the base of my neck.

"I'm too impatient to stretch you enough for both of us," Rook growls in my ear, his fingers leaving me. "So he's just going to have to wait." Oliver, though it seems he's thrilled about that, jerks himself to hardness, leaving streaks of blood along his length, as Rook slams into me, making me cry out. I reach forward, needing Oliver as well, and when he kisses me, it's with a mouth that tastes of blood and death and *perfection*.

He kisses Rook next, crowding close enough that he can

grab my knee and lift it off the ground. I balance on my other foot while Rook fucks me, drowning in pleasure, losing myself in the fire that rages through every part of me.

Do other people ever feel like this? So intensely alive that it feels like they're burning up on the spot like a dying, brilliant star?

I love you, I almost say, when Oliver's teeth find my throat and bite so hard I know I'll wear the mark for a while.

I fucking love you! I almost howl as Rook slams into me for a final time and snarls as he comes, the sounds swallowed by Oliver.

Then he's slipping out of me, leaving me empty, as Oliver readjusts his grip so that Rook can bear more of my weight. He gazes at me, those crazy, adorable, perfect eyes under his long lashes looking like gorgeous emeralds in his tanned face.

"You're perfect," he murmurs, and slams into me just as hard as Rook had, causing me to *scream* in pleasure and dig my nails into his shoulders. Rook grips me tight, devouring my mouth, then Oliver's, marking me with his nails and his lips so I know that I'll wear both bruises and blood tomorrow without fail.

But I *want* their marks. I want this feral side of them, the brutality that oozes from them and soaks into me. I've never needed anything more in my life; neverending pleas leave my lips, dribbling like drops of blood against Rook's jaw as Oliver fucks me closer and closer to my edge.

He comes with a snarl, much like Rook, and I cry out as well, digging my nails into his shoulders and dragging downward, just like I plan to do to Rook's chest the moment I get the chance.

I've never come harder than this. Trapped between them with nowhere to go, aching from desire and covered in blood, I see stars as my orgasm tears through me with rampant aban-don, nearly knocking me out in its intensity.

"I love you," I think I say, though it may be a fever dream. It comes out in breathless panting, my words slurred and prob-ably unintelligible. Neither of them says anything, so I'm sure after a moment they haven't heard me, or understood what I said.

And maybe, for now, that's a good thing. Especially when we have to at least get cleaned up enough to go to bed, and I have to ask what we'll do with Langhorn's body when it cools, before the faraway neighbors can notice.

But that's a problem for tomorrow. A fact that's made abundantly clear when Rook scoops me into his arms and carries me into a bedroom where he can pour me onto the bed and come down on top of me, trapping me against the mattress with a growl and smearing the sheets with blood as he thrusts my thighs apart and grins at me in warning.

It's clear he isn't done. Neither is Oliver, judging by the way he kisses me with a hand around my throat.

But that suits me perfectly.

CHAPTER 29

There's something wrong with me.

I'm covered in blood that sticks to my skin, and both bodies that surround me on the mattress of the cabin are similarly splashed with red, dried blood.

I flex my fingers when I roll onto my back, staring as I raise my hands up toward the ceiling. Twenty or thirty feet away is a cooling body, and I know for a fact today's cleanup is going to suck. I'm not going to make the boys do it all, obviously. But I've never cleaned up a body before.

Every part of me aches, but that's not exactly a shock—the murder and the feral fucking are to blame for that. Every time I close my eyes, I *revel* in the memories from last night.

It had been perfect.

The weight of the knife in my hand had been everything I thought it would be. And the drag of it across Langhorn's throat?

It had been the best thing that I'd ever experienced. Aside from Rook and Oliver, in their entirety. *They're* the definition of perfect. *They're* what's gotten me here, in some shape and form. Well, I amend thoughtfully. They're not what got me in the situation to *need* this.

But they are the reason I'm here instead, between them, covered in blood. And more comfortable in my own skin than I've been in a long time, rather than having spiraled dangerously and ended up in jail.

And that's what makes me realize that something is oh-so-wrong.

I shouldn't be this complacent, this content. I shouldn't be lying here on a bed with two serial killers, covered in the blood of my first victim, who I'd taken immense pleasure in killing. And yet... I don't *feel* like there's something wrong with me. I feel like everything has fallen into place over the last day, and I don't want to go back to how things were before.

Not *ever.*

Another hand reaches up beside mine, and Rook rolls in against my back, twining his fingers with my own. "Are you okay, darling girl?" he murmurs, his sticky, blood-stained skin brushing against mine. He's not wearing anything either, reminding me how absolutely wild we'd all become last night, once Langhorn was dead and his blood was staining all of us.

"I'm... more than okay," I admit in a whisper as Oliver continues to snore. "But I think something's wrong with me."

"Because you're more than okay?" There's a touch of bemusement in his voice, and he pulls my hand back down, pressing it to his chest, then urges me to roll to face him until my knees tangle with his under the sheets. "That sounds like it doesn't add up."

"I killed someone," I whisper, like it's a secret. "I *murdered* someone last night."

A sigh from behind me meets my ears, and Oliver uncurls, stretching out his knees and pushing his toes toward the bottom of the bed. He rolls over and wraps an arm around my shoulders, nuzzling his face against my throat. "You were *savage* last night," he agrees. "You did exactly what he deserved. *Exactly*. Fuck, it was so hot." It's clear he's more excited than he should be just waking up, because I can feel his length brush against my ass.

"Oh stop," I chastise, slapping at his hand. "I can't fuck you right now. I need at least an hour to shower off this blood." Last night it was hot. It had been such a turn-on for all of us to be dripping with Langhorn's blood. Especially the way Oliver's eyes had glittered when he'd wiped his hand against his face and left dark red, crimson streaks of it.

God, both of them are so insanely attractive that it's unreal. Especially when they're in murder mode, which I never would've expected could be so much of a turn-on.

"Then shower with me," Rook purrs in my ear. "We should conserve water, you know? It would be the responsible thing to do."

"Right, because we're such responsible people," I agree, tilting my head back towards Rook. "We're such—"

He cuts me off by catching my lips in a kiss, and his hand slides up to press between my shoulder blades to keep me in place. Oliver's hand comes up as well, curling around my throat and pulling me back just a little.

It's a perfect push and pull, it's an even better tug-of-war as they both fight to claim my mouth while also kissing each other. I make sure to find both of their lips, nipping at them, begging for entrance and getting what I want easily from both of my gorgeous men.

"Okay, okay." I laugh finally, when Oliver's hand curves down my thigh to reach between them, close enough to my clit that I know what his intentions are without needing to guess. Then again, Oliver seems to be hornier than a teenager, and ready to go at most times.

It occurs to me I've never asked how often they have sex. Every other day? Every day? *Multiple* times a day? It wouldn't shock me, honestly. Not with how they look at each other like they're always hungry for each other's touch.

But fuck, I'm sure I'm getting to that point as well. I know I'm desperate for them at the best of times, and if they wanted to fuck more than once a day, I won't be the one to complain.

"I need to shower," I repeat, getting to my feet at the foot of the bed. It's easy to look back at them, to stare at them as Rook snags Oliver's arm and jerks him over to his side of the bed.

"Come find us when you're done," my professor purrs, eyes glittering when he leans down to fasten his teeth into the juncture of Oliver's neck and shoulder. "I'll have him a little more manageable by then. He's just bratty in the morning." Already Oliver is letting out a low, grating noise, and his head is tipped back as if begging Rook for more.

It's so hard to walk away. Almost too hard, but I manage in the end. My steps take me past the main room, where Langhorn is still spread out in pieces waiting to be cleaned up. Rook had been smart when he'd laid down a tarp that stretches almost the entire room. I'd thought it was a bit extreme last night. I'd thought surely there was no way we would get that much blood all over things. But I'd been desperately wrong. I stop at the last minute to glance back at the scene, none of it turning my stomach even a little.

How can it, when I was the one responsible for so much of the gore staining the sheet and the spatters of blood along the plastic? My teeth sink into my lower lip as I take it in, but I force myself to keep moving. To find the shower and submerge myself in hot water.

Maybe guilt will find me there.

Like Rook's main house, the cabin is elegant and lavish, even in its rather rustic simplicity. The bathroom is fully furnished, with both a shower and a tub, and is built to show how much money he spent on this place.

I wonder if he bought it as-is, or had it renovated.

Neither possibility matters right now. Not when I'm more interested in finding towels in the cabinet and spreading them on the floor around the shower stall that looks like it was built for three or four people.

Once the water is nearly scalding, I step under the spray, groaning when it hits my tight muscles. The waterfall-like spray cascades over me, and I crack my eyes open to stare down at the white tile floor below me.

I hadn't turned the lights on, so in the light from the window I can see streams of dark mixing with clear. Together, they swirl around the drain like a vortex, filtering down it and taking away all evidence of the things I've done. I lift my hands to my face, staring at them as the blood runs off of my skin, dripping down my arms and finding its way down the drain.

Is it really this easy? To just get rid of all the evidence and the physical stain on me? It feels like it should require more scrubbing. And while I will have to scrub off some of the more resilient bits of blood on my skin, most of it just... fades away in the water.

There's something so wrong with me.

But it isn't because I killed Langhorn. Sure, that's part of it. And maybe I wouldn't be this way if he hadn't assaulted me in that office almost four weeks ago. But I'd thought when he was dead that this feeling would go away. That I'd go back to normal, sane Blair who makes mostly good decisions, except when it comes to men.

Unfortunately, that doesn't seem to be the case at all. I still feel the same urge, the same darkness in me that has me thinking about heading to the bars with a blade in my pocket and a helpless, miserable look on my face.

There's something so fucking wrong with me, because I want to kill again. I want to sink my fingers into a wound I've created and rip it wider, to see what's gone wrong with men who think they can take advantage of others. Surely if I keep digging, I'll find a commonality between them.

Maybe I can show it to them before they die, with my hands covered in blood from digging around in their bodies.

And maybe I'm just really, really fucked up right now.

I step out of the shower still streaming water, and barely manage to wrap a towel around myself before I'm walking through the house again, barefoot, until I'm back in front of the bed, watching as Rook runs his fingers up and down Oliver's spine.

Oliver really does seem more settled now, but he cracks open his eyes to look at me from under his lashes. "Are you okay?" he murmurs, reaching one hand out to me in invitation.

I take it, but I don't get back under the blankets with them. I sit between them, still dripping water from my long blonde hair, and stare at the stained sheets below me.

"I think I'm broken," I admit to them, glancing from Rook's face to Oliver's. "I think there's something really wrong with me."

"Because you like all this blood?" Oliver assumes, scratching his arm and watching it flake off from his skin. "I like it too, before it dries. You still have some on you, by the way. In... a lot of places, actually."

I shake my head at him, frowning. Is it not obvious? It *feels* obvious to me, like I'm wearing a big neon sign that points out exactly what's going on.

"Because you want to do it again." Rook's words aren't a question, but the accuracy of them has me looking up at him, not quite startled.

"Yes," I whisper, clutching the towel I have wrapped

around me. "So you see what I mean about something being wrong with me?"

"Maybe," he agrees, thinking. "But if you're going to say something is wrong with you, then I assume you think something is wrong with *us*."

Objectively... yeah. Absolutely. I've always thought something was wrong with them for wanting to kill people. That they were born different, or born without something in them that would have given them a better moral compass.

But what if they're just like me?

"Well, I mean, if we're being honest." I raise a brow and look between them. "You guys probably aren't the textbook definition of normal."

"And who wants to be?" agrees Oliver, wrinkling his nose. "So what if we like to kill people, wonder girl? So what if *you* want to kill people? Where's the problem in that?"

There are a lot of problems with that, aside from the obvious few. But every time I try to grip one so that I can express the reason, it slips through my fingers like blood running down the drain.

"God," I mutter, a soft laugh trickling out from my lips. "I'm so fucked up. I blame you guys for this, by the way. For being bad role models."

"The worst," Rook agrees, throwing off the blankets and coming around to rest a hand on my head. Oliver, not wanting to be left out, crawls toward me as well, until he's half in my lap like a finicky house cat.

"I take full responsibility for being awful," Oliver purrs, nuzzling my thigh. "And I support you killing again. You were so good at it."

That doesn't feel like a compliment I should want. My fingers clench in my towel, but before I have a chance to really dwell on my worries, Rook tilts my head back so that I have to meet his gaze.

"Well then, our pretty little killer," he murmurs, his gaze never leaving mine. "Better put some clothes on. It's time for you to learn how to clean up after yourself so you don't end up in jail."

"Is it going to take long?"

"Yeah, Blair," he laughs. "It's going to take all day. You brought some old clothes, right? So there's no getting out of this. If you're going to kill with us, you're going to clean up with us. I won't let you go around being irresponsible." He looks at Oliver when he says it, making the latter snort.

"He's just trying to make a point about how much I don't like cleanup," Oliver teases, getting to his feet. "Come on, Blair. Let's get you something to wear that's already stained beyond repair." When he leaves the room, I follow, stopping once again to stare at the mess we'd made.

It only takes a few seconds for Oliver to come back to me, and he rests his chin on my shoulder, arms wrapped around my waist as he looks at it, too. Rook is next, ambling out toward the bathroom and stopping when he sees us.

"I really did this," I murmur, staring at the scene in front of me in the proper light of day. "And I'd really do it again. Doesn't that make you worry?" I'm not sure who I'm asking, or *why*. But I need their answers like I need to breathe.

"No, darling girl," Rook murmurs, pressing his face against mine and leaning forward to kiss my jaw.

It's Oliver that finishes his thought, with his mouth close to my other ear and his voice as low as sin, "*It excites us.*"

ABOUT THE AUTHOR

AJ Merlin would rather write epic love stories than live them. I mean, who wants to limit themselves to only falling in love once? She is obsessed with dark fantasy, true crime, and also dogs. From serial killers to voyeurs all the way down to the devil himself, AJ's specialty is in writing irredeemable heroes who somehow still manage to captivate their heroines (and her readers).

Made in the USA
Monee, IL
14 January 2024

51758645R00168